William Stickney

Memorial Sketch of William Soule Stickney

William Stickney

Memorial Sketch of William Soule Stickney

ISBN/EAN: 9783337097004

Printed in Europe, USA, Canada, Australia, Japan

Cover: Foto ©Raphael Reischuk / pixelio.de

More available books at **www.hansebooks.com**

MEMORIAL SKETCH

OF

WILLIAM SOULE STICKNEY

By HIS FATHER.

FOR PRIVATE CIRCULATION.

A youth to whom was given
So much of earth, so much of Heaven.—WORDSWORTH.

WASHINGTON, D. C.
"SCHOOL OF MUSIC" PRESS.
1881.

PRINTED AT THE "SCHOOL OF MUSIC,"

707 Eighth street, N. W.,

Washington, District of Columbia.

IN MEMORY OF

WILLIAM SOULE STICKNEY

Who Died in Los Pinos, Colorado,

July 20, 1880,

WHILE SERVING AS SECRETARY AND DISBURSING OFFICER

OF THE UTE COMMISSION.

———

Οὐ διακονηθῆναι, ἀλλὰ διακονῆσαι.

Not to be ministered to, but to minister.— MATTHEW, 20: 28.

Ἡγεῖτο γὰρ αὐτῶν ἕκαστος οὐχὶ τῷ πατρὶ καὶ τῇ μητρὶ μόνον γεγενῆσθαι, ἀλλὰ καὶ τῇ πατρίδι.

For each of them considered that not for his father and mother only was he born, but for his fatherland.

— DEMOSTHENES, "De Corona."

INTRODUCTION.

Or dost thou warn poor mortals left behind,
A task well suited to thy gentle mind?
Oh, if sometimes thy spotless form descend,
To me thine aid, thou guardian genius, lend,
When rage misguides me, or when fear alarms,
When pain distresses, or when pleasure charms,
In silent whisperings purer thoughts impart,
And turn from ill a frail and feeble heart;
Lead through the paths thy virtue trod before,
Till bliss shall join, nor death can part us more.

TICKELL.

To the Members of the Calvary Baptist, Calvary Mission, and Kendall Chapel Sunday Schools.

DEAR FRIENDS—

The warm affection cherished by you towards my beloved son, and the absorbing interest he felt in the prosperity of these three schools, with which he had been so long identified, have prompted me to place before you, principally by means of his own writings, the gradual development of a character, the possession of which in such symmetry and beauty made him so great a favorite with his friends, and won for him "a good testimony from those without." Two motives control me: first, a desire to perpetuate his memory; secondly, the hope that a study of his many virtues, noble spirit, and self-sacrificing devotion to the cause of Christianity, may lead you—and all who may peruse this volume—to the Source and Inspiration of his life, that you too may cultivate those manly qualities of head and heart, which were so conspicuous in him.

My object has not been to write a panegyric. You who knew him best will agree

Reasons for publishing the Memoir.

No need of Eulogy.

with our worthy Pastor: "He needs no eulogy; his record is his best eulogy."

I scarcely need disclaim, in the preparation of this imperfect sketch, any attempts at literary excellence in style or composition; nor perhaps is it necessary to apologize for the insertion of letters, youthful compositions, or other matters, which, to a general reader, might appear too trivial for publication.

As the doll, the top, or other playthings of childhood are invested with an interest almost sacred in the eyes of the parent, after their dear ones have been removed by death, so to me, and I doubt not; to some extent, at least, to you also, the letters, words, and acts of our dear one, of little significance it may be, when written, spoken, or performed, are now recalled with tender interest, and are enshrined in the memory as precious treasures.

Many of you have asked for some memento of our dear boy. Accept this Memorial Sketch of his life with the earnest desire that its perusal may not only recall to your memory his manly form, cheerful countenance, courteous bearing, Christian spirit, unselfish

Reasons for inserting letters and youthful compositions.

Desire of friends for some memento.

devotion to the happiness of others, purity of heart and life, but also inspire and nurture in you a resolute purpose, by God's help, to leave behind a memory equally fragrant in kind words and good deeds.

CHAPTER I.

BIRTH AND CHILDHOOD.

HEAVEN lies about us in our infancy.—WORDSWORTH.

> YET hath thy spirit left on me
> An impress Time has worn not out,
> And something of myself in thee,
> A shadow from the past, I see,
> Lingering, even yet, thy way about:
> Not wholly can the heart unlearn
> That lesson of its better hours,
> Not yet has Time's dull footsteps worn
> To common dust that path of flowers.—WHITTIER.

" OUR PET "

at the age of one year

WILLIAM SOULE STICKNEY, son of
William and Jeannie K. Stickney,
was born at the residence of his grandfather,
Amos Kendall, in the "old house" at Kendall
Green, District of Columbia, October 24, 1852.

Birth.

This property, with the farm, was subsequently purchased by the Government for
the use of the Deaf and Dumb Institution.

On his father's side he was a descendant
of William Stickney, who emigrated to Massachusetts in 1636 from the town of Stickney
on the eastern coast of England.

Ancestors.

His progenitor on his mother's side came
from the town of Kendall,—derived from
Kent's dale,—a city of considerable importance in England.

His middle name was the maiden name
of his grandmother Stickney.

The second and only other child of his
parents was born in 1854 and died at the age
of six months.

The day of Will's birth was the day on
which America's greatest statesman died.
This coincidence was sometimes pleasantly
referred to as a favorable omen that the
mantle of the great Daniel Webster would
fall on his shoulders.

Obedience to parents.

Though he was an only child, and the pride of his parents, they were never so indulgent as to permit him to grow up without seeking to instil into his young mind and heart those principles of obedience, and respect for their wishes, which they considered essential to a true and manly character.

From early childhood it was his mother's habit to pray daily with and for him, he following with a prayer of his own. This practice was continued until he left home for school, and we believe was blessed to his good.

Two or three times only did his mother have occasion to use the rod, and in each instance the punishment was occasioned by disobedience. The last time resort was had to this method of discipline was when Will was four or five years of age. The incident

Conscientiousness.

illustrates the conscientiousness of the boy—always a conspicuous trait in his character. Bringing to his mother a little switch, he said, in answer to her question of surprise: "What shall mamma do with the switch?" "Mamma must whip Willie. Mamma said I must not eat cherries, and I have been eating them." His mother said, Yes, she was very sorry, but she would have to whip him. After the light punishment, which the little fellow received without a tear, he desired her to kneel down and ask God to forgive him, which she did. Then he followed in a sweet, childish prayer of his own, asking his Heavenly Father's forgiveness, after which he threw his little arms about his mother's neck and sought her forgiveness, promising ever after obedience to all her wishes. **Prayer for forgiveness.**

The promise was faithfully kept, and the sweet spirit of the child was never lost in the after life of the youth and the man.

Another of his noble characteristics which endeared him to all who were acquainted with his young life and which was a part of his nature was the moral courage to stand up for the right. This trait exhibited itself when he was a child of about nine years. **Moral courage.**

The family were accustomed to ride to Washington, a distance of about two miles, to attend church. Often, when returning home, Will would leave the carriage and walk, sometimes by fleetness of foot reaching his father's house first. One Sabbath, as the carriage approached the gate leading to Ken-

Incident.

dall Green, his parents saw him talking earnestly to three German boys, all considerably larger than himself; as the carriage drew near these lads walked away. When Will was questioned about the matter he said he found the boys fighting, and, said he, "Mamma, I asked them if they did not know it was wicked; that God had commanded them to remember the Sabbath day to keep it holy. Then one of the boys called another a fool, and I said to him, Do you know that the Bible says,—'Whosoever says, Thou fool, shall be in danger of hell fire.'" This Scripture quotation caused them to separate, wondering, probably, at the spirit which possessed the little peacemaker.

Memory of the Sermon on the Mount.

More than a year before this incident Will had committed to memory the Sermon on the Mount which he often repeated without missing a word.

The boy was father of the man, for never in his after life did he hesitate by word and example, manfully and sometimes heroically, to express his convictions of what was noble and true.

During this period of his early childhood Will, having no young associates, found his out-door society with his dogs and chickens, and occasionally a pet rabbit or squirrel.

Playmates

If the colored servants on the place had children of about his own age, he loved to teach them some Sunday School lesson or lead them in singing, with all the gravity of a master. Sunday afternoon was the favorite time for these exercises. Often have I seen him with a class of colored children, some older and some younger than himself, trying to teach them out of God's Word, earnestly exhorting them to be true and honest if they would enter heaven.

Early efforts to teach the Word of God.

His talent for music developed at an early age, and at eight years he commenced taking lessons on the piano, while pursuing the elementary branches of knowledge under his parents' instruction. At the age of thirteen he entered the Rittenhouse Academy in Washington, for the first time going regularly to school.

Talent for Music.

Enters Rittenhouse Academy.

About this time the members of the Calvary Baptist Church were canvassing for subscriptions for the erection of a house of worship. His grandfather asked Will what he was going to subscribe. He replied, he had no money. On being asked if he would like to

2

earn some for that purpose, he expressed the pleasure it would give him to do so. His grandfather then promised him five cents for every load of gravel he would spread, as the hired men were then employed in repairing the roads. Will eagerly accepted the proposition, and soon received a dollar and fifty cents, as the pay for his labor, which he gladly subscribed and paid into the building fund of the church. He said afterwards. when thinking of his grandfather's remark, "that he owned a brick in the church," he "sometimes watched the workmen as they prosecuted their labors on the church, and wondered which of the bricks was owned by him!"

In the autumn of 1859, Will had his first sickness which produced anxiety in the minds of his parents. It was a mild form of typhoid fever, which confined him to his bed for about two weeks. He gradually recovered, but was never of a robust constitution. He was possessed of a delicate organization, a nervous temperament, and keen sensibilities, a gentle spirit, sensitive to any intentional wrong. and quick to forgive an injury. Though application to study was never disagreeable, he showed no more fondness for books than is common among most boys.

He commenced Latin at nine years, and, though his progress was not rapid, he understood what he went over. Though never quick to learn, he yet held fast the ground he went over, seldom giving but one perusal of his lessons in preparation for review.

After writing compositions upon "The Horse," "The Cow," "The Dog," and "The Cat," his next subject was "Life," written at the age of nine. I give it precisely as it lies before me from his pen:

Early compositions.

LIFE.

I will tell you something about life. Life is long or short whichever God permits. Some persons die when babes, others live a few years longer, and some to an old age. This is a beautiful subject to write about.

On "Life."

Sometimes people live to a great age. Methuselah lived to be nine hundred and sixty-nine years. He was the oldest man in the world. Many others are mentioned in the Bible who lived to a great age. Enoch, Noah, and many others.

What would this world be without life?

Desolation of earthwithout life.

The trees, flowers, and grass that look so beautiful in the spring and summer, all are given to us by our Heavenly Father, but do not live forever, even they all die.

Life more beautiful in heaven.

Life is very beautiful on earth, but far more beautiful in heaven. If you wish to reach this happy place, you must not swear, nor steal, and God says that he will not have liars in heaven. How thankful should we be to Him for His goodness to us!

WILLIE SOULE STICKNEY.

His next composition written January 15, 1862,

BE KIND TO THE POOR.

On kindness to the poor.

There are but few people who care for the poor. God teaches us to be kind to everybody. You must hunt up the poor and ask if they wont come with you to church, or Sunday-school, and learn to be good.

The way to be kind.

You must be kind to the poor and get all the old clothes you can and ask your neighbors if they have n't some, for many are suffering with the cold, and a great many poor people die or starve for want of care.

You must look after your own children

first, and the poor next, for you must love the poor.

I cannot say much more on this subject, but there is one thing I forgot to say about the poor, you should visit them when they are sick and, if you can, take to them what they need to do them good.

I have now ended my composition.

W. S. STICKNEY.

How he practised in after life these precepts of charity and benevolence, they who knew him best can testify.

Early letters.

The following is one of his early letters.

Washington, April 25, 1863.

MY DEAR FATHER—

I have looked in the geography, as you told me, and have found that the distance from the earth to the sun is 95,000,000 of miles, and the distance from the earth to the moon is 240 thousand miles.

Study of geography

Geography is a description of the earth's surface. The circumference of the earth is about 25,000 miles and the diameter of the earth is about 8,000 miles. The diameter of anything is the distance through it.

Day and night are caused by the earth going around on its axis. The earth goes around on its axis once in 24 hours, and the earth goes around the sun once in 365 days and 6 hours. The seasons are caused by the earth going around the sun with its axis inclined to the plane of its orbit, always pointing to the North Star.

The shape of the earth is that of an oblate spheroid.

Father, I studied that, that you told me, and then I sat down and wrote this.

From your affectionate son,

WILLIE S. STICKNEY.

Rockville, Ct., June 30, 1863.

DEAR GRANDPA—

Letter to his grandfather.

How are you? and how is grandma? I got a nice hat yesterday, and I have a cash-book and I expect to send a copy of it soon to father.

Grandpa I am having a nice time up here—the mornings are beautiful and pleasant.

Tell Berta that I will send her a little letter. I will inclose a little letter to Emilie—but grandpa, are they good? for if they aint I don't believe I can write them, and is Emi-

lie as sweet as ever, for if she is good she
must be sweet.

Please tell me how the dogs are, especially Zip.

I want to see every body that I know.
Tell every body that there is a little boy in
Rockville that sends his love to them. His
name is Willie S. Stickney. Write soon.

From your affectionate grandson,
WILLIE S. STICKNEY.

The cash account came in his next letter.
It contains the items for traveling expenses
to Rockville, with small investments for
"Oranges," "Candy," "Lickerish," "Contributions," "Rockets," "Roman Candles," &c.,
written in the round hand of an eleven-year-
old boy, but balanced to a penny.

This methodical habit of rendering an
account to his father for all the moneys received, he carefully adhered to until he finished his college course. His accounts are
models of neatness and accuracy, giving a
truthful statement of all his expenditures.

Rockville, July 30, 1863.

DEAR PAPA—As I have nothing else to
do I thought I would write you a few lines.

*Cash ac-
count*

Yesterday uncle John put on an old pair of boots, and an old shaker hat, and he went out and poured some hot water right on a swarm of hornets, and I think they are about gone now. I have been stung by another hornet right on the cheek.

Witch, a little kitten, ran right through a nest of hornets, and then she ran first one way, and then another, and then she tumbled down stairs, and then she stopped and began a scratching, and then a hornet came up between her ears and then she ran away.

But I must stop. Write soon.

From your affectionate son,

WILLIE SOULE STICKNEY.

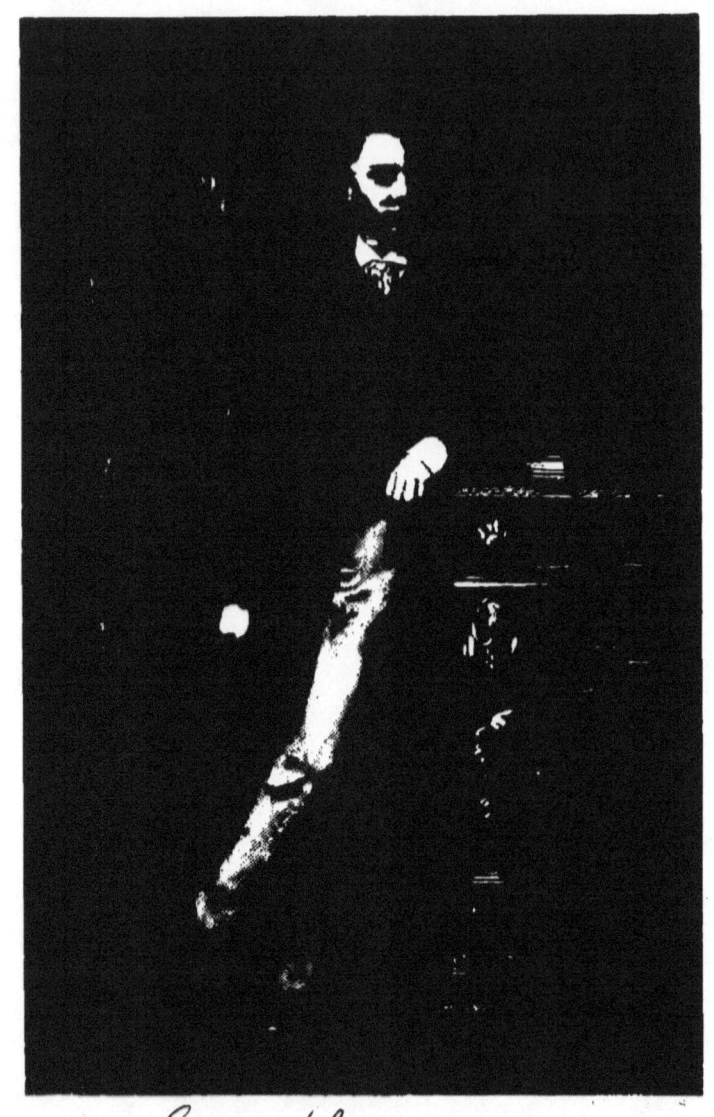

may God bless, and protect
you and bring you back safe
to your Son
Willie

Paris, 1866.

CHAPTER II.

A TOUR ABROAD.

TRAVEL, in the younger soul, is a part of education; in the elder a part of experience. He that traveleth into a country before he hath some entrance into the language, goeth to school and not to travel.

When a traveler returneth home, let him not leave the countries where he hath traveled altogether behind him.

Let it appear that he doth not change his country manners for those of foreign parts, but only put some flowers of that he hath learned abroad into the customs of his own country.— BACON.

ten, or, if never known before, was now
gained at every step, and in a way to make
the most lasting impression upon the mind.

Will had formed the plan early in our
travels to procure books that treated particularly of the subjects or persons for which the
places visited were celebrated. At Rouen he
had the life of Joan of Arc; at Pompeii, Bul-
wer's "Last Days;" at Wittenburg he studied
Luther; at Constance, Jerome of Prague and
Huss, and thus he acquired a vast store of
information to be obtained so effectually in
no other way.

Europe,
Asia, and
Africa.

All the principal cities in Great Britain.
France, Belgium, Germany, Austria, Holland,
Italy, Greece, and Turkey, in Europe; Alexan-
dria, Cairo, the islands of Cyprus and Rhodes,
the Red Sea, and Isthmus of Suez, in Africa;
Joppa, Jerusalem, Damascus, the Dead Sea
and Jordan, and the principal Bible lands in
Asia were leisurely visited, and many of them
carefully studied. Every new place was a
fruitful theme for conversation and reading.
New sources of knowledge were constantly
opening up to us, which were explored with
avidity and delight.

A winter in Florence gave Will an opportunity for taking music lessons under an eminent master, and afforded us time for studying the Italian tongue. Will and myself regularly recited our lessons, and carried on much of our conversation in that language. The daily paper we soon learned to read without difficulty, and made fair progress in conversation.

In France Will gave himself to the study of the French language, which his knowledge of Latin made easy for him to acquire.

But it was in Palestine that we entered into the highest possible enjoyment of the great treasures in store for us. Spending a few days at Joppa, we started thence with our tents and horses, making the journey in the oriental style of the country.

Leaving Joppa about noon we took an easy ride to Ramleh (Arimathea), eighteen miles distant, where we arrived in about four hours. A ride of eight hours the next day brought us to Kirgeth Jarem, where we pitched our tents for the night. This place we left the next morning about nine, and at noon entered the Holy City.

"Beautiful for situation, the joy of the

Music lessons in Florence.

Study of the Italian language.

Visits Jerusalem.

whole earth, is Mount Zion, on the sides of the North, the City of the Great King."

We engaged rooms at a small German hotel and gave ourselves up to the enjoyment of the wondrous treasures scattered on every side.

Calvary, the Holy Sepulchre, the Pools, Olivet, Bethany, Bethlehem, Jordan, Jericho, the Dead Sea, Shechem, Shiloh, Bethel, Damascus, Beirout, and many other places of sacred interest were visited. At every step we found the confirmation of the truth of the Bible. Palestine seemed a fifth Gospel, so abundant were the evidences of the truth of the sacred record.

Palestine a fifth Gospel.

As the key fits the wards of the lock, so everywhere were the most striking and convincing proofs of the wonderful events narrated in the New Testament.

Of course upon Will, as upon the rest of us, these facts made a deep impression. No shadow of doubt existed in our minds, after our forty days sojourn in the Holy Land, of the reality of all those marvelous events so minutely recorded by the Evangelists. It seems as if the very stones at our feet cried out in confirmation of them. With

Influence upon the mind.

our Bibles in our hands we traversed the places where the feet of the Son of Man had trod, looked upon the scenes upon which His eyes had once rested, and came away, as fully persuaded as it was possible for us to be, of the truths of revelation.

After visiting Greece, its ruins and its Marathon, and Constantinople, we crossed a portion of the Black Sea, entered the Danube at its mouth, and, through the Iron Gates, steamed to Prague, and thence to Vienna.

In October, 1867, we returned home in good health, having given sixteen months to travel and visited many of the most interesting places on the globe. Our pleasure had been marred by no accident, and no serious sickness disturbed or interrupted our enjoyment.

Returning to our home at Kendall Green, we were agreeably surprised to find the grounds beautifully illuminated, and a transparency at the gate in burning letters giving us a "Welcome Home."

To each of us the trip had been full of pleasure and profit, but it was evident that the advantages to Will would be incalculable. He had traveled with eyes and ears

Visits Greece and Austria.

Returns home.

Reception at Kendall Green.

Benefits of the trip.

open, had made friends everywhere by his
intelligence and polite bearing. The drago-
man in Syria, the Arab guides in Egypt,
showed. in many ways their friendship. He
had seen the principal galleries of art and
studied their master-pieces and the lives of
their authors; had heard the greatest living
musical performers and studied many of
their own compositions; had heard England's
greatest statesmen in the Houses of Parlia-
ment and her most eminent preachers from
their own pulpits; had seen the leading men
of France as they stirred their countrymen
from the Tribune at the Corps Legislatif;
had visited the venerable and classic seat
of learning at Oxford; read the Odes of Horace among the olives and oleanders of Tivoli
and the Alban Hills; explored the ruins of
Cæsar's palace; looked upon the glories of
Mont Blanc and Jungfrau; climbed the Py-
rennees; crossed the Alps; gazed down the
crater of Vesuvius; surveyed the Campagna
from the summit of Brunelleschi's dome;
threaded the gloomy catacombs of Rome; visited the fields of Waterloo and Marathon;
feasted upon the beauties of the Rhine, of Co-
mo, and Maggiore; studied the ancient civili-

zation from Egyptian monuments; witnessed
the splendors of all the principal courts in Europe, with their kings and emperors; explored
the museums, libraries, and galleries of art;
visited the cathedrals; ventured across the
Mer de Glace; sat by Jacob's well; traversed
the valley of Ebal and Gerizim; clambered
among the ruins of Baalbeck; studied the
lives of Savonarola, Michael Angelo, and
Galileo at Florence, "where he stood at night
to take the vision of the stars"; of Knox at
Edinburgh; of Calvin and D'Aubigné at Geneva; of Luther at Wittenberg, Erfurt and
Wartburg castle; of Zwingle at Zürich; of
Napoleon and Josephine at Fontainbleau; of
Frederick and Voltaire at Sans Souci; witnessed the King's fête at Venice, "the bride
of the sea"; stood upon the Acropolis; traversed the Roman forum; and with an intelligent apprehension of what he had seen, returned to make his new acquisitions useful in
the development and growth of his future life.

Though not at this time a professed
christian, no one could be more exemplary in
all the varied and sometimes trying experiences of this long journey than he. On the
Sabbath it was our invariable practice to at-

Observ-
ance of the
Sabbath.

SOON after his return from abroad he again entered the Rittenhouse Academy in Washington, where he continued to attend until the middle of 1868. The quarterly reports of his principal, Mr. O. C. Wight, show him to have been perfect in his studies and deportment during this period, with scarcely an exception.

Re - enters Rittenhouse Academy.

In August, 1868, he entered a private school in Philadelphia. Under date of August 15, he writes:

Enters a private school in Philadelphia.

"I commenced going to school yesterday; recited six lines in Virgil. I have taken up Greek and ancient history, besides spelling, Latin, geography, algebra, arithmetic, reading, and writing, so you see my time is pretty well occupied. I have practised on the piano this afternoon one good hour, and have yet to get three pages and a half in Greek grammar and a good lesson in Virgil.

"I am very comfortably situated, have a beautiful room, very nicely furnished. Went to Sunday School last Sunday afternoon. The large room in the basement had about 350 in it. They use the Sabbath Carols, and a miserable, poor book it is. In the first place the children did not sing with a *will*,

Goes to Sunday School.

and in the next place the good *new* tunes are few and far between.

"I am in pretty good health. The other day I went to market with Mr. K. I felt very restless, and while crossing the street in front of the house I became as blind as a bat for a few seconds, but I got hold of Hampton, and after stumbling over the curb, I reached the steps, and then my eyesight began to return slowly. After resting for a while on the sofa, I was soon well enough to be about, but I have had slight touches of the attack ever since.

Suddenly taken ill in the street.

"Remember me to Wesley [the coach-man], and tell him to take the very best care of Nellie" [buggy horse.]

BECOMES A CHRISTIAN.

Philadelphia, Feb. 23, 1869.

DEAR MOTHER—

Your letters of 10th and 22d inst., as also one from father received.

Especially am I glad to hear so many young persons are coming to their blessed Savior. You may be surprised to read this from my pen, but, dear mother, the film has been removed from my eyes, the temple curtain has been rent and the face of my Lord and Master is no longer hidden from my eyes. I rejoice in the strength of the Lord. He is mine and I am his. The change came over me last Saturday afternoon. I now take comfort in prayer, and pleasure in reading my Bible. I have gone right to work in the vineyard of Jesus. I am now using all the influence I possess to bring sinners to Christ. Mother, is n't it singular that I have put off my salvation so long? I used to think it was hard to become a christian, but oh, if I had only read my Bible more I would have discovered the delusion under which I was laboring. Tell all my unconverted friends to "Come to Jesus;" tell them what peace I have found. What shall I do in respect to relating my experience, and being baptized? Do you want me to wait a little while? I believe that my sins are all forgiven, and I am ready to tell the people what God has done for me, next Friday night, and be buried in the baptismal water next Sunday morning. Mr. Kennard says that he dont see as there is any cause for delay on my part. Please advise me immediately. I should like to be baptized here, for there are a good many

Becomes a christian.

Wishes to be baptized.

young friends of mine that begin to feel anxious about their sinful condition, and I think my example would encourage them; but it is as you say.

Give my love to grandpa, father, and all who love me.

Write soon to

      Your christian son   WILLIE.

He was baptized by Rev. J. S. Kennard, in the Tenth Baptist Church in Philadelphia, on the 14th March, 1869. His parents and grandfather had the satisfaction of being present, greatly to the joy of the obedient young christian.

Notwithstanding this radical change of heart wrought by the Divine Spirit, no marked change was perceptible or possible in his outward conduct.

Hitherto Will had been greatly blessed by the constant and intimate association with his grandfather Kendall, who watched with tender interest the development of his grandson's character.

Mr. Kendall united with the Calvary Baptist Church, in Washington, April 2, 1865, and now had the happiness of seeing

Grand-father Kendall.

his grandson following his steps in the sacred ordinance, administered by him at whose
hands he had received it four years before.
He was an earnest, consistent member, laboring with cheerful zeal in the Sunday
Schools, attending the public and devotional
meetings, sometimes at great sacrifice of personal comfort, always ready with his word
of testimony, full of the missionary spirit,
devoted to the prosperity of the church, making its interests paramount to all other considerations.

Such a life, of necessity, exercises an
almost controlling influence over those in
contact with it.

Mr. Kendall had attained his eightieth
year; his increasing infirmities admonished
him and his friends that his time was short.
After a confinement to the house of about
four months, during which his strength was
perceptibly failing, though his mind continued
perfectly clear, apparently gaining in vigor,
as his physical weakness increased, on the
12th of November, 1869, his spirit took its
flight. A few hours before his death he called
Will to his bedside and gave him the following words of admonition:

Christian
Influence.

MR. KENDALL'S DYING WORDS TO HIS GRAND-SON W. S. STICKNEY, NOV. 11, 1869.

"You have been a good child; be faithful. Do all God enables you to in his cause, not only in the Calvary Baptist Church, but *everywhere;* for this religion is not confined to persons or individuals; but *whatever* your duty is. I hope you may ever be able to perform it.

"In the first place, comply with all your moral duties in the Old and New Testaments; fulfil your duties to your fellow-men; do not deceive them for any purpose, but go through life an honest man as your grandfather has endeavored to do. What I would add to

that is christian faith, which is the only assurance we can have for any immortality at all. Be true. Be useful and honest with your fellow men. Be true and faithful to your christian profession. Do all you can in every proper way to promote Christ's kingdom here on earth while you live. Be honest; go straight forward. There is one point upon which you cannot deviate: whatever you have belongs to your creditors, if you get in debt, rather than to yourself. First satisfy them; conceal nothing; be direct and honest.

"Be honest—honest first and last. No man can be a true christian who is not in all his transactions truthful and honest. If we cannot get along according to the principles of the Bible, we cannot get along at all."

Honest first and last.

The solemn and impressive circumstances under which these words were spoken by the dying saint of eighty years, were well calculated to impress the heart of the christian boy of seventeen. That scene and those words he never forgot.

Solemn impressions produced.

His profound respect and reverence for the character of his grandfather gave them additional force. He had witnessed his daily walk as it illustrated and confirmed his profession, and his young heart was impressed with the conviction that there was an intense reality in a truly christian life.

Whatever resolutions he made, or prayers he offered then and there, were never known; but his life, with all its energies and possibilities, was unreservedly and joyfully consecrated to the triumphs of the gospel. Every thought, purpose, and plan were subordinate to this great, absorbing consideration. In study and pleasure, at home and abroad, with friends or strangers, wherever he was, and whatever his circumstances, the great purpose of his life was ever kept prominently in view—to honor the name of his Master and promote the triumphs of his cause.

Returns home.

The school in Philadelphia was closed on account of ill health of the principal. Will returned home, and in the autumn of 1869 entered the private school of Mr. Young on Fourteenth street. Here he applied himself to study, entering with zest upon his duties, keeping along in music, taking an active part in church and Sunday School work, until June, 1871, when he was admitted to the Freshman class of the University of Rochester, as he tells us in the following letter:

Admitted to college.

Osborn House, Rochester, June 26, 1871.

DEAR FATHER—

I have just returned from the University, having passed the examination *without a condition.* Will probably leave here next Thursday for Hartford and Rockville.

If not too much trouble, please tell Mr. Young of my success.

Your affectionate son   WILLIE.

From Rochester he went to visit friends at Southport, Conn., whose acquaintance he made abroad. From there he writes:

Visits Southport Conn.

Southport, July 10, 1871.

DEAR FATHER—

My sojourn here has been very pleasant. Mr. M. and Miss J. do all they can to make it pleasant for me. I expect to leave next Wednesday, the 12th instant, for Rockville. Uncle John and Aunt Mary want me to make a visit there, so I will go Wednesday.

Yesterday I attended service at the Congregational church. The preacher gave us a *moral discourse*, prefacing it by the affirmation, "I am a Republican," and taking for his subject—"Take care of No. 1." His text was the 4th verse of the 2d chapter of Phillippians.

Comments on Sunday services.

After church I stayed to Sunday School. After singing from the "Happy Voices," prayer was offered, but it was impossible to understand more than half that was said.

The Asst. Supt. gave me a class of two boys, but they only distinguished themselves by their remarkable dullness. I asked "What happened 1871 years ago?" Quite a pause

Teaches a class in Sabbath School.

ensued, when one of them said, "I know";
and upon further inquiry said, "The flood"!
The classes were continually interrupted by
the Librarian, Superintendent, and Treasurer.

With much love, I remain

Your affectionate son   WILLIE.

Southport, July 18, 1871.

DEAR MOTHER—

Your letter of the 14th came duly to hand.
You may be surprised to see that I am still
here; but it is Mr. M.'s doings. He expects
to leave Thursday for Newport, and he wanted me to stay until he went; so we all expect
to start then. Mr. M. and Miss J. for Newport, and *Mr. S.* for Rockville. I should be
most happy to welcome father, if he finds
that the Council can just as well adjourn.

If you are so hungry for music, why
do n't you feed yourself? The piano is all
ready to respond if you desire it and use the
proper means.

Yesterday morning I took my *first* swim.

Please ask father to bring "Religion and
Chemistry," by Cook, when he comes on.

How are the Missions getting along? Sunday I was requested to take charge of the

organ, but declined. The music is very poor, the preaching not much better. I do long to hear a good sermon.

But the carriage is ready for us all to go riding, so I must say Good-bye.

Give love to father, and write soon to
Your affectionate son   WILLIE.

From Southport he visited friends at Weston, near Boston.

Speaking of the great organ, he writes:

"Last Wednesday I went to hear the great organ, and I do n't know when I have enjoyed an hour so much. I can't understand why some people, highly educated and cultivated, do not enjoy music. Just think of an instrument with 108 stops and 4 keyboards! but you have heard it, and can appreciate my feelings. I could not refrain from lifting up my heart in thankfulness to God that he had permitted man to enjoy and to have such delightful music.

"Now I guess you would like to know how I occupy my time, and what I am reading. Well, I read four chapters in the Bible every day—three in the O. T. and one in the N. T. You do n't know how much easier it

Visits Boston.

At Music Hall.

Reading.

is for me to live a christian life, since I have
made myself more familiar with God's Word.
I am also reading Freeman's 'Early English
History,' and that is very interesting as well
as instructive. I practice nearly every day
on the piano."

Value of
his letters.
Inasmuch as the life of our son, while at
college, is to be revealed by his own letters,
it seems fitting that a word or two should be
said with reference to them. In the first
place, then, we give them just as they came
to us — the familiar, open - hearted utterances
of a child, in whom there was never the least
appearance of deceit, to parents the joy of
whose life was their perfect confidence in
their boy, that, whether under their immediate watch - care, or far absent from home, he
would be true to their honor, and the profession of his faith. In the second place, these
letters, which could not have been written
with the least thought that they would appear in print, are invaluable for the unsought
testimony they give to his true character.

Returning to Rochester at the beginning
of the term, in September, 1871, he gives the
following account of himself:

Rochester, Saturday, Sept. 23, 1871.

DEAR FATHER —

Yours of the 16th inst. was duly received. Do n't be afraid of my studying *too* hard. I understand some of my friends have ranked me among the "smart men" of the class of '75, but I have not obtained such credit from hard study. Latin and Greek *translations* are easy, but grammar is a bugbear; sometimes I feel almost ashamed to think I am not posted. I retire at ten o'clock and get up at six or half past. After dressing, play on the piano (which arrived in good condition last Tuesday), and at seven go next door to breakfast, after which I read over Livy and Xenophon with Messrs. Milne and Adams (who live next door) — the former is the best man in the class. At 9 we report at the chapel for prayers; directly after which we recite to Prof. Sage (Latin), then to Prof. Robinson (algebra), and finally, to Prof. Mixer (Greek.)

At 12½ we dine, and then Milne and Adams either come in here, or I go in there, and we study until 4½, and then I go to St. Peter's church and practise on the organ till 5½. At 6 the tea-bell rings. After tea Adams and I

Reputation as a scholar.

Outline of the labor of the day.

6

generally go to the Post Office, and take a walk, getting home about 8, and we spend the remainder of the time either singing or playing—Adams accompanying me on the piano with his flute. So you see I have something to do, and do something all the time. My health is good, and I am feeling *well*. My headaches, I hope, have departed, never to return. My organ teacher is said by all to be the first organist in the city.

Society question.

There is one thing I wish to leave entirely to you, and that is the society question. There are only two good societies in the University. [Here follows his opinion of the two societies, not necessary to copy.]

With love to mother and all inquiring friends. Your aff. son   WILLIE.

The following requires a word of explanation.

Will had informed me that his landlady had complained that he and his companions had offended her by their boisterous singing and late hours. Not knowing the character of his associates, and fearing he might be tempted to neglect more important duties, and give too much time to serenading, I

Under censure.

wrote the letter to which the following is a reply.

His letter convinced me that my criticism was unnecessarily harsh.

Rochester, Oct. 13, 1871.

MY DEAR FATHER—

Your letter of the 10 inst. is before me. I was surprised, and sorry, to find that I had in any way displeased you.

· Father, I think you are rather severe, when you say, "You are so unmindful of what you are in Rochester for, as to join sere- nading parties." You must remember that it was on a *Friday* night. We have *no* lessons Saturday, hence, by going out serenading, I neglected no studies. Friday afternoon I studied my Latin and Greek for Monday, and it was easy to get algebra on Saturday; so you are convinced no studies were neg- lected. You speak as if I intended to make a habit of serenading. In that you are mis- taken. There are five of us, who sing to- gether about every week, on *Friday* even- ings, and as our music is as well adapted to serenades as any thing else, we sung a few of them the other night.

Defence.

I think if you were here you would think I made "music a recreation." My practice on the organ is certainly a rest, after studying from half-past one to four without stopping. In the evening, I take your advice, and, when weary of study, I wake up the echoes of the piano.

Your wishes in regard to taking an organ will be heeded.

In the foregoing, please do n't think me impudent or presumptuous; I have no such idea; I only want to explain things to you, that you may not think your son is spending his time in follies, rather than in study. I will try to do better in the future. I 'm sorry that you have been obliged to say that you are "disappointed" in me. Rest assured that it will be my earnest endeavor, during the remainder of my life, so to conduct myself that you will never again be able to make such a statement.

This week has been very pleasant at the University. Every thing has passed off well. We have tough lessons in mathematics, but Latin and Greek are easy.

The Sophomores have tried several times to get the Freshmen into a fight, but we

Noble resolution.

have kept very cool. Yesterday a party of them stood at the gate and refused to let us pass, but we all went through after a good deal of pulling.

Prex was at the recitation in mathematics yesterday and to-day. He gave us quite a talk about the Chicago calamity, which was very instructive. He speaks to me occasionally.

At the next covenant meeting of the church, please ask for my letter to the First Baptist Church here; Dr. Robbins, pastor.

Seeks his letter to join church in Rochester.

I am in Dr. Kendrick's class in S. S., and it is as good as a sermon to hear him. The first day I heard him was communion Sabbath, and then I made his acquaintance. The people appear very cordial, and I think it will make me a good church home.

My reading is confined to McKensie's "Life of Dickens," in which I am very much interested. With much love to you and mother, I remain, affectionately,

Reading.

Your *would be* dutiful son   WILLIE.

Rochester, Nov. 5, 1871.

MY DEAR FATHER—

I suppose by this time you have returned from your north-western trip.

Prof. Gilmore asked me to come to the Bethlehem Mission last night, and I went. They have just organized a church with eighty members, and wanted me to play the organ (cabinet), so I consented. Service is held in the morning, and prayer-meeting in the evening.

This A. M. Dr. Anderson (Prex) preached the first sermon. His ideas were deep, and evidently the result of much study. The church was nearly full. This afternoon I went to the mission, and my boys were very good. Mr. Phillips, the Supt., put the singing in my charge; so you see I have all at once taken quite a responsibility upon me, and you may rest assured I will try to acquit myself in a manner that will be creditable to myself as well as to those who gave me the position. But I must go to supper, and thence to teachers' meeting and church.

I have just returned from church, and I don't know when I have been made to feel my situation here as a stranger as to-night. But two members spoke to me, and what they said seemed to be a concentration of an abridgement, so few and precise were their utterances.

At work in Mission Sunday School.

Feels himself to be a stranger.

If any young strangers come into your meetings, father, please speak to them. You have no idea how lonesome one feels, when neglected by those from whom he should most expect attention.

Please give much love to mother. Hoping you are both feeling the better for your trip, I am

Your affectionate son   WILLIE.

Rochester, Nov. 21, 1871.

MY DEAR FATHER—

Yours of the 11th inst. was duly received, and would have been answered sooner, but I have been hard at work most of the time; the spirit was willing, but the flesh was weak.

I am having grand times at the East Ave. Church, and I have good news for you, viz.: Fassett told me yesterday he had found his Savior. You may imagine my feelings, when you know we are together most all the time. What a pleasant surprise it will be to his parents! At present there is a good deal of religious feeling among the students—"our class," especially.

Dr. Buckland preaches at the church, and a great many students attend. My class are

Grand times at East Ave. Church.

Conversions.

improving. I am not prepared to say how many, if any, will go home with me Xmas. It seems a good way off. Sometimes I think the wheels of time are running down, it moves so slowly; but at other, 't is almost impossible to keep up with it.

Years ago I thought there was a great deal of romance connected with college life, but I have found all such ideas to be groundless; it's no jest, but stern reality. This is the first time I have been under the necessity of being my own man. Home is too far off to retreat to, and the little squalls, seemingly large to an inexperienced voyager, must be brunted.

Many times I have had occasion to thank God for my early christian training, and my present faith in Him. A student that is a christian is doubly marked: first, by the community, as a student, and second, by his fellows, as a christian. Yet I have never enjoyed my religion so much as I do at the present time.

Last week the hebdomadal epistle did not go at its wonted period; the reason was, that I put it in the back part of my Bible, expecting I would think to mail it when I passed

Hard study.

Thanks for early Christian training.

the box, but it flattened down so that I did
not see it until it accidentally fell out while I
was reading. Love to you and mother.

Affectionately, your son WILLIAM.

W. Stickney,

Washington, D. C.,

U. S. A., N. A., West. Hem., Tem. Zone.

Rochester, Nov. 27, 1871.

DEAR FATHER—

Your letter of 24th inst. came to hand
this morning, just before I started for college.
I can't find words in which to express my
thanks for it.

The past week has been one of particular
interest in the college, and out of it, as regards religious matters.

Our class is getting waked up, and we
are having grand good times at our prayer-
meetings. Last Saturday some christians
spoke who have not opened their lips before,
concerning Christ, since their connection with
the University. The meeting was protracted
for the purpose of praying for our classmates.
At the church (East Ave.), last night, two
said that, during the past week, they felt as
if the burden of sin had rolled from their

Good
times.

7

backs, and quite a number asked the prayers of God's people. I really think that God is with us. It seems the older I become, the more do I appreciate the blessings with which I am surrounded, and the more do I have of God's love. Yet, as I said to one of the boys the other day, the more fully do I realize my responsibilities as a christian.

Yesterday morning Professor Gilmore preached about St. Paul as a man of *one idea*, and held him up as a model. In the P. M. I went to the S. S., and my boys were unusually good. One remained after the exercises were over, and I had quite a long talk with him about the importance of being a christian. Father, pray for that boy, as well as for his teacher.

Anxiety for the conversion of his Sunday School scholars.

Success to you in the preparation of the cantata. Don't work too hard; let each do his share.

Opinion of Tammany.

You speak of "Tammany." That's a thing of the past; its stronghold is weakened, its leaders are palsied, and it is fast going to ruin. I think it would not be inappropriate to hold a special day of thanksgiving over its destruction. The habitation of the wicked shall not stand, but will fall as a house built upon the sand. New York should "Praise God" till the heavens ring with the echoes, so great a scourge have they been released from.

How is Dr. Parker's health? I suppose he is hard at work in the church. Are the salaries of the pastor and sexton paid up regularly? I think one reason why our church dont have souls converted in it, is *because it dont pay its debts.* If the members are not sufficiently interested to pay their pew-rents, are they, can they be very much interested in the enlargement of Christ's church. I think it is just as much a duty for us to pay our debts as it is to pray.

Concern for the church at home.

Each member of the church and congregation here is expected to pay something per quarter.

Mr. Phillips handed me the inclosed card *for you.* They are very nice people. They asked me in yesterday P. M., and it seemed *almost* like home. We sat around the piano and I played, and we all sung those good old tunes you like so much — Hamburg, Rockingham, Duke Street, &c.

I wish I could be with you and help eat the Thanksgiving turkey; but for the *first time* my seat must be vacant. I expect my dinner will be very much as that upon other days.

Impressions of the earthly great.

.Not long since I met Mr. ——, [a member of his church]; he spoke, and that was all. I should like to know him, but *boys* must n't have too high aspirations.

My health is first rate, and with much love to you and mother, I am

      Your affectionate son   WILL.

           Looneyville, Dec. 1, 1871.

DEAR FATHER—

You must n't think I have fetched up at the insane asylum; but I concluded to accept the invitation of my friend Ed. Adams, and spend Thanksgiving-day with him.

Thanksgivingday.

Yesterday I went to church, and heard a Methodist minister. He advanced some good ideas. His sermon was orthodox, and seemed to please the people.

Ed. and I sung in the choir, and *of course* the singing was good—Federal Street, Eltham, Doxology, and a Thanksgiving Anthem. The *last* was *first* rate.

In the afternoon we had a very good dinner, and afterwards spent the evening at one of the neighbors, and had a splendid time.

I am writing in Ed.'s school, which is four miles from his home. He teaches to make money to pay his way through college. I have enjoyed this day, and think I will return better able to appreciate the blessings with which I am surrounded.

Mr. and Mrs. A. are very pleasant people, and do all they can to make me enjoy myself. While I write it is snowing quite hard. It seems odd to see so much snow at this season of the year. The mercury has been down to 10°, and I find myself able to stand the cold as well as the residents here.

But Ed. is having a spelling-match, and I must see the fun.

Will write more soon.

Give much love to mother.

Write soon, to

    Your affectionate son   WILL.

The following letter shows that the young student was entering upon that stage of college life so full of the spirit of destructive criticism—one of the most dangerous periods of youth—when, with the enlargement of

A critical period.

the mental vision, more than one side of
some great principle, or truth, or fact is
seen, without ability to discern their essential unity. It is just here that two ways
meet—the one leading to scepticism, the
other to humble, and devout, and resolute
faith. Over which of these two ways his
feet traveled, his own letters shall bear testimony. They show the victory that overcometh the world—even his faith.

Rochester, Dec. 5, 1871.

MY DEAR FATHER—

I arrived safely from my Thanksgiving
trip Saturday night. Sunday morning it
was very cold, and thinking it would continue so, I went out without my rubbers, but
by noon the snow and ice had thawed, and I
returned with wet feet. I tried to dry them
before S. S., but when night came, I had a
severe cold accompanied with a headache.
Monday morning I could hardly speak, so
I kept house. This morning my throat was
sore, but it is now better, and I hope to go to
college to-morrow, D. V.

It is very stormy; the wind has been blowing hard all day, and at the same time snowing.

Lately I have been thinking a good deal about the immortality of the soul. 1st Timothy, 6th chapter, and 16th verse, says, that Christ *only* hath immortality; and in 17th verse of 1st ch., it speaks of Christ as immortal, and implies to my mind that immortality was the property of God, excluding mankind. Yet, in the 10th vs. of 1st ch. of 2d Tim., it speaks of immortality being *brought to light* through the Gospel. What does that mean? In the 13th vs. of the 3d ch. of John, we read, that no man ascended up to heaven but the Son of man. Now how can we reconcile that with the 11th vs. of 2d ch. of 2d Kings, which says, Elijah went up by a whirlwind into heaven? And where did Moses and Elias come from when they appeared at the Mount of Transfiguration?

Again, in the 16th vs. of the 6th ch. of 1st Tim., what does it mean by saying, that no one can approach unto the light in which God dwells, unless it be that *no one dwells* in his presence?

Do n't you think the theory that there is a place of rest for departed spirits, before the final resurrection, is a plausible one? because it says, in 31st vs. of 2d ch. of Acts, that

Immortality.

Speculation.

Christ, at his resurrection, was not in hell,
nor was his flesh permitted to see corruption;
and in the 17th vs. of the 20th ch. of John, it
states, that Christ had not yet ascended to
heaven. So where was he?

Father, I ask these questions, *not* because I doubt the religion I profess, for I
love it more and more every day, but because I want to know where I stand, and
what I believe.

With my limited knowledge of the Bible,
I am unable to answer these questions as
they from time to time present themselves to
my mind. So please enlighten me.

One more question: Do you recall what
caused the "Dark day," in 1780? (I think
that was the year.) I was asked whether
it could be accounted for by science, and
was unable to answer.

Social re-
cognition.When I returned from my Thanksgiving
trip, I found invitations to dine with the
Prex, Prof. Gilmore, Mr. Morse, Mr. Bene-
dict, and Mrs. Gorton. Was not that pretty
well for a Freshman? Cash account inclosed. When you see "contributions, one
dollar," you may exclaim, "Charity covereth
a multitude of sins"; but I am old enough to

know that honesty is the best policy. But I must say, Good night. Give much love to mother, and write soon to

Your affectionate son WILLIE.

Rochester, Tuesday night,
Dec. 19, 1871.

DEAR FATHER —

You will have to excuse the brevity of this epistle, as we have an examination in Greek to-morrow, and I am reading over the work of the term. I have just finished the Anabasis, and will go to work at once at my Greek grammar. On Thursday, I will find out what I *do n't* know of algebra, and Friday will make us stand around in Latin. Next time I will write more at length. I hope to be with you before long.

Give love to mother, and accept much for yourself,

From your affectionate son WILLIAM.

At the close of the term, Will came to Washington, and passed a happy Christmas.

January sixth, he advised us of his safe arrival in Rochester, and warm greetings by many friends.

Christmas at Washington and then back to Rochester.

Rochester, Jan'y 10, 1872.

MY DEAR FATHER—

I propose to take part of my time this morning, and inform you how I have prospered since my return.

Sunday morning brought to us a capital sermon from Dr. Buckland, on the "manner and results of the workings of the Holy Spirit." It was instructive and interesting.

At S. S., in the afternoon, my boys were attentive, and seemed to be interested, on account of which I felt very much encouraged; but you know the best is saved to the last of the feast, so in this case, for in the evening Prof. Gilmore baptized six persons — three ladies and three gentlemen. The house was crowded, and the meeting was interesting. Monday afternoon fourteen rose for prayer, and we have indications that the spirit of God is resting on our city. Last night I attended a prayer-meeting at East Ave. Ch., and it was pleasant to be there. To-day is set apart for the day of prayer for colleges.

Give much love to mother, remember me kindly to all inquiring friends, and write soon to your aff. son   WILL.

Baptisms.

Rochester, Jan'y 16, 1872.

DEAR FATHER—

As I have studied my lessons, and finished my reading, I will proceed to answer your letter of the 11th inst., which came duly to hand.

The beneficial influences of a teachers' meeting are not mine to boast of. The lessons are not what I desire for my class. The boys know nothing of the life and teachings of Christ, and I think it is preposterous to teach any thing before the pupils have even a crude idea of the Hero of the Bible.

Sunday evening I remained at home, and prepared a few questions on the "Life of Christ," from the first and second chapters of Matt. They are simple, and I think will be interesting. I propose to copy them—one for each boy in the class—and see if I can persuade them to study them.

Prepares questions on Life of Christ for his class in Sunday School.

It always seemed strange to me that a christian could be so glib in business meetings, and so *very* quiet in prayer-meetings. What we want is men of clear, sensible ideas, who are not afraid to speak them.

Much obliged for your good opinion of my account.

I am about to send you a keg of winter-green cider. The cider is a present from Mr. Gorton, the *keg from me.* You know we must n't despise small things, and if it was not for the keg, you could n't have the cider!

Let me congratulate you on seeing another Jan'y 15. [The anniversary of his parents' marriage.] May He who rules the universe, and directs the affairs of men as well, permit you to see many more years of conjugal happiness. In the past the Lord has dealt with us with a bountiful hand. and may it not close, nor his blessings cease, as you approach the meridian of life. And may the love of the Lord increase in your hearts till they will hold no more.

Give much love to mother. not forgetting to appropriate your share.

It is nearly half-past ten—time for a student to rest. So good night.

Affectionately, your son   WILLIE.

Rochester, Feb'y 25, 1872,
Sunday night.

MY DEAR MOTHER—

As I have nearly an hour before church, I will devote it to you.

Father's letter, enclosing check, was duly received, and I would return many thanks for it.

Things are just about as usual, though the monotony was disturbed two or three weeks ago by the expressman bringing me *two* boxes. Their contents were soon displaced, and you would have laughed to see me *going through* them. I am ever so much obliged. The books were all right, and the picture and paper-rack both sound. The picture is right over my piano, and I enjoy looking at it very much. How kind of you and father to think of my wants, and things that were not wants.

Presents from home

* * * * *

I never knew how much I loved you and father until I came here. Everything is so different from home.

What's father so busy about, that he can't write a good old-fashioned letter? How prospers the Women's Christian Association? It is first and foremost, as ever, in your thoughts, I suppose.

I was asked if I would take an organ at four hundred a year. I declined. The bells are ringing, and I must to meeting.

Love to all inquiring friends, especially to father.

Write soon, to your affectionate son

WILLIE.

Rochester, March 16, 1872.

MY DEAR FATHER—

Your letter, written just one week ago, lies before me.

Ill health.

I have not felt very well lately; my head has troubled me more or less, and my practice has been to go to bed as soon as my lessons were learned—and often before. Have not been to college the last two or three days. There is nothing in particular the matter, but a good deal in general; and· that's the worst of it, because I don't know what to do for myself. I have just such a turn as I had in Jan'y, 1871, when I stayed away from school a week or so. To-day I feel better for my rest. Next week will be spent in preparing myself for examinations, and so soon as they are over, I propose to take the first train for home. At the class election, held recently, I was unanimously elected secretary.

During the past month I have heard

Punchon and Collyer lecture, and Madame Diehl Randall read. The first two were interesting, but the last was considerably below par.

I celebrated the 22d ult. by listening to Wendell Phillips on "Labor and Capital." His arguments were forcible.

In my cash account you will find several items for purchase of books (my weakness,) viz.: works on "Phonography," "Words and their Uses," by R. G. White; "Legends of the Old Testament," by Gould; "Classic Atlas," by Long; "Correct Pronunciation," Soule and Wheeler; "Smallest Ed. of Shakspeare," and "Bartlett's Quotations."

Mr. and Mrs. Gorton have treated me with marked kindness. In all my experience away from home, I have never received so much attention.

The church is progressing, and we are all hard at work.

Love to mother, and accept much for yourself, from your affectionate son

WILLIE.

After a brief visit home, he is again at his post.

Lectures and reading.

Rochester, April 11, 1872.

MY DEAR FATHER—

You see that I have arrived, and it only remains for me to add, safe and sound. On our way we—Geo. Ordway and I—stopped at the Fifth Ave. Hotel, N. Y. Tuesday we went down street on Banner [for S. S.] business. Finding myself in the vicinity of Mr. L.'s office, I called in. Receiving a polite invitation to visit Staten Island, at one o'clock I took the boat, and met a cordial reception, stopping to dinner. All wished to be remembered to you and mother.

This is your birthday. Let me congratulate you with the hope that your years of usefulness and happiness may be many, and you may ripen into a good old age. I feel, in the coming years, as I grow older, I may be of more assistance to you, and may serve you as becomes a son.

"Adieu." Much love to mother, and write soon to

Your affectionate son   WILLIE.

Rochester, April 26, 1872.

MY DEAR FATHER—

Yours of 24th inst. is received. I would

have written before, but we have had just as much as we could do.

I am glad to hear of Nellie's [buggy horse] improvement. Hope you will not loan her to any one to use during your absence from the city. ·

By reëlecting their former President, the Council showed their wisdom.

I have adopted your suggetion, and every day exercise an hour at the gymnasium. I feel better for it.

I have been elected leader of the singing in S. S., and chorister in the church. The choir will sing their first anthem next Sunday. My college duties must not suffer from these new duties. So soon as I feel they do, I will resign.

This morning the Prex gave us a good political talk.

Friday night the Sophomore class buried "Calculus." The members of the class were dressed in white sheets, and wore masks, except the Priest, who was in black. They had a coffin, in which the conquered study was placed. After a funeral sermon, and some singing, the coffin was placed on a pyre and reduced to ashes, which were then

Elected chorister at the church.

Burial of Calculus.

gathered up, placed in an urn, and buried. The grave is marked by a cross board, bearing the inscription,—"'74 Calculus. Died March 27, 1872."

Tell mother that wearing a stove-pipe hat has a good effect upon her son.

Much love to mother and yourself, from
Your affectionate son   WILLIE.

Rochester, Tuesday, May 21, 1872.
MY DEAR FATHER—

Every thing is moving in the even tenor of its ways here, and the monotony of college life remains unbroken.

Thursday I thoroughly enjoyed a ride to the lake. Saturday we had a shower. Sunday it rained, and yesterday it *poured.*

Work.

We are all very busy, as this is our hardest term, and it requires *hard work* to keep up a good standing in the class.

If any of my friends complain of my silence, please tell them our days are bounded on all sides by hard work.

Tell mother she must not work too hard in the W. C. A.

Please send my fishing-pole and tackle. You will find reel, corks, sinkers, and rod in the south closet of my room. Yesterday Ed., "Deacon" Rowley, and I went to the lake, and caught two dozen black bass. This morning at breakfast we did ample justice to them. Ed. sings out, "Remember me to your mother"; so please deliver the message, with much love to mother and you. Bon nuit.

Recreation.

Your affectionate son   WILLIE.

Rochester, June 15, 1872.

MY DEAR FATHER —

Yours of 3d inst., enclosing check, has been received; for both of which, many thanks.

I suppose you have received the paper containing an account of the doings of '75. We had a grand time, and though not good for much the next day, the class was benefited.

The 8th inst. was "Class day." I sent you an account of that, also, in the "Union." I was disappointed in the manner in which the exercises were conducted. The senior forgot his speech, and many of the graduates acted more like boys than young men preparing to battle with the hardships of the world.

Class day.

College Jokes.

Just before "Class day," a notice appeared on the Bulletin board of rather a mystical character, and the next day the flagpole was lying on the ground. A few days ago another similar notice was seen, and on the following day the Juniors did not recite in mathematics, as the blackboards were greased from end to end. To-day another notice was posted, so I expect we will have more of these silly performances. On Wednesday, the 26th, examinations commence, and Friday will close our apprenticeship as Freshmen, and we ascend one step—no "*more*" fools. Much love to mother.

Affectionately, your son   WILLIE.

Rochester, June 27, 1872.

MY DEAR FATHER—

Examinations.

Yesterday we had an examination in *Livy*. Inclosed, you will find the paper. I answered every question to the 6th section, and just then Prof. Morey informed us "time was up," so I had to stop.

This P. M. we have a Greek oral examination, with Dr. Kendrick. I expect to get through all right. To-morrow mathematics, and I can safely say I dread it.

Please meet me at the St. James, in Boston, the 4th prox.

With much love to mother, and hoping to see you both soon, I remain

Your affectionate son   WILL.

After a pleasant tour to the White Mountains, and a visit to his friends in Southport, Will returned to his studies.

Visits the White Mountains

44 Park Ave., Rochester, Oct. 5, 1872.
MY DEAR FATHER—

Your letter of 1st inst. came to hand, and was very welcome.

At this end of the line every thing is progressing favorably.

Yesterday Dr. Anderson called me aside and suggested that I ride on horseback, because, he said, he noticed I did not look very vigorous. I thanked him for his interest. This A. M. he repeated the suggestion, advising me to ride three or four times a week. Think I will try it.

The other day I made out my cash acc't for June, *et seq.*

Cash account.

My expenses for Freshman year were $1,103.21. Doing pretty well, was n't it, to get rid of so much money?

In your last you signed yourself, "Affectionately your son." Much obliged; but I
guess you mistook the person.

The supper bell warns me I am wanted
below. Much love to mother.

　　　Affectionately, *your* son   WILLIE.

　　　　　　Rochester, Nov. 20, 1872.
MY DEAR MOTHER—

Your nice letter of the 16th is before me.
The braces are upon my back, and my carriage is more erect. They feel very comfortable. The jacket, too, is much admired.
Heretofore I have only worn it on Sundays,
because it is so short it reveals the seat of
my every-day pants, which are somewhat
dilapidated. I was measured yesterday for
a new pair. The study-lamp you sent goes
first rate. I hardly know what to think of
my head, which gives me a good deal of
trouble. Dr. Anderson says I have dyspep-
sia. I have done little or no studying the
past month, except in French. I am now
some better, and expect to work hard in
preparation for examination. Mrs. Douglass
is very kind, and says, if I am too sick to
write, she will.

I have purchased a chromo, called a "Highland Lake," which is the gem of my "gallery."

The other night I was initiated into the Delta Kappa Epsilon Society, which is a *very literary* one.

The other day the Latin Professor called up a student, whom I will call P., and asked him to give the subject of the 1st Satire, in 2d book of Horace. P. was silent. Prof. then called for the first sentence. P. replied, he could not read *that*. As a *dernier resort*, the Prof. called for the *second*. P. replied, he could not read *that*. Prof. then said P. reminded him of the honest negro, who told his master one of his own oxen was dead, and after a short pause, added, the other was dead, also. He said he did not like to tell it all at once, for fear the *shock would be too great*. We thought that a pretty good joke on P.

We have commenced analytical geometry and calculus. — *Tough*. But "Pranzo pronto subito."

With an indefinite (on account of its large quantity) supply of love, I am

Your loving son   WILLIE.

A considerate student.

P. S. May you enjoy your Thanksgiving.
Wᴍ. Sᴏʙᴇʀ Sɪᴅᴇs.

Rochester, Dec. 2, 1872.

MY DEAR MOTHER—

Although I do n't owe you a letter, I am going to be very generous to-day and tell you what a nice time I have had during the past few days. Friday I left Clarence — where I wrote father's letter—and after the four mile ride in the sleigh, took the cars for Buffalo. The further west we went, the more snow we met, so that when we reached our destination, we found good sleighing. George S. and Marcus H., classmates, were waiting for us, and seemed to be real glad to see us. George took us to his home. His mother is a real nice woman—reminding me very much of you. His father is a fine-looking man, very particular in his dress, conversation, &c. That evening we called on one of the young lady friends of the boys. We had a pleasant time, but did not stay long, as she had an engagement.

Saturday morning, after breakfast, we went to the Synagogue, to please H. The prayers and readings were in Hebrew, the

Buffalo.

singing and sermon in German, so that, to me, every thing was unintelligible. The Rabbi chose for his text, the death of Horace Greeley. I spent the sermon time in reading the preface to the Prayer - Book (Jewish.) From that I learned that the Reform Jews do not expect to return to Jerusalem; also, that they look for a Messianic *Era*—not a Messiah in person. They also believe the souls of the dead are affected by the prayers of those on earth. I never knew these things before.

We took dinner with H., and had a regular Jewish meal. The meat had been inspected, and all the veins removed, and the blood allowed to drip out. We had no butter, as it is not permitted to have butter and meat at the same time. At dinner they generally have what they call "the meat dishes," and for tea, "the milk dishes;" and it is contrary to their law to use the same dishes (plates, &c.,) for one meal that they have for another.

After dinner we visited the Young Men's Library, also the Grosvenor Library. The former contains about 25,000, and the latter about twelve thousand vols. The former

Jewish synagogue

Jewish meal.

10

is self-supporting, while the latter is endowed.

Sunday morning I attended church. The minister did pretty well, considering he graduated from Andover only last Sept. Singing poor—no choir. We boys sung almost as much as all the rest put together.

In the evening we went to the M. E. church—dedicatory service of a new edifice. They raised yesterday morning twenty thousand dollars. Last night they made another effort to pay the debt. We left at ten, and they were then fifteen hundred short.

George goes home with me Christmas; so you must be on the lookout for us. But I can't put much more on this sheet, so will say Good-bye.

Give lots of love to father, and write soon to

   Your affectionate son   WILLIE.

        Rochester, Dec. 14, 1872.
MY DEAR FATHER—

I thought you and mother would be glad to know I passed my examination in "Ancient History," this morning, all right. No mistake of omission or commission; conse-

quently I feel quite happy. But this is only a foretaste. Next week we have Latin,
French, and mathematics. During the present week I have worked hard, and expect
to be very busy next week. We are having
sleighing, and the bells make merry with
their tintinnabulations. There are some fine
horses on the streets, but I would not give
"Nellie" for any of them.

I expect Geo. Stearns will spend Christmas with me. He stands "A No. 1" in his
class, and sings bass. We anticipate great
pleasure.

David and Theo keep me pretty well
posted about general affairs.

Dr. A. expressed pleasure at the receipt
of the Autobiography. He continues a pa-
ternal care over me, and occasionally permits me to come into his awful presence, for
the purpose of asking after my health.

Love to mother, and kind remembrances
to all inquiring friends.

Affectionately, your son WILLIE.

After a happy Christmas at home, with
his friend Stearns, Will returned to the University.

Rochester, Jan'y 11, 1873.

MY DEAR FATHER—

Yours of the 8th is received. Every thing here is progressing as usual. Last Monday we paid our respects to Dr. Kendrick—"Demosthenes' orations against Phillip," and "on the Crown;" Prof. Mixer—"Sprechen sie Deutsch;" and Prof. Quimby—"Calculus." As to this last, it is almost like casting pearls before swine, to set before *us* the beauties (?) of calculus. We can't see 'em.

So far, our class has been signally blessed by Death passing us by. But one of our boys is now very sick with erysipelas. I have doubts of his recovery. I called on him yesterday, and found him delirious. We boys don't half appreciate the blessings God gives us in life and health.

Before leaving home I accidentally broke one of the windows in the door of the coupé, and forgot to mention it.

Mr. Morehouse, *our pastor*, has come. and preached first-rate last Sunday, from Eph. 6: 19, 20. There is considerable religious interest in the S. S., and we hope for an abundant blessing.

I must not forget to tell you that the

Prof. of Higher Mathematics told the Faculty I passed a very creditable examination, considering the disadvantages under which I labored. I feel it was just, but almost too good to be true. Love to mother.

Affectionately, your son   WILLIE.

Among the papers found since my son's death, is a composition upon the "Authenticity of Ossian's Poems," written in college about this time. It bears evidence of thorough study of his subject, and was highly commended by his teacher. An eminent scholar, who recently read the paper, returned it with a note, saying: "It shows great merit, and independence of judgment, in such a young writer. Besides, his decision in the matter is *decidedly* right."

AUTHENTICITY OF OSSIAN'S POEMS.

For First Term. Soph. Year.

In the latter part of the eighteenth century the literary circles of England were stirred by the publication of what purported to be a translation and compilation of some "Gaelic Poems" written in the fourth century.

Jas. Macpherson.

The Highlander.

Fragments of Ancient Poetry.

Fingal.

The "translator," James Macpherson, was born at Kingussie, in 1738, was intended for the church, and received the necessary education at Aberdeen. At the age of twenty he published the "Highlander," which proved at once his ambition and his incapacity. It was a miserable production.

In 1760 he published another volume — "Fragments of Ancient Poetry," translated from the Gaelic or Erse language. These "fragments" he professed to have obtained from his countrymen, whom he had heard rehearse portions of ancient poems.

This publication created such an interest, that a subscription was made to enable the author to visit the highlands and collect such other poems as he might be able to find. The tour proved quite successful, for in 1762 an Epic Poem, in six books, called "Fingal," was published, and the next year another Epic, of eight books, was given to the public.

These poems attracted general attention, and were universally read, but not without some misgivings as to their authenticity.

Mr. Taine's statement will apply as well to the prevailing opinion of that time as to the present. Alluding to Mr. Macpherson, he says: "A Scotchman, of not overmuch wit, having written, to his cost, an unsuccessful rhapsody, wished to recover himself, went to the mountains of his country, gathered picturesque images, collected fragments of legends, plastered over the whole with an abundance of eloquence and rhetoric, and created a Celtic Homer, Ossian."

Taine's opinion.

Critics tell us that the plot of "Fingal" is the same as that of the "Highlander," but that the names of individuals and places are changed, and that the poem has been embellished with some fragments of Gaelic legends.

The nearest approach to the "Temora." that can be found, is in the "Death of Oscar," a ballad of sixty stanzas, but the resemblance is so faint as to be hardly recognizable.

On account of the controversy that arose in regard to the genuineness of these poems. the "Highland Society" of Edinboro' appointed a committee of inquiry to investigate the subject; and in their report the committee stated that they had "not been able to obtain any one poem the same in title and tenor."

Committee of inquiry.

Who is
Ossian?

It will be remembered, that Mr. Macpherson makes Ossian a Scotchman, but tradition represents him as an Irishman—the son of Fionn or Fingal Mac Cumhal.

In the *Chronicon Scotorum,* no mention is made of King Fingal, and although the genealogy of the clans has been pushed to the utmost, not a single family has been found to be derived from the Fions. They were unknown to Monro in his genealogies of the clans, and are mentioned in Buchanan's Surnames as an Irish militia, commanded by Fion Macoel, concerning which, "divers rude rhymes are retained by the Irish and some of the highlanders."

But even granting that Ossian was a Scotchman, there is left a wide field for argument.

Historical
discrepancies.

First, it would be well to notice some historical discrepancies, which are sufficiently glaring to be considered.

Beginning about the year two hundred, we find that Comhall, the grandfather of Ossian, burnt Balclutha, the Alcluith of Bede, and the Dumbarton of more modern times. But Laing, in his history of Scotland, tells us that this place was built by

the Romans, in 308, and called by them The-
odosia, in honor of Theodosius, General of
Valentia; and as more conclusive evidence
of the non-existence of this town during the
time of Comhall, Ptolemy, in his enumera-
tion of the towns of each nation, makes no
mention of this.

Again, in Comala, we read of Fingal,
the father of Ossian, encountering Caracalla
on the banks of the Carron, which would
seem to conflict with Mr. Laing's statement,
that it was not until 258 that the Scots, under
the leadership of Fergus MacErth, came to
Scotland.

In describing the Orkney islands, Mr.
Macpherson would have us believe that they
were peopled by the Scandinavians, and that
the scenery was varied with "aged trees,"
and that a "rock, with all its echoing wood"
and "flaming oaks," were also there; whereas, history informs us that they were possessed by the Picts; and Solinus, a cotem-
porary of Fingal, describes the islands as
"orcades numero tres, vacant homines, non
habent sylvas, tantum junceis herbis inhor-
rescunt cetera earum nudæ arenæ et rupes
tenent."

Quotation
from
Solinus.

11

Errors not
confined
to Ancient
History.

Errors are not by any means confined to *Ancient* History. Messrs. Shaw and Hill, also Dr. Young, searched the highlands, but could discover nothing concerning "Swaran," but of Magnus Barefoot, who, seizing Cantire and the adjacent isles, was killed in the beginning of the twelfth century, and who, with an anachronism not uncommon in traditions, is represented in some rude ballads, as encountering Fingal.

In the first "fragments" of Fingal, Swaran was called "Garva," a literal translation of "Magnus" into Erse; but the fictitious Swaran was afterwards substituted.

Thus do we find the *historical* portion of Mr. Macpherson's so-called translations untrustworthy. Still another test would we suggest, and that is to compare the manners and customs of Ossian's time, as set forth by Mr. Macpherson, with the opinions of historians.

Comparison with historians.

In "Ossian" we read of generous heroes clad in complete steel, and of chivalric knights quaffing the wine from sparkling shells in the halls of mossy towers, and traversing the restless waters of the Northern Ocean in large ships.

But Dio, Herodian, and Hume seem to differ from him. They tell us that the natives discarded any helmet or mail, but, armed only with a narrow shield, a lance, and a short sword, they kept up the guerilla warfare in which they took so much delight; that they dwelt in booths, and subsisted on pasturage and hunting.

Discrepancies.

Solinus informs us that they had no means of navigation, except by currachs, which cross the Irish channel during a few days only of the summer solstice.

The next question is, if Mr. Macpherson did not have any poems to *translate*, where did he obtain his poetical ideas and expressions? for the "Highlander" certainly proved that he did not have the genius to originate such poetry.

Mr. Shaw answers the question, when he alludes to "the numerous passages in these works evidently plagiarized from the whole range of literature, from the Bible and Homer down to Shakspeare, Milton, and even Thomson."

Plagiarism.

One example will serve to illustrate this statement. A portion of Ossian's *Address to the Sun* is as follows: "The moon is lost in heaven, but thou art forever the same, rejoicing in the strength of thy course. But to Ossian thou lookest in vain, for he beholdeth thy beams no more."

In Milton's "Paradise Lost," we find the same idea, expressed in similar language:

> "But thou
> Revisit'st not these eyes that roll in vain
> To find thy piercing ray."

Again, in "Samson Agonistes," we read:

> "The sun to me is dark
> And silent as the moon,
> When she deserts the night,
> Hid in her interlunar cave."

Job, also, uses the words, "He rejoiceth in his strength."

When the poems were first published, Mr. Macpherson, untaught by that best of teachers, experience, unwisely incorporated the following in his preface:

"Poetry, like virtue, receives its reward after death. His [the poet's] foibles, however, are obliterated by death, and his better part, his writings, remain. His character is formed from them, and he that was no extraordinary man in his own time, becomes the wonder of succeeding ages. Their virtues remain, but the vices which were once blended with their virtues, have died with themselves. This consideration might induce a man diffident of his abilities to ascribe his own compositions to a person whose remote antiquity, and whose situation when alive, might well answer for faults which would be inexcusable in a writer from this age."

These allusions were certainly uncalled for, unless *their* author was also the author of the poems. They were withdrawn from subsequent editions.

In view of the foregoing, the most natural conclusion would seem to be, that the names of Fingal and Ossian are known among the Irish, and perhaps among the highlanders to a limited extent, as heroes that existed in almost prehistoric times.

But that over twenty thousand verses, with numberless historical facts, could have been preserved by oral tradition for fourteen centuries, seems preposterous.

Mr. Wordsworth denies the authenticity of the poems, and David Hume wrote Dr. Blair, that he had heard "them totally rejected as a palpable and most impudent

Conclusion.

Gigantic
fraud.

forgery. This opinion has, indeed, become very prevalent among the men of letters in London." So that we are not alone in turning our backs upon this gigantic fraud practised upon the whole literary world.

Feb'y 8, 1873.

W. S. STICKNEY,
Class '75, U. of R.

Rochester, Feb'y 17, 1873.

MY DEAR MOTHER—

Let me congratulate you upon the return of this, your birth day. It may bring with it some regrets, but the blessings of God are so numerous, that I know you have not forgotten them. Then the day is sunshiny, and the air is balmy, harbingers of good. May you have, during the year just entered upon, all the pleasures, and none of the sorrows, of the past year.

Sociables
and recep-
tions.

I had a grand time last Friday night. The sociable of Mr. Brown's church was to be held at Dr. Anderson's residence, and having received several invitations I went. Mrs. A. gave me a kind reception, and I had a good time.

At half-past ten I took my departure

for the reception of Mr. Hiram Sibley, Jr., and Mrs. S., *née* Harper. The house was packed, and the bride was beautifully dressed in white satin. The presents were handsome and costly. Many of the guests wore powdered hair, à la Marie Antoinette. Dr. Anderson was there, and very agreeable. One other student, besides myself, graced the company. ✦George sends love.

Affectionately, your son   WILLIE.

Rochester, March 1, 1873.

MY DEAR FATHER—

It has been a long while since I have heard from home. It may be all true, that "no news is good news," but it makes a body feel more comfortable to have *some* news, even if it be but little.

We have been jogging along as usual. at the rate of seven days a week.

Day before yesterday the "Social Union" had a meeting, but I did not feel able to attend.

Last week Prof. Gilmore had the Faculty of the University, Drs. Strong and Buckland, of the seminary, the Revs. Brown and Morehouse, and Gen. Rathburn at his house to

Society.

spend the evening. All who had wives brought them. Of course, in such a select company, it was absolutely necessary for your son to be present, and I have reason to believe he was there; and, judging from his remarks upon the subject, I think he had a pretty good time. Why not? The supper was excellent, and the ladies were very agreeable.

Lecture.

Last night I heard a splendid lecture by Wendell Phillips, upon "Froude and the Irish Question," spiced with jokes which greatly tickled the audience, who were evidently sorry when he finished.

How prosper the church and S. S.? We have first-rate sermons from our pastor, and the school is increasing. Two expect to be baptized to-morrow.

Love to mother.

    Your loving son   WILLIE.

        Rochester, March 24, 1873.

DEAR FATHER—

Yours, inclosing check, received.

Saturday we had examination in history, and, although I hesitated about going in, as I felt rather miserable, I had the satisfaction of seeing the Prof. mark my work 10. To-day we have Greek, under Dr. Kendrick.

What time I have left after college studies and the paper, is given mostly to church meetings, S. S. lessons, and rehearsals.

I have here cast my first ballot. I tried to vote honestly; so, after inquiring about the candidates, found there was not much choice. Of all the evils, I chose the least. My ticket was democratic, liberal republican, and republican, and, as it happened, the very men I voted for were elected. Casts his first ballot

Many thanks for the check. Will be home, D. V., the last of this week.

Love to mother.

Affectionately, your son   WILLIE.

Rochester, June 19, 1873.

MY DEAR FATHER—

Yours of 2d inst, enclosing check, programme, and report of organ concert, and law-school invitations, *all* duly to hand.

I have not written, because we are now reviewing, and, owing to my absence at the beginning of the term, for me it is all advance. Since half-past twelve (it is now six) I have read five pages Wm. Tell, seven Reviewing.

12

of French selections, and nine in Tacitus. Every day I have reason to be thankful that I regained my strength before returning, for at no other time in my college course have I been able to do so much work.

Class Supper.
Friday, the 5th, we had class-supper, and it was a success, of course. All the boys, except one, went, and we had a thoroughly delightful time. We serenaded Dr. Kendrick and Prof. Gilmore, received speeches from each, and a collation, in addition, from the latter.

Our excursion club have decided to *do* the White Mts., instead of the Adirondacks.

In a few days you will receive prospectus of a college paper we ('75) propose to start, and would be glad for an *ad.* of Columbia Law-School. Love to mother.

Affectionately, your son WILLIE.

Rochester, June 27, 1873.

MY DEAR FATHER—

Yours of 23d received. The White Mountain trip includes the Franconia Notch, Crawford Notch, and Mt. Washington, towards Lake Umbagog. Most of the traveling will be done on foot.

I cannot leave before the middle of next month, as I attend the convention of the Y. M. C. A., at Po'keepsie, as a delegate, commencing the 9th.

Wednesday, had examination in Latin. Prof. Morey said I "passed splendidly."— Yesterday in French, to-day German. I passed pretty well in the last two; and now my work is about finished for this year.

This is the half-way house. We are no longer reckoned among the "lower-class men," but take our stand as Juniors.

Half-way house.

It does n't seem possible that two years have passed, but they are gone, to come up again at the last day. In thinking over the past, there is no question in my mind, that I 've grown; but whether my advancement has been as rapid and as steady as it should have been, is another thing. My health has heretofore been poor, but now is thoroughly good, and, with all the blessings a mortal can have, I hope to make greater strides onward in the future.

Last Friday night we had a rich joke on the Fresh. They went to have their class-supper. It is usual to serenade the Faculty after the repast. We (Sophs.) col-

Sophomores' joke on the Freshmen.

lected, and, having found the Fresh. songs, sang them to the Profs. Dr. Kendrick came out and talked to us about '76, and praised us sky high, never suspecting any thing wrong. We then went to Prof. Gilmore's, and he thanked us for our kindness, and lauded the class of '76. We then went to Dr. K.'s, and hid. Pretty soon the Fresh. came and sang, and *sang*, and SANG; finally the Dr. came to the *window*, and said, "'76 again! '76 is all glorious!" Whereupon we relieved the Fresh. of their astonishment by showing ourselves. They did not serenade any more that night.

Love to mother and yourself.

Your affectionate son　　　WILLIE.

Luzerne, N. Y., Aug. 1, 1873.

MY DEAR MOTHER—

I expect you begin to wonder what has become of your boy. Well, you see we are in the "stupidest place in the world," to use the language of the proprietor of our "Wayside Inn." It may be stupid, but it is a relief after being at Saratoga.

We are surrounded by a spur of the Adirondacks, and at a stone's throw from the hotel is Lake Luzerne, a small but very beautiful sheet of water, where ladies and children amuse themselves by rowing and fishing.

Though the "Lake of the Four Cantons" is suggested by the name, there is no resemblance between them. The high hills and small mountains, far and near, are very thickly wooded, softening the landscape, and varying it by different shades of green. Close by is a pine grove so dense the rays of the sun seldom penetrate it. This is a favorite resort for the ladies, to keep cool and sniff the aromatic air. This A. M. father and I fished for a little while in the Hudson, ten minutes' walk distant. We were told it was a splendid place for "fishing," and we found it so—but did not have a nibble. The hotel is comfortable, has *no bar*, and is a nice place for drinking copious draughts of pure, fresh air, and for reading the book of Nature from the works of God, so extensively spread out before us.

Fishing.

I expect to visit my friend George Ordway, at Waterloo.

We did n't go to the White Mts., after all. As the trip was abandoned, father sent

Interest in
the church
and chapel

me word to meet him in Saratoga, and we
have been together ever since—both in excellent health, and both wish you were with
us.

How come on the church, S. S., and Kendall Chapel? Father sends "lots of love,"
and take "lots more" from

Your affectionate son　　WILLIE.

Camp on Kearsarge Mountain, N. H.,
Aug. 13, 1873.

DEAR FATHER—

Will leave for New Market Junction
Monday, and will be with you at Bangor
Tuesday, if nothing happens. We are having a splendid time—cooking our own meals,
sleeping on spruce boughs, &c.

With love, your son　　WILLIE.

Waterloo, N. H., Aug. 15, 1873.

MY DEAR MOTHER—

You see I am still here, but to-morrow
expect to go to Fisherville, leaving there
Monday, and reaching Bangor Tuesday at
seven A. M., if all is well.

We "broke camp" on Mount Kearsarge
day before yesterday. I have had a splen-

did time; but I must tell you about it. Last Thursday, before I was at this house two hours, one of the boys drove up to the door, saluting me with, "You are the very fellow I want." I retired to my room, but soon appeared in a bluish-gray shirt, old pair of pants stuck in my boot legs, and to crown my "classic brow," my old felt hat (your delight ?); no vest or coat — the flannel shirt being sufficiently warm to keep me comfortable. In our wagon could be found ice, baked beans, coffee, sugar, etc., etc.

About ten o'clock, after a six mile ride, we reached our destination. The boys heard I was coming, and came down the hill and gave me a hearty, and I think, sincere welcome. A cup of coffee was soon made, and in the bright moonlight, with the mountains in silent grandeur looking down upon us, we took our evening meal. The tent was close by, and we soon retired to it. Spruce boughs formed our mattress, and over us we had a number of "comfortables." I slept soundly.

The next day we took turns washing dishes and doing the necessary chores about the camp. One day we took a tramp of thirteen miles, fishing and gunning. The

In camp.

Recrea-
tion.
views were magnificent. The scenery here is not grand, but the views are beautiful, and, by the dim light of the moon, are almost sublime.

Wednesday we concluded to descend to civilization. Accordingly, our camp was struck, and we have resumed our white shirts, collars, cuffs, and blackèd boots.

I had some headache yesterday, but feel rather better to-day. My visit here, at Mr. and Mrs. Ordways', has been very pleasant.

You have doubtless read of the sad affair of the Wawasset. What a blessing it is to know that He who made us, said, "I am with you alway." Those words have volumes of meaning, and worlds of comfort to me.

Take good care of your health, and do not forget, God wants the work of our bodies when they are in their *best* condition—our best work. With love.

Your affectionate son   WILLIE.

Returns to
college.
After a pleasant visit to Maine, Will returned, in good condition, to his studies, somewhat hastened by his duties as Secretary of the Board of Editors of the college paper.

Rochester, Sept. 23, 1873.

DEAR FATHER—

Having studied all my lessons since six o'clock, I have yet a few moments before breakfast. My health is good, and we are *very* busy. Seventy have been examined—about fifty in Freshman class.

Please send on the *ad.* for the Col. University soon as possible. Our paper goes to press Saturday, but will not be issued till Tuesday. Make the Law department prominent.

I am reading in college, Sophocles' Ajax, and studying Philosophy and Logic—enough to keep us very busy. All seemed glad to see me, when I made my appearance at church last Sunday.

The bell has rung. Give love to mother. Write soon, to

    Your affectionate son   WILLIE.

Rochester, Oct. 1, 1873.

MY DEAR MOTHER—

I believe this is my first letter to you this term. You must take the will for the deed. We are very busy unraveling hard problems in mechanics, cracking hard nuts of logic,

Study.

13

College
paper.

and digging up Greek roots. Besides this, we are to publish "The University Record." But the paper has gone to press, and I've finished copying my notes in logic and philosophy, and Dr. Kendrick will not be here to-morrow, so I have plenty of time to write to-day.

The first number of our paper will be out Friday. Receiving no *ad.* from father for the University, I wrote one myself, giving, as a compliment, two squares to the Law-school, in the first issue, whereas they only engaged one.

Tell father I have about given up the boat idea, as a useless expense. It costs less to *hire* than to *build.*

Met Uncle John, from Rockville, yesterday, on his way home from A. B. C. F. M. Went about with him some, and dined with him at the Osborn. He left at three P. M.

With love to yourself and father, and kind regards to friends,

Your affectionate son   WILLIE.

Rochester, Oct. 25, 1873.

MY DEAR FATHER—

This morning the expressman came up

and announced "a box" for me. I was expecting it, for mother's letter, received last night, announced its coming. Of course it was soon opened, and from the hay and paper emerged the beautiful present. I had no idea it would be so elegant, so I was the more surprised. The figures came in good shape, except the arm of Plato was cracked.

Gifts from home.

And now let me thank you and mother for your gifts. I am VERY much obliged, and will try to prove myself worthy of them. I think I really want to do only that which is right, but sometimes I forget myself, and utterly fail.

I do n't know as I felt very different yesterday [his 21st birthday] in entering the 2d Act of my life, from what I usually do. I have no desire to be different in any respect, except to grow in my christian life. All that I am, I know I owe to God and my parents, and my earnest desire and purpose is, that neither may be dishonored nor disgraced. What I have done in times past that was wrong or annoying to you, I 'm sorry for, and hope you will forget it, knowing you have forgiven.

Twenty-first birthday.

My health, now, is very good, so I do

my share of the work, which is quite a good deal. The second issue of the paper will soon appear.

With love to you and mother, I am

Your affectionate son   WILLIE.

Rochester, Nov. 28, 1873.

MY DEAR MOTHER—

Friday afternoon has again come around, and I take pleasure in writing you all the news. The box, with its contents, came all right. Many thanks.

Thanksgiving.

Thanksgiving day has come and gone. I took dinner here with four or five of the boys. After dinner, which was a good one, we sang the inclosed programme. At the second "music" I presided at the piano. The church was full. Prof. read, among other things, Jean Ingelow's "Divided." If you have it, please read it; I think you will like it. After the Sociable, about forty of us adjourned to the house of one of the Trustees, as a surprise (?) party. There we had a good time, and enjoyed a fine collation.

Oral dissertation.

This A. M. I had to deliver an "oral dissertation" before the class, on the "Musicians of England." Prof. Gilmore, and a good many of the boys, complimented me on my performance.

My health is first rate. I have been thinking how much we have to be thankful for; and, in looking over the year, I could n't wish any thing God had given me different from what it was. I try to do right, and live very near to my Savior, but sometimes, I know, I wander. How important to watch and pray. Review of the year.

Lots of love to you and father.

Your affectionate son   WILLIE.

A pleasant Christmas home, in company with his friend Stearns, and Will again returned to college.

Rochester, Jan'y 15, 1874.

[The anniversary of his parents' marriage.]

MY DEAR MOTHER—

Twenty-two years ago to-day —— well, I wont say any more, except to offer to you and father my sincere congratulations, with the hope you may see 'many anniversaries of this day.

We are crowding a great deal of work in a very little time, and, as it is all occupied, the days seem short. At work in college and in church.

Revival.

Our class is gradually losing its men. Ordway expects to leave for a position in Washington. Church matters are prospering; prayer meetings last week, this, and next. Last Sunday I received many compliments from my church friends for my playing.

College matters moving along as usual. "The [college] days of life are sisters—all alike, none just the same."

I must tell a joke on a sub-Fresh., who went to see the Dr. Having heard him spoken of as *Prex*, he addressed him as "Professor Prex." He said afterward, he thought " the Professor" had a very peculiar expression on his face !

With love to father.

Your affectionate son   WILLIE.

Rochester, Feb'y 13, 1874.

MY DEAR MOTHER—

Yours of the 9th inst. came to me while at prayer meeting, night before last, and it made my "cup full to running over." At the meeting, a young lady for whom I had prayed earnestly, said she had found her Savior. I will tell you why I was so much interested in her. There has been a good deal of interest in the S. S., and my scholars being all christians, I endeavored to set them to work. Prof. G., seeing I was pretty well waked up, put two classes in my charge. This was last Sunday. I was introduced to the girls—from 12 to 16 years of age. I talked seriously with them, and one promised to give up *every thing* for Jesus.

Monday night I went to the inquiry meeting. I hunted up this one of my protégés, and the first words she said to me were, "I love Jesus." *I* was very happy; and did I not have reason to be? Nine of my "Parish," as Prof. calls it, are now serving Jesus. Ten more yet to come. Pray for them and for me. About sixty have been converted in the past few weeks. Last Sunday night eleven were baptized. Many families are being completed. God is blessing us abundantly.

Tell father to read the leading editorial in the next issue of our paper, and tell me what he thinks of it.

It is the first of my productions that has been complimented by the President. He read it before it was put in type.

Conversion of his Sabbath School scholars.

Love to father and yourself.

Your affectionate son   WILLIE.

Rochester, March 14, 1874.

MY DEAR MOTHER—

Saturday night yours of 12th inst. was received. ·Was surprised to hear of uncle George Kendall's death.

> " 'T is sweet, as year by year we lose
> Friends out of sight, in faith to muse
> How grows in Paradise our store."

I hope you will reap abundant harvest for all the work done, and prayers offered at Calvary Church.

Is there any religious interest in the Missions? I am glad Eva is at work. I feel more and more that we can do effectual work every day, letting our love for the Savior manifest itself in the various situations in which we are placed.

College will probably close next week. I expect to be home Saturday night, to stay just a week.

Love to father.

Your affectionate son   WILLIE.

Anxiety for religious interest at home.

Rochester, June 26, 1874.

MY DEAR FATHER—

To-day closes another year's work. This A. M. we passed our last Junior examination, so now we are SENIORS ! !

Enters Senior class.

Yesterday was examination in astronomy, in which I scored 10. Wednesday I worked from 9 in the morning till 9½ at night on my astronomy, and even then I trembled a little, when the time came—so much of it was advance to me. But I went through splendidly. To-day we have had a "written" in Cicero "de Officiis." I answered all the questions.

Our class makes its first appearance in public next Monday—Class day. We sing a song to the "Bone-man" (a skeleton), which the graduating class presents to us. I am leader of the singing.

Song to the "Bone-man."

What is the projective point for the summer—Bolton or Delaware Water-Gap?

My health is again first rate. I have but little headache. I have been elected Pres't of the College Y. M. C. A., and reëlected Editor of the Record for first six months of next year. Love to mother.

Pres't of College Y. M. C. A.

Affectionately, your son   WILLIE.

Rochester, Nov. 17, 1874.

MY DEAR FATHER—

Am glad Mr. Hall thought so well of my efforts as a delegate at Syracuse Y. M. C. A. Convention.   Dr. A. made *the* speech of the meeting.

Last week a College Glee Club was organized, and I was made Director.   The Y. M. C. A. flourishes.   I wish churches and christians generally would pray more for the young men in college.

Our church has lately been considerably exercised by the pastor's having received two calls.   He has decided to acquiesce in the wishes of the church, and remain.   There is much interest here, and we hope to see good work done for the Master this fall and winter.

Affectionately, your son   WILLIE.

Rochester, Dec. 11, 1874.

MY DEAR MOTHER—

I suppose you think it is most time for "the boy" to write.   Well, I 've been pretty busy lately in preparation for examinations. This A. M. I passed examination in Dr. Anderson's department—Intellectual Philosophy, and received 9, though I did not make a single mistake. Did the Rogers group come all right? I must tell you about it. Thanksgiving day I took dinner with Stearns in Buffalo, returning in the P. M., to be ready for college the next day.

That night there was a sociable in the church. The room was full. I went late. We had some singing, and then the pastor brought out, with the assistance of another, the group, "The Favored Scholar." I admired it, of course; listened, not very attentively, to the preliminary remarks of the pastor, and was never more surprised than to hear my name announced as the favored one. My reply was brief. It is the first gift I ever received from comparative strangers, and I prize it very highly. [This handsome present was made in recognition of his efficient services as conductor of the church choir.]

Gift for services as chorister at the church.

My health is good, when I am careful of my diet; but I'll be glad to get home from here. Be it ever so lonely, (?) there's no place like home.

Love to mother.

Affectionately, your son WILLIE.

Rochester, Jan'y 15, 1875.

MY DEAR FATHER—

Away nearly two weeks, and not a word from home. I hope to hear very soon.

I have been very busy the past week studying Roman Law, Physical Geography, and Mental Philosophy, in college, and the Vatican Decrees, for Society debate.

The more I study the Roman Law, the better I like it. These crystallizations of men's thoughts in regard to the relations of *meum* and *tuum* are grand. With the lectures that the Professor dictates, we read in Justinian's Institutes.

Mental Philosophy is about as uncertain as Rochester weather—sometimes clear, and then foggy.

My reading on the Vatican Decrees is quite extensive and benefiting. I have had to study English, French, and German History, to understand the subject at all. Last night I had about me seven books of reference while studying Gladstone's Expostulations. I am learning how to use books— "reading across," as Dr. Anderson calls it: studying by subjects, not by books.

Please send me "Hadley's Lectures on

Study of Roman law.

Reading.

Roman Law." You will find it in my book-case. I carried it home last May, and left it there.

Remember me kindly to inquiring friends. and give love to mother. *Write soon* to

Your affectionate son   WILLIE.

This habit of "reading across" was never lost; for he was not only choice in the selection of his reading, but also careful to get at the meaning of the author, and to make the knowledge thus acquired of service to him. Hence the note-book was his constant companion. In the wild regions of the Indian Territory, when a member of the Ute Commission, he found time not only to read, but also to fill his book with notes of what he had read.

Note book

Himself so intelligent and pure in his reading, it was not strange that he should have been desirous that all who were under his care and instruction should be equally so. For this reason, he exercised a judicious care over the library of the Sunday School of which he was superintendent, and sought to create in the scholars a taste for the best classes of literature, as well as to lead them

Sunday reading.

in the choice of their reading to remember
the Sabbath day to keep it holy.

Communion with the beautiful in the works of nature.

In reading his letters, one is impressed
with his deep and constant communion with
the beautiful in the works of Nature, as well
as in the realm of mind and of morals. No
one had a heartier appreciation of the unity
thus indicated in the 19th Psalm, when David turns from the contemplation of the perfectness of the law of the material world to
find its counterpart in the law of spirit-ex-
istence. Hence to him the book of Nature,
as well as the book of revelation, declared
the glory of God. To the one, as to the
other, he turned for the refreshment of his
mind, in the exhaustion caused by hard
study.

Recreation.

Indeed, it may be said of him, in a general sense, that, in seeking recreation, he
always gave the preference to those methods
to which evil did not attach, even in appearance, and which informed and strengthened
the mind, rather than dissipated it. For this
reason, in many of the amusements to which
youth resorts, he had no interest. Among
his papers was found, after his death, a
game of Proverbs, the object of which was

not only to furnish diversion, but also, at the same time, to lead to memorizing of this portion of the Word of God.

Rochester, Feb'y 15, 1875.

MY DEAR FATHER—

Many thanks for yours of the 11th inst., with its inclosure.

Since my last, I have been on a little excursion. Not feeling particularly bright last Thursday, I persuaded Ordway to go with me to the Falls. We left on the 10:05 train. At Lockport I ran across our fellow-traveler, met on the St. Lawrence on H. M. S. S. "Secret," Mr. McCollum. We had a pleasant chat.

At two we reached the Falls—the weather we hoped to leave in R. coming with us. First, dinner at the Spencer House, and then hunt for a sleigh. Finally engaged one for the P. M., for $2.50. Our first visit was to Prospect Point. Imagine our appearance— an old hack on runners, two poor horses, three robes over our knees, and the snow blowing and eddying around us, and in our faces, sometimes almost blinding us; and yet we enjoyed it.

Visits Niagara Falls.

Winter
landscape.

On the Point the trees and foliage were covered with iced snow. The pavilion was wreathed in the same pure alabaster-like covering, looking as beautiful and forsaken as the Palace at Versailles when we saw it, or the royal residences at Schönbrunnen.

We next crossed the rapids to Goat Island, and went to Luna Island. Here we gained our best view of the American Fall. The centre was obstructed by ice, which extended in huge icicles to the bottom of the Fall. Many of these were split up into several, when near the bottom, making "fringes" and "open work" of singular beauty. At the bottom of the Fall were large "mounds," from beneath which the water pours, as we saw it at Gründelwald and the Mer de Glace.

Our next stopping place was on the Tower-side of the island. There was less ice on the Canada Fall, and the mounds were not so large. The view up the river was strikingly desolate.

We crossed the new bridge, the wind blowing the sleigh against the railing, and producing an undulating motion to the bridge, that made a foot-passenger, crossing at the same time we did, quite sea-sick.

From the Canada shore the view was very grand. The river below was frozen, and huge masses were piled up to an enormous size and height. While looking at this Fall some large pieces of ice came over, producing a noise like the booming of distant cannon.

Purchasing a few photos, we returned to the Spencer, well pleased with our sight-seeing. At 8 took the return train; stormed several snow drifts, causing a shock to the whole train, and reached R. safely at midnight.

Love to mother, kind regards to Mr. and Mrs. J., and Jeannie R.

Your affectionate son   WILLIE.

The foregoing closes Will's correspondence while in the University at Rochester.

His parents had the pleasure of being present at the commencement exercises in Corinthian Hall, Rochester, Wednesday, June 30, 1875, and were never more proud of their boy than when listening to his manly oration on that occasion.

His subject was, "Why should the State Educate?" His oration displayed excellence

Graduation.

15

both of style and composition; originality of thought; and a grasp of the subject seldom attained in one of his years. His delivery was elegant and graceful, eliciting general applause from his immense audience.

His parents were equally gratified to find their son enjoyed the friendship of a large circle of acquaintances, who were lavish in their praises of his usefulness, his purity of life, and nobility of character.

He had passed through this critical period, not only without reproach, but had won the confidence and esteem of all with whom he had associated—an honor, in the estimation of his parents, far outweighing in value that of a diploma from his Alma Mater, highly as they prized that.

Though diligent search has been made among his papers, we have been unable to find a copy of his oration.

The following "rough draft," copied from his notes, gives an imperfect idea of the finished oration, but covers its essential points:

WHY SHOULD THE STATE EDUCATE?

It is the function of the State to enforce respect for the rights of property and protect human life.

Function of the State.

It is clearly the privilege of the State to maintain its own existence.

If these propositions are admitted, it follows that it is the duty of the State to elevate the substrata of society, that never-failing source of peril to life, property, and the very existence of the State, by providing them the means for a certain degree of intellectual training; not with the State an end in itself, but simply a means to an end.

Duty of the State.

There can be no question that every individual needs a certain amount of education, that he may intelligently perform the functions of citizenship.

Education necessary to intelligent citizenship.

The prosperity of the *individual* is the prosperity of the *State*.

Even under despotic governments this principle is recognized and acted upon.

There can be no doubt that one's manhood is promoted, and his independence of character asserted, by affording him this means of intellectual training.

Education promotes manhood.

The truth of this proposition appears self-evident. Where the masses are suffered to grow up in ignorance, they are at all times liable to become the dupes of wily politicians and unscrupulous demagogues.

Another reason for State education.

Another reason why the State should educate, exists in the fact that we are annually receiving, by immigration, an army of foreigners, essentially un-American in tastes and habits.

This vast aggregation of humanity can in no way be absorbed and assimilated in our national life, and become thoroughly Americanized so effectively, as by placing within their reach the means of instruction.

How far should the State educate?

If it be asked, "How far is the State warranted in carrying the education of its citizens?" the reply is not difficult.

The object should be kept steadily in view, viz.: to make good, intelligent citizens, able to understand our form of government and comprehend its laws.

To accomplish this, a man is not obliged to be familiar with Lecky on Morals, or puzzle his brain over law books. The rudiments of an education, or what is usually known as the common, elementary branches of knowledge, are all that is required.

Certain visionary schemers contend that it is the duty of the State to maintain colleges and technical schools. This is clearly beyond the province of the State. With higher education it has no more to do than it has with religion.

The State should not maintain colleges.

It may, and should, educate sufficiently for self-protection—for this an ornamental education is not essential.

Ornamental education not essential.

If this view is correct, the State clearly has no right to appropriate money for college buildings, or Professors' salaries. Such legislation is usurpation. It is using the money of *the people* for the higher education of a privileged class, inasmuch as a large majority of the youth of school age can never reap the benefit of a college education. even if provided at the public expense.

If a common school education is sufficient to meet the demands of the State. the State education should there stop.

Common schools.

If it is necessary for the State to train teachers for common schools. let this be done; but. at the same time. let care be taken that all the people should share directly in the benefits.

Erroneous
views.

Misled by the notion that a republic contemplates not merely the political, but the social and intellectual equality of its citizens, the champions of public colleges claim that every boy in the land must be furnished, at public cost, with facilities for studying chemistry, farming, engineering, and even the dead languages. Such views are anti-republican, and wholly at variance with the spirit of our institutions.

Must not
educate a
few at the
expense of
the many.

No logic, however subtle, can make it consistent with the true ideas of a republic to confer upon the State the duty or right to educate the few at the expense of the many.

Aristocra-
cy.

Such a policy consists better with aristocracy than democracy.

After spending a few months in recreation, Will returned once more to his home, to prosecute his studies for the legal profession. He entered, with his accustomed zeal, into all activities of the church and Sunday School, never growing weary of them, never faltering, but devoting to them all the energies of his being.

He presided at the piano in the Home school, with such skill and good taste, as made him an universal favorite; he was teacher of a class in the Home school, in the morning, and in Kendall Chapel, in the afternoon. Constant in his attendance upon meetings; ready to contribute to his utmost in promoting their usefulness; always prompt in offering his services where they might be the most useful; liberal in his pecuniary contributions to every benevolent and worthy object; cheerful in rendering assistance to his father by every means in his power, he sought, unselfishly and unostentatiously, to devote himself to the Church of Christ and the good of his fellow-men.

In October, 1876, he entered the junior class in the Law School of Columbian University, and, at the same time, enrolled himself among the students of the Washington Business College for a year's study in practical business methods.

In June, 1876, he graduated from the college, with the honor of the Valedictory. He acquired a leading influence over his fellow-students, and won the respect and confidence of his teachers, who expressed a

Abounding in church work.

Enters Law School and Business College.

Graduates from Business College.

strong desire to have him remain in the college as an instructor.

His Valedictory, on the occasion of his graduation from the Business College, delivered at Lincoln Hall, Thursday night, June 1, 1876, was as follows:

VALEDICTORY BY W. S. STICKNEY.

Valedic-
tory.

The ship, about to enter upon a perilous voyage, with sails spread to the favoring wind, dismisses the pilot whose skill has directed her course through the intricacies of the harbor, and so breaks the only remaining link that binds her to her native land.

Voyage of
life.

We, the graduating class of this college, started on our course by skillful navigators, to-night cast off our moorings, and, with buoyant hopes, enter upon the voyage of life, fraught with perils, but full of grand possibilities.

To-night past scenes crowd our memories, and, while our minds are filled with pleasing reminiscences, we are forced to the reality that henceforth new experiences, new associations, and new duties await us. The pleasures of memory, however, are still ours to enjoy and cherish; photographed on the mind by a process more beautiful and more mysterious than man's philosophy ever devised, and with a distinctness that time itself cannot efface, we bear them with us, precious treasures, mementoes of the days that are past.

Our attachment to this Business College is no sentiment, no figment of the imagination, but true and genuine, founded, as it is, upon the knowledge experience gives us of its great influence and importance. Let it be understood we are not of those who decry the importance of classical learning, of culture, and all the adornments of a finished education. But life is, now-a-days, emphatically, a struggle; a thorough knowledge of affairs is absolutely necessary to him who would cope successfully with the exigencies and difficulties to be encountered.

Importance of classical training.

Practical knowledge.

The foundation must be deep and solid if the superstructure would survive. A business training is to a business man what discipline is to an army.

Our banks and mercantile houses are full of cripples, who go limping through life, when a few years of study in the Business College would have rendered them efficient and successful.

16

Methods.

With our school-room divided into streets and squares, the real estate agent finds ample opportunity to ply his vocation and realize handsome profits.

The College Bank, instituted on the true Jackson theory of hard money, discounts notes with good endorsers, fears no suspension, draws its bills of exchange, and issues its notes redeemable at maturity. Its capital is unimpaired, its management honest, its assets always exceeding its liabilities.

Our transportation and commission business, successfully conducted on a sound basis, leads one into all the intricacies of trade and commerce.

Neither is the art preservative of all arts here neglected. The newspaper taxes the brain and calls into exercise the talent of him who would enlighten his fellow-students upon the current questions of the times.

These are but an outline of the methods and processes by which a student can, in a brief space, furnish himself with the means of usefulness and success.

As the great mass of mankind hurries restlessly on, ever seeking and never satisfied, the inefficient and the sluggard are rudely thrust aside or are trodden down. Selfishness loves few and pities none. Although each may persuade himself he is seeking the "greatest good of the greatest number," the "greatest number" is generally number one, and the "greatest good" his own aggrandizement.

The merchant of to-day has the whole world for his market, and all its inhabitants for customers. The iron horse has supplanted the slow coaches in which our ancestors rode. The lightning has been civilized, and is now our swift-winged messenger, annihilating time and space. The ends of the earth are within speaking distance, and its most remote inhabitant is our neighbor. With all these advantages, the *sine qua non* of the business man of to-day is energy and brains. Taught how to use his brains, and all directed by a true morality, a young man's possibilities are as illimitable as truth, as sublime as immortality.

The graduating class of '76 is the Centennial offering of the Washington Business College. 'T is ours to enter upon the active duties of life with greater responsibilities and greater advantages than were ever

Progress.

Business qualities.

Centenni-
al offering.

given to man before. There is laid at our feet the experience of the grandest century in the history of the world. A period marked by no such peaceful grandeur as characterized the Augustan age, or the Elizabethan era—but one eminent for its mighty men, for its advance in physical and metaphysical research, and for the development of an idea at once sublime and God-like; the idea, cherished by every American heart, that all men are created free and equal. Inaugurated when John Hancock and his compatriots signed the immortal Declaration of Independence, consummated when Abraham Lincoln gave to the world the Proclamation of Emancipation.

As Newton stood on Kepler's shoulders, it will be expected of us that, resting on the experience and knowledge of the past, we will reach up still higher, grasp grander truths, solve mightier problems, and so help enlarge the horizon of human knowledge.

We leave our halls of study and pleasure with regret. We linger to say good-bye to you whose genius has directed our studies and inspired us with a noble ambition. We shall endeavor to profit by your counsel, and

bring no discredit upon our college. May
you be spared these many years as faithful
guides to the young of Washington; and
when these days draw to a close may they
be radiant with a beauty that shall be a
promise of the joy and happiness beyond.

Good
wishes.

To you, ladies and gentlemen, who have
so kindly listened to our exercises, we extend
our thanks. We commend to your care and
good-will the Business College of Washington. Honored by the lives of its former
graduates, may its reputation be still further
enhanced by those now taking their leave.

From the Business College we graduate
into the great common school of life. We
enter with you in the race for success, and,
seeking it on the basis of truth, we know we
shall succeed, for though

> "Truth is ever on the scaffold,
>   And Wrong is ever on the throne,
> Yet that scaffold sways the future;
>   And behind the great unknown
> Standeth God within the shadow,
>   Keeping watch above His own."

Will continued his studies at the Law-school, giving, also, much time in assisting his father.

Useful-ness.

He seemed to derive real pleasure in being useful to others, though far from enjoying good health.

Zeal as a student.

His anxiety to sustain himself among his fellow law-students, often kept him at his studies when he should have been in the open air, seeking recreation.

Health.

Many a night, when poring over his books till a late hour, has he been told to lay them aside and go to bed. But though of weak constitution, he was seldom totally disabled by sickness. He was generally able to attend recitation at Law-school, and seldom, or never, absent from church or Sunday School.

He mingled but little in society, and had but a limited circle of acquaintance outside the church.

Literary Club.

He had joined a literary club, in whose meetings he took great pleasure.

Music.

Music, vocal and instrumental, always afforded him recreation and satisfaction. He was always happy, when, with four or five of his musical friends about him, he would lead them on the piano in rendering some favorite glee, anthem, or song.

On June, 13, 1877, he was graduated with his class from the Law-school, and received his degree of Bachelor of Laws.

He immediately joined with others in forming a post-graduate class, for one year more of advanced study, and would have been graduated with his class, receiving a degree of Master of Laws, but for his absence in the west. He was admitted to practice at the bar of the District of Columbia July 2, 1877.

Saratoga Springs, N. Y., Aug. 1, 1877.
MY DEAR MOTHER—

I will answer yours of the 25th, and father's of the 30th, together.

The indefiniteness of your plans is refreshing. You know, here, it is, get up in the morning, drink spring-water, eat breakfast, read awhile, spring-water, eat, more reading, spring-water, eat, spring-water, and to bed—so, to have to do with something not fixed by any rule. is very refreshing.

Mrs. H. has just asked, "When do you

expect your father and mother?" Mrs. B.
asked the same question. Mr. and Mrs. H.
repeated the same interrogatory. The last
time I saw Mr. and Mrs. R. I enlightened
their minds on the subject. Dr. A. and Dr.
K., from Rochester, Dr. and Mrs. F., from
Bangor, and numerous other friends, are in
pursuit of similar information.

I have busied myself in investigating
causes of pauperism and modes of relief.

Sunday I met Drs. Anderson and Kendrick at church. Dr. A. is on his way to
Ovid, N. Y., to examine an insane asylum;
so I accompanied him, with three other
members of the State Board of Charities.

At Geneva we took a boat and went
down Seneca Lake twenty miles to the asylum. It is beautifully located on a large
farm on the shore of the lake — high ground,
which commands a fine view of the lake and
surrounding country.

I wish you would come here, that way,
via Balt. and Harrisburg to Watkins, thence
by boat, forty miles, to Geneva; from there
by rail to Schenectady here.

We reached the asylum yesterday A. M.,
about 10:30. This is a receptacle for the

*Visits in-
sane asy-
lum at
Ovid, N. Y.*

worst forms of disease in all the county hospitals. 1,250 inmates.

The buildings are in groups of about five two-story brick wards. An eighth of a mile separates the two sexes. It seemed almost too bad to put nature's deformities where her beauties were so striking; but it is right they should be made as happy as possible. I do n't think I should make a good Insane Hosp. Supt.

Dr. Anderson has returned to Rochester; left regards for you and father.

Please send some more religious papers. Love to father.

Affectionately, your son

WILL S. STICKNEY.

In October, 1875, he was elected President of the Calvary Christian League, an organization composed principally of the young people of the church and Sunday School, for mutual improvement and social intercourse.

President of Calvary Christian League.

At the expiration of the first year, he was reëlected for another term. In accepting the position, he delivered a brief address, defining the object of the organization.

Reëlected.

17

Among his papers was found the following "points" of his speech:

"Analyze the name—Calvary Christian League. Name is the body, the idea is the soul. The body demands respect as it furnishes· a habitation for the soul. Give brief sketch of the life of Christ, whose birth was heralded by notes of joy, chanted by angelic choirs, ravishing the ears of the wondering shepherds on Bethlehem's plain. Christ a paragon of excellence, the personification of Truth and Virtue. We are His representatives, and if true disciples, must illustrate His life in our lives. The League was not formed for pleasure merely; to tie it to such limits, would make it unworthy the name."

On retiring from office, at the expiration of his second term, 1877, he expressed a strong desire for the future prosperity and usefulness of the League. He called particular attention to the name of the organization, defining the word "Christian" as embracing all the intellectual, social, and moral qualities of man's nature. He considered growth, a principle of the christian life— when development ceases, decay begins; this is as true of an organization like this as of an individual.

During the last year of his administration, thirty-five new members were added, and $227.76 was received. This money was appropriated for the benefit of the poor in the S. S., for foreign missions, sewing-circle, repairing church furniture, &c.

Results.

In the early part of 1877, the President approved a bill appropriating $20,000 for the relief of the destitute poor of the city of Washington. A commission was appointed to carry it into effect. During the following months of the winter and spring, Will gave the whole of his time to aid the commission, of which his father had been made President. As indicative not only of his zeal in every good work, but also of his administrative ability, a portion of the report he made to the board is here given.

Relief Commission.

EXTRACT FROM REPORT OF W. S. STICKNEY TO THE RELIEF COMMISSION.

Report to the Commission.

"Since our city is the seat of Government, it presents the singular appearance of a metropolis without manufacturing or commercial interests. It has little or no interest, outside of the local trades and government patronage, that are essential to comfortable living. Its population comprises many nonresidents, allured· from comfortable homes by the *ignis fatuus* of a government office. Discharged from the departments, their means of subsistence are cut off, and large numbers are thus thrown upon the tender mercies of the charitable for relief.

"Besides these, there is another large class, too ignorant and lazy to make themselves useful to themselves or any one else, who stand at our doors appealing for assistance. This class, so erroneously and unfortunately called the 'nation's wards,' comprises nearly one-third of our population, and received over eighty per cent. of the help given by the Relief Commission during the past year.

"Since the late war of the rebellion our city has been the head-quarters for these people, and, since in prosperous seasons they can with difficulty take care of themselves, in these 'hard times' the relief office is besieged for bread and clothing for men, wo-

men, and children in every grade of want
and destitution.

"These are the principal classes that
demanded our attention and assistance during the past year.

*   *   *   *   *   *

"On the 5th of Feb'y, 1877, the President
of the U. S. approved a bill appropriating
twenty thousand dollars for the 'destitute
poor of this city,' to be disbursed by the
Relief Commission.

"Such a large sum of money doubtless
attracted some who had previously managed
to do without aid. But the absence of any
law of settlement, or authority to send immi-
grant paupers home, made it difficult to dis-
criminate between those who had moved
into the city to avail themselves of this aid.
and our own needy citizens.

"The commission endeavored to prevent
this immigration by adopting a rule, which
the visitors were instructed to see enforced,
that no application should be received from
any who had not resided at least a month in
the city.

"The number of those who received aid
from the twenty thousand dollars appropria-

Appropri-
ation for
the poor.

Aid given.

ted by Congress, was 14,358.   Number of families helped, 8,191.

*   *   *   *   *   *

Proper mode of giving aid.

"The primary object of all charitable organizations, should be to relieve distress, and, at the same time, to administer relief in such a way as to diminish pauperism.

"There is nothing incompatible with this idea in the granting of out-door relief, if it is bestowed judiciously and systematically. But it should be so given, that the applicants will be compelled to resort to *other* means of obtaining a living than the monthly rations provided by the city.

Principal cause of poverty.

"The principal cause of pauperism in our city, directly or indirectly, is intemperance, greatly aggravated by the want of employment.

"It would be more economical to support the paupers in the work-house, and provide for the children industrial schools and homes, thus relieving the pauper class of those who would otherwise follow the example of their parents in idleness and vice, and thus training them to habits of industry and usefulness.

"We do not endorse the opinion lately

adopted by many social economists, that pauperism is hereditary. Men and women are not constitutionally paupers, but become such from their surroundings or environment. Improve these, and the evil is greatly diminished, if not effectually cured.

Pauperism not inherited.

"Most of the families applying for aid have in them able-bodied men, who either cannot find employment, or are determined not to work.

"We would not recommend, as a measure of charity, the employment by the government of those temporarily without work, at *their full value.* The disastrous operations of such a system have been too fully demonstrated in France, during the last hundred years, to call for adoption here.

A French mistake.

"The evil of the *Ateliers nationaux* was, that they *attracted* laborers, by paying the full value of their service; so that what was intended as a charity, many came to demand as a *right.*

"If fifty cents a day were given to such employées, the objection to the French system would be obviated. For, while this would be sufficient to supply a family with bread and fuel, it would not be enough to tempt laborers from other work, or to hold them, if any other employment could be obtained.

Premium on idleness.

"When the applicant is assisted by public charity, he is regarded, and regards himself, as a public dependent. His shiftlessness is encouraged, and his children taught the lesson — once learned, never forgotten — that the government virtually pays a premium for idleness.

"It has been hinted, that some families move into the city to avail themselves of the aid given to the poor. This immigration should be discouraged, and to accomplish this, the city government should have authority to send these people back to their homes. This plan works well in other places, and deserves a trial here.

Misdirected charity.

"During the past year it came to our knowledge that several families were actually relieved from work by the aid given by the various relief societies. They were *supported* by charity. Such a system is worse than none, as it conceals the imposter and encourages the lazy.

"To prevent such frauds, all societies granting out - door relief, should send to some central office, daily, the names and residences of those assisted the day before.

"Whatever is done for the poor, should be of a permanent character. Owing to the want of powers of the Commission, many last year were helped only to be helped again. If they are confirmed paupers, not able to take care of themselves, they should be put by themselves. The welfare of society demands it. If they are only temporarily distressed, it is the interest of society to help them on their feet again, without pauperizing them.

"Oftentimes the visitors find applicants too old and infirm to work. It would seem to be the dictates of true charity and humanity, that these poor, old and disabled people should be sent to the poor-house, where they may have more of the comforts of life.

"Children are sometimes found, who, with no friends to care for them, depend entirely upon begging for their daily subsistence. They are waifs, exposed to every form of vice and crime, and will eventually be found in our gaols and penitentiaries.

*   *   *   *   *   *

"In conclusion, allow me to recapitulate

Suggestion.

Children.

Recommendations.

the recommendations presented in the foregoing:

"1. The District Government should establish a 'Labor Bureau' for the employment of men whose families apply for aid—the wages being considerably below the usual rate, but sufficient for maintaining subsistence.

"2. That orders be given, that any applicant for aid, having a legal settlement elsewhere, be sent to his home.

"3. That all societies granting out-door relief, be requested to send to the central office, daily, a list of the names and residences of those assisted the previous day.

"4. For every five hundred dollars appropriated by Congress to benevolent institutions in this District, the Relief Commission be entitled to send one inmate for one year.

"5. That the Relief Commission be constituted a visiting board, to visit *all* the charitable institutions in the District, at least once a year, to examine the condition and management of such institutions, and report the same to the city government. This system is found to work well in the State of New York.

"In these suggestions no extra expense would be involved, except, perhaps, in the labor bureau, and, in that case, the benefit would more than compensate for the outlay.

"Respectfully submitted.

"W. S. STICKNEY."

Feasibility of these suggestions.

CHAPTER IV.

FIRST UTE COMMISSION.

"Not the place honors the man, but the man the place."

The day is short, and the work is great. It is not incumbent upon thee to complete the work; but thou must not, therefore, cease from it. If thou hast worked much, great shall be thy reward; for the Master who employed thee is faithful in his payments. But know that the true reward is not of this world. —Talmud.

CONGRESS passed a law, approved May 3, 1878, for the appointment of a Special Commission to negotiate with the Ute Indians in Colorado, for the consolidation of all the bands into one agency, and for the extinguishment of their right to the southern portion of their reservation. Gen. Edward Hatch, of the army, N. C. McFarland, of Kansas, and Wm. Stickney, of Washington, constituted the commission. W. S. Stickney was appointed Secretary and Disbursing Officer.

The Commission met and organized at Manitou, near Pike's Peak, Colorado, July 30, 1878.

The unusual altitude or peculiar climatic conditions of this region so affected me, that, fearing I should be an obstruction to the work of the Commission, and meeting ex-Governor Morrill, of Maine, at Manitou, with his consent, I telegraphed the President, suggesting that he be appointed in my place, at the same time announcing my resignation on account of ill health. This change was immediately effected.

Gen. Clinton B. Fisk was present, representing the Board of Indian Commissioners.

Ute Commission.

Appointment.

Change.

Eclipse of
the sun.

After remaining several days at Manitou,
where we had the intense satisfaction of
witnessing the total eclipse of the sun on the
30th of July, the Commission, accompanied
by Gen. Fisk and myself, proceeded to Alamosa, the terminus of the Denver and Rio
Grande R. R., crossing, en route, the celebrated Veta Pass.

We remained at Alamosa a day or two,
waiting for the military escort which was to
accompany the Commission to Los Pinos and
other points in southern Colorado.

Journey-
ing.

The Commission started on their long
journey over mountains, plains, and valleys,
while Gen. Fisk and I returned east, stopping to visit the Indian Territory on our way.

The following extracts from a letter of
my son, gives interesting incidents and impressions by the way:

Glimpses
of glorious
things.

"Since my last letter, which was from
Manitou, our camp has moved all through
the famous San Juan mining country. I can
give you but glimpses of the glorious things
we saw in that almost unknown land. The
ride to Alamosa, over the narrow-guage
(gouge it should be called, for charging ten

cents a mile), was rather devoid of interest,
excepting the Veta Pass. This R. R. feat
our Colorado friends seem never to tire talking about. Not having money enough to
tunnel the mountain, the railroad company
went over it. The summit is 9,339 feet above
the sea, and the average grade for 21½ miles
is 211 feet to the mile. One sharp curve of
30 degrees, with a radius of 193 feet, called
the 'mule shoe,' is one of the sights. As a
piece of engineering, this is no great wonder,
as the road sticks close to the mountain side,
and the certainty of reaching the top only
depends on the strength of the locomotive.
But the view down the valley is very fine— *View down the valley.*
the Spanish peaks looming up on the foot-
hills five or six thousand feet and overlook-
ing the prairie plains that extend as far as
the eye can reach. The ride down the *Rapid transit.*
mountain was on the double-quick, but a
heavy shower and thick, black clouds prevented our seeing any thing of the country.

"Alamosa, the present terminus of the
road, affords two hotels. We stopped at the
Perry House. The proprietor, Joe Perry, as
he is familiarly called, came originally from
Chester, N. Y. The chief end of his life

appears to be to 'keep a first-class hotel on the frontier.' He has already built sixteen hotels, following the western terminus of the Kansas Pacific, Atchison, Topeka and Santa Fé, and now of the Denver and Rio Grande Railroad. On the 23d of last June his guests took breakfast in his hotel at Garland City, and tea in the same house at Alamosa, 30 miles beyond. After breakfast the house was taken apart in sections, loaded on fifteen cars, transferred to the new town, and rëerected.

"We reached Alamosa the 7th of August. The town was then two months old, with a population of six or eight hundred. The town was in process of construction. Houses almost finished, half built, some with only the foundations laid, could be seen all around. Prairie schooners brought families from Del Norte, thirty miles beyond, to locáte in the new town; and a few came directly from the east. Freight trains loaded with houses, the owners sitting on top, steamed in from Garland. All about the town were tents and covered wagons, serving as houses till more substantial ones could be roofed in.

Prairie schooners

"The town is located in the middle of the Rio Grande valley, about a mile west of the river. The valley is sixty miles wide, and four hundred long; is skirted by high mountains, and is covered with a luxuriant growth of sage brush, grease wood, and cactus. It is said, that, with 'irrigation,' this valley may be made to blossom as the rose. A friend—a Colorado enthusiast—would picture us picking bananas, oranges, and other tropical fruits from the groves of San Luis Park—*Nous verrons.* The dust is an inch or two deep, and so filled with alkali that it is especially disagreeable to the eyes. Its presence in such quantities is accounted for on the theory that the rocks on the mountains have become disintegrated and blown into the valley. No gardens have been started yet; hence living is expensive. Most of the vegetables come by rail from Kansas, thirty-six hours distant, and are re-shipped at Pueblo. The Texas herds furnish most of the meat. We observed several Chinese, in their national costume and the inevitable pig-tail, who seemed to be doing a good business.

"There we bade farewell to what civili-

Rio Grande valley.

Dust.

Farewell to civilization.

The General.

The Judge

The Governor.

The Doctor:

The Captain.

The Colonel.

zation there was, and started for the mountains. Before beginning the trip, you must know something of the party.

"First, came the 'General,' [Hatch] full of war stories; always ready for a hunt or a fish; generally good-natured, but a thorough military man. Then there was the 'Judge,' [McFarland] tall and slim, about six feet two, unused to rough roads and 'irregular meals;' but, with the aid of his quinine pills and the ambulance cushions, he managed to survive his 'new sensations.' The 'Governor,' [Morrill] started in well, but the roads were too much for him, and we had to send him back. We were all sorry to lose his genial face and pleasant company; but camp is a poor place for being sick. The 'Doctor,' [Park] went along for his health. It would certainly have improved fifty per cent. more if his wife and babies had been with him. *His* correspondence alone discounted all the rest put together. The 'Captain' did not go far; Uncle Sam wanted him in New York, and that settled it. The 'Colonel' turned the scale at 200, was always in a hurry, good company, and an acquisition to the party. The 'Lieutenant,' commander of the escort,

is a Pennsylvania boy, sent here to die; but
mountain air would n't let him.   He does
little of every thing; collects flowers; bottles
spring-water; keeps an accurate register of
the thermometer and barometer (when he
thinks of it); measures the marches with an
adometer; and then tells us about them all.
and lots of other things.   Then the 'Secretary,' [W. S. S.] who needs no description,
an escort of ten men, and Col. Pfeiffer, the
interpreter, a veteran Indian fighter.   For
many years he was the warrior-chief of the
Utes, and even now it is sometimes difficult
to tell which he likes best, the Indians or the
whites.

The Lieu-tenant.

The Secre-tary.

The Inter-preter.

  "The business of these gentlemen was to
visit the Ute Indians in south-western Colorado, and purchase, if possible. a part of
their territory.   At the lower end of the
Reservation is a strip of land about 200 miles
long by 15 wide, on which the whites are all
the time encroaching, and it was feared the
Indians would resist these encroachments.
and so cause trouble.

Object.

  "To carry the outfit, required ten covered ambulances, a buckboard, and four
wagons, with thirty mules to draw them.

Outfit.

"The Commission had four wall tents, which were generally arranged in the form of a hollow square, and over the centre a large awning, under which was the dinner table. The escort and interpreter had their tents on one side, making altogether quite a camp.

"It would be too great an undertaking to describe in detail each day's journeying, so we will only notice the principal points passed on the trip to the Southern Ute agency, and the general pow-wow held there with Ignacio and his warriors.   .

First day.

"The beginning of the first day's ride was, the first part, over an exceedingly dusty road, but toward the last we came to the 'bad land,' where it looks as if a great stream of lava and scoria had poured down over the valley. The first camp was on the Conejos river, near a town of the same name.

Mexican town.

"The second day we passed through Conejos; and as it is a thoroughly Mexican town, I will tell you something of it. It is built in the shape of a square, with a church and monastery on one side, and adobe houses on the other three. There is really but one

house to a side of this public square, though
that is divided into many apartments, which
are used for various public and private purposes. The whole is so constructed as to
have a square court in the centre. It is a
square bounded with squares — one of the
few things the Mexicans do on the square!
These courts have their only entrance from
the great public square. In them are the
stables and store-houses. They are the
back yards of a Mexican town.

"Leaving Conejos, our road was along
a very pretty valley under some cultivation.
dotted with Mexican houses. One house
was being repaired by a couple of women,
who were on the roof plastering up the holes,
while the pater familias was on the ground
bossing the job and stirring up the mud
mortar. Close by each house is the bake-
oven, a conical-shaped mound of earth about
three feet high. All our surroundings were
so un-American, it seemed as if we must be
traveling in the Orient."

Woman's wrongs.

Notwithstanding the discomforts to which
they were exposed, their destination was
finally reached in safety.

Saturday, August 10, 1878.

In Camp on Los Pinos Creek.

MY DEAR FATHER—

Rain, rain, rain. I'm so glad, on your account, that you are not along. We remain here till it stops raining.

Yesterday the Governor complained of not feeling well. I did the best I could for him, and this A. M. he feels a little easier, but is afraid to go on. McCauley takes him back to Fort Garland, and the rest of us will keep on. The Judge says, though the weakest man of the party, he has already beaten two men.

Rubber coat and shoes come in first rate. We live very comfortably. Dr. and I tent together. He appears happy, and improving in health. I am very well this A. M., though yesterday my head had a very decided inclination to go where my heels are.

Love to mother.

Affectionately,   WILL.

Los Pinos Agency,

Thursday, Aug. 29, 1878.

MY DEAR FATHER—

I feel almost like complaining a little,

that I have not received any letter from you or mother. Not a word have I heard since we parted at Alamosa. The rest have all had mail, but nothing for me.

The Commission toil on. The Council at the Southern Ute agency, so far, has been of no avail. The Indians refused to come here, and declined to go to White River.

We used one of the letters to agent Weaver, granting permission to spend $1,000, and bought calicoes, knives, caps, handkerchiefs, scarfs, &c., and gave them to the Indians. Four hundred and ninety-six men, women, and children squatted on the ground together, and received their portions of the spoils. It did n't take very well, for the Indians stubbornly refused the next day to do any thing the Commission asked. We left the interpreter there, and he may succeed in doing something.

Distribution of gifts to Indians.

The road up here we found very rough. From Animas to Silverton the road was so narrow, in places, that the river had but three or four inches to spare. We deserted the wagons, preferring to walk most of the way alongside of Cascade Creek. The scenery is very fine. The valley is about a mile

Rough roads.

wide, and at each end a sentinel mountain, the walls from one to three thousand feet high, forming a suitable frame for the picture.

At Silverton we left the wagons, and took horses to cross the Red Mountain trail to Ouray. The wagons go round by Lake City; our baggage was mounted on donkeys, and came with us.

Mines.

On our way we passed several mining works. The road was steep in some places, but not dangerous. From the summit the view was magnificent. Coming down, the way was in some places very steep and dangerous. We frequently dismounted and took it on foot. We were all glad to reach Ouray. Just before arriving there, we crossed a regular *mauvais pas*—none of us had the courage to ride across.

Ouray.

Ouray is beautifully located at the head of a valley, high mountains on three sides, the fourth opening north toward the agency. From our hotel, the Dixon House, we could see a waterfall, reminding me of Staubach, though not so beautiful.

Yesterday we took a wagon and came here. The Indians have been sent for, and we hope to get away to-morrow or next day, and then push on to Alamosa. We will all be glad to get out of this country. It's rough, and there is no pleasure in being surrounded by miners and Indians.

Love to mother and yourself, and do n't forget to write soon.

Affectionately, your son WILL.

Los Pinos Agency,
Saturday, Aug. 31, 1878.

MY DEAR FATHER—

Yours of the 22d inst. just received. I do n't understand why the $25,000 "could not be done." It's strange we can't have an *honest* policy towards the Indians.

We met the Indians in council yesterday. The Commission offered $10,000 in cash for the four mile square. They declined at first, but afterwards adjourned till to-day, to consider it.

With few exceptions, the Indians do not work, but spend their time in loafing and hunting. The northern bands are superior to the southern.

Just outside of my window, in full sight, are about a dozen Indians, all well armed

Honest policy.

Indians.

with revolvers, one or two with rifles, and one old fellow is playing with his tomahawk. One chief refused to shake hands with Col. Watkins—demanding his credentials!

Issue of beef.

I went to see the issue of beef this P. M. The steers were put in the corral, and the Indians sat on the fence and fired away at them. Sometimes they killed at the first shot, but frequently three or four bullets would be put into the poor animals before they fell. Just as soon as the last one fell, women, boys, and men all rushed to the dead cattle, and commenced cutting them up. The Judge and I voted it a great and unnecessary cruelty.

We start to-morrow for Lake City, thence to Del Norte, Alamosa, and Garland to White River.

Affectionately, with love to mother,

Your son   WILL.

Denver, Col., Sept. 1, 1878.

MY DEAR FATHER—

Vitality of Commission low.

The Commission still lives, though vitality seems low. Gov. Morrill has gone to Washington, to see if Prest. Hayes and Secretary Schurz approve of putting the Indians on the head waters of the San Juan, Navajo, Blanca, and Piedra.

Judge McFarland is going home. Gen. Hatch is off in a few days to Santa Fé, to look after "border troubles," "approve contracts," &c.; and McCauley and I are to go to White River, to inspect the country, consult the Indians, and report. I suppose (one never *knows* on this Commission) we will leave to-morrow; will postal card you from Fort Steele or Rawlins. About the 30th we expect to have our final council.

By the way, I want you and mother to decide what you wish in regard to my settling in Des Moines. Whatever I do, I want to feel that you and mother are *perfectly* satisfied. If you think you will need me at home, say so, and that will settle the question. I will disregard entirely my own preferences, and do gladly just what you and mother say. So I expect you to have it all decided by the time I reach home.

I have been so busy running around over the country, that I may appear to have neglected writing my friends. Remember me to all. Love to mother.

Affectionately, your son WILL.

What to do in the future.

Salt Lake City, Sept. 30, 1878.

MY DEAR MOTHER —

How I should like to see your face when you read this letter heading. You did n't know the Utes were in this part of the country, did you? Where should we find them, but at *Ute-tah?* The Uintah Indians are all Utes, and are part owners of the land we want to purchase, and I am here to obtain their consent.

We arrived here last Wednesday, and started Friday for the agency, 225 miles off, with a good team, and what seemed to be a strong wagon, expecting to reach it in four days. After making twenty-five miles, the right hind wheel became disgruntled, the spokes had a falling out, and brought us to a halt. We repaired damages as well as we could, and under difficulties continued our journey to Park City, ten miles beyond. I, to lighten the wagon, took passage with a Mormon, who happened along just in time. He was a skillful driver, found every stone in the road, which gave me a good bouncing. We had not gone far before we met Col. Watkins, who said the road beyond was impassable; that no wagon could ever reach

Ute-tah.

Break-down.

the agency. He said he had mentioned to the Indians the object of my visit, and it would only be necessary to write a letter, and send it by a courier. I immediately decided what to do. We went on to Park City, hired a horse, and dispatched our driver as courier.

This driver is quite a character—Smith, by name—and a Mormon. He said his father had two wives. I asked him if he called the one who was not his mother, mother No. 2? He said he called one mother, and the other "aunt Mary"; that aunt Mary, had always lived with them, and his father thought he might as well marry her. He says the Mormons believe baptism is a saving ordinance—that it is efficacious for the dead.

A character.

We stayed over night at a Mr. Kimball's. Mr. K. has 104 brothers and sisters, and, I was about to say, thirteen mothers. I wonder if the father gives all the children Christmas presents!

A numerous family.

Saturday we returned to this place. Yesterday morning McCauley and I started for church, but found there would be no Gentile service till twelve o'clock. We went to the

Temper-
ance.

Methodist church. Met a Mr. Kaighn (pronounced Cain), who remembered seeing you
in '76. The pastor introduced "Bro. Allen,"
a temperance reformer—a kind of Gough
No. 2—lately from San Francisco. I could
not see much of his face, for the hair and
whiskers. He was fifty-five minutes going
through his violent gymnastics.

Mormon
meeting.

At two o'clock we attended the Taber-
nacle. You remember what a queer, turtle-
shaped building it is. We were three minutes early, and there were about five thousand present. The organ is large and very
harsh. *On dit*—it requires four men to
blow it. The singing was poor, and the
preaching intolerable. The service opened
with communion, and was so devoid of so-
lemnity, that it seemed more like a free
lunch. While the bread was being passed,
a Bro. Hart spoke in defence of Latter-day-
Saintism. He said he had been an Episco-
palian, but that did not satisfy him. He
then joined the Baptists, and was ready to
cry "Eureka," but found *that* was not what
he needed; at last he became a Latter-day-
Saint, and was happy. The house of the
Lord was to be built in the last days on

the tops of the mountains. This was that church. The little stone that was cut out of the *mountain* was the church of the L.-d.-Saints. When the water was passed to him, he stopped preaching, and took a good drink. He seemed to be very thirsty; at any rate, his preaching was dry enough. He was followed by several other speakers; the last of whom compared Christ with Joseph Smith, making the latter equal in sinlessness, inspiration, and righteousness to the blessed Savior. The people seemed to be the scum of the earth, who had floated to Salt Lake City. I did not go out at night.

The Wasatch Mountains, their peaks all covered with snow, and the bright sun shining on them, look beautiful from my window. I expect to await the return of my courier, which will probably be by the last of the week.

Waiting for the courier.

Called on Gov. and Mrs. Emery Saturday night. They remembered you, and wished to be remembered when I wrote.

Love to father and all inquiring friends. If I can be spared for a few days, intend to take a look at San Francisco.

Affectionately, your son WILL.

21

Fort Fred Steele, Wy. Ter'y.
Oct. 15, 1878.

MY DEAR FATHER—

The courier despatched to the Uintahs returned, and reported that the Indians were all off hunting, and would not return before 1st prox. Agent Critchlow, a good and reliable man, has offered to see them for me.

California.

Having received permission to visit San Francisco, I lost no time in starting. Thursday we rode to the Cliff. I had not expected

Ocean of Peace.

to see the "Ocean of Peace" so soon. The fact that I was on its banks interested me much more than the seals and Cliff House. The Golden Gate could hardly have looked better. The sky was blue, and the sun was bright. Returning to the city, we were received very cordially by Mr. Harmon, who invited us to dine the day following.

In the evening, with a Mr. Barstow. Capt. Stone, chief of the detective force, Danezin, Chinese agent of Wells, Fargo & Co., and Mr. Jennings, patrolman of Chinese quarters, McCauley, Woog, and Major Lockwood, of the Interior Dep., and two other gentlemen, we set out on a visit to Chinatown. First came the restaurant, where we drank some very good Oolong tea, and attempted the chop sticks; then visited a merchant, and were interested by the rapidity with which he counted on the abacus. Next, was a "respectable" opium den, comfortably fitted up with an easy divan for two smokers. We then proceeded to a "low" opium den, and though it was dirty, and, in its approaches, filthy, I could not but feel that the quiet, deceptive slumber of the poppy was preferable to the senseless laugh, or bestial stupor of the whiskey drinker. It *may* be possible for a man to smoke opium and be respectable, but there is nothing respectable in being a whiskey drinker. The joss house was dark and dingy; the idols shapeless and without expression. We saw the gods of Wealth and Protection, and the god of Women. A small lamp was hung before each idol, kept constantly burning.

We then visited the theatre. House full; about 1,200 present. Of all the jargon I ever heard, this was the worst. I could see no sense in the play, though the costumes, embroidered in silk, were rich. After the first act, there were tumbling and fencing; the latter deftly done. After taking a look at a

China town.

Opium.

Music.

fourteen thousand dollar orchestrion, and hearing a few selections from "Lucia," we returned to the hotel.

Friday, in company with Etta and her father, I rode about the town, and we dined together. Saturday we started eastward. stopping here for things left behind.

Next Saturday we take a wagon and start for the southern country again for another council.

Please have a chair for me at the Thanksgiving dinner. It is snowing hard.

Love to you and mother.

  Affectionately,   WILL.

    Cheyenne, Wy., Oct. 18, 1878.

MY DEAR MOTHER—

Eastward.

You see I'm inclining toward home. McCauley and I left Fort Steele yesterday A. M., intending to take the Denver Pacific R. R. here for Denver, but the train had gone, and we now expect to leave at 3:15 for D.

I had a delightful visit at Fort Steele. It almost seemed like home. We were the guests of Mrs. Major Thornburg. The Major is now after the Cheyennes. Mrs. T. spared no .pains to make our stay as pleasant as possible. I was *about* used up from my trips about the country—tired and nervous—so I stopped over one day, and our hostess could scarcely 'have treated us with more kindly attention if we had been her own brothers.

Resting.

This P. M. I hope to be at Denver; to-morrow night, if all is well, in Alamosa, ready to start Monday for the south again.

I have been kept pretty busy; part of the time having to carry considerable money, but no harm has yet reached me. I trust it will not overtake us.

Love to father and yourself.

Affectionately, your son   WILL.

Lake City, Oct. 26, 1878.

MY DEAR FATHER—

Just arrived from Alamosa. Left there last night, with two thousand dollars in specie, and the same amount in checks, to be given Ouray's Indians in pursuance of instructions from the Int. Dept. As the stage company declined to take any responsibility for the safety of the treasure, I did n't sleep a wink, expecting a call from some of the Mexican population; but I was ready for them with an "eight-shooter Colt." But had no trouble, and to-night the cash is safely lodged in the express office.

Birthday.

Celebrated my birthday by riding on a stage, then a wagon, and lastly, a buckboard. My health is good, except a little cold. I weigh 150!!

I am very tired, so will not write more. Love to mother and yourself.

Affectionately, your son   WILLIE.

Los Pinos, November 1, 1878.

MY DEAR FATHER—

Wilderness.

Here I am again at the agency of the Wilderness.

My instructions from the Commission direct me to secure the consent of the Indians to the sale of their land south and west of the San Juan, and the little four mile square of Uncompahgre Park.

At present most of the Indians are out on a hunt; couriers have been sent for them, and I expect them in a week or ten days. I had a talk with a chief yesterday. He said the Indians did not want to sell their land, and suggested that a delegation of the principal men be sent to Washington to talk with the Great Father. He would not look at the money; said he did not want it.

Yesterday I wrote Gen. Hatch for authority to take three or four of them on, if necessary, as a *dernier resort*, provided the band would authorize the delegation to make sale of the land. Dernier resort.

I believe the impression they would receive from the extent of our country, and its great population, would make them more tractable; and I confess I am ready to undertake the job.

To-day the Gen'l and Judge meet the Southern Utes at Pagosa Springs, to agree on the price to be paid for that lower country. As I have secured the consent of all the other bands, this is all that is necessary to make our summer's work a success.

If the Indians are to be kept on the frontier country, they should be isolated from the whites; or, if they must mingle with the whites, they should be taken east, where the society is not composed of cutthroats, respectable (!) defaulters, and men who do not dare live any where else. Companions of Indians.

My health, as a rule, is very good. Love to mother. Affectionately, your son WILL.

Los Pinos Agency, Colorado,
Sunday, Nov. 3, 1878.

Mrs. Wm. Stickney,
Washington, D. C.

MY DEAR MOTHER—

A postal from Lieut. McCauley informs me a letter from home is waiting for me at the post office. It will probably arrive in a day or two.

Newspapers.

The last few days I have been able to keep up with the outside world—Mr. Abbott, the agent, having Boston papers sent to him daily; the latest is Oct. 22d; but that is better than none.

I expect to remain here about two weeks longer, and then —— go somewhere else.

Delegation to Washington.

The Indians seem set on going to Washington, and if permitted to take charge of them, I shall be satisfied. I know them pretty well, and think we could get along well together. They have been so badly deceived, that I do n't blame them for wanting to see and talk with the President.

How I wish the Gov't would make it an object for a real first-rate man to be Indian agent; pay him enough to live on, and then not require him to ask permission to take an

extra breath of fresh air. Some of the Dept.
rules sent to this agency, are simply ridicu-
lous. These people are not understood; they
are nomadic; as much so, probably, as the
wildest Indians in the country. To-day
they are here, to-morrow you can't find
them. Their religion teaches that work is
dishonorable and degrading; and about here,
to accomplish any thing, an intelligent farmer is indispensable. Some of the less difficult
things they can do. A few will dig potatoes
or pull corn; but the agency farmer must
plant, cultivate, and irrigate.

Indian farming.

As to their mental vision, they are children; they do not understand what is best for
them. They command, and it is done; and
it is difficult for them to see why the Great
Father, with all his boasted power, can't
keep his word. They are honest and faithful
in their pledges. In all this tribe, number-
ing, may be, three or four thousand, only
about a dozen thieves are known.

Chief Sapovoneri is in the room now—
about 5 ft. 7 in., heavy frame, old, white,
felt hat, with a small black feather *sewed* in;
hair to the top of his shirt collar, black vest,
blue, striped cotton shirt, buckskin leggings

Sapovo-neri.

and shoes, leather belt about the waist, to hold up a red, Indian blanket—a good, reliable, trustworthy man.

Indian
self-sac-
rifice.

Though he'would like to go to Washington, he says it is best he should remain here, lest some trouble might arise in his absence; an exhibition of self-sacrifice creditable to Indian or white man.

It is about 3:30 with you. My S. S. is just getting under way; how I wish I could be there. Kindest regards to the teachers you may meet, and love to father.

Affectionately, your son

WILL S. STICKNEY.

Los Pinos Indian Agency,

Monday morning, Nov. 2, 1878.

MY DEAR FATHER—

Many thanks for yours of 24th ult., with inclosure.

Though the country here is considered healthy, there are some diseases peculiar to it.

High
altitude.

The Doctor here, told me the majority of cases treated, is for giddiness and headache, caused by the high altitude. Mr. Abbott, the agent, is troubled in the same way. If you were in some of these places about here.

I fear you would n't have any head left. Mine has sometimes spun like a top, but no serious inconvenience has resulted from it.

Nothing new here. Indians not yet in. They, to a man, are opposed to transfer. They hate the soldiers almost as much as they do the white settlers; but if the transfer is not made, a broader, more comprehensive, and intelligent policy is necessary.

Among other improvements, I would suggest that the Indians should have a code of local laws, and some way of enforcing them. At present the Deputy Marshal and the U. S. Commissioner have to be called in, and from this agency they are twenty-five miles distant. At the White River, two hundred. Something might be invented to apply to these Indians, when they are bad, without the use of so much red tape, and such long delays.

Love to mother.

Affectionately, your son   WILL.

Laws for Indians.

Los Pinos Indian Agency, Colorado,
Tuesday, Nov. 5, 1878.

Mrs. Wm. Stickney,
Washington City, D. C.

MY DEAR MOTHER—

Since my last, nothing new has occurred, save a visit of some of the Navajos to their late friends — five men and one woman. Their faces resembled the lower class of Italians more than I have yet seen among any Indians. I wish I had a picture of them to send you; but a description will have to suffice. The leader was quite tall, with a dark-red handkerchief tied about his head, à la brigand; his long hair was tied and twisted at the back of his head, something after the water-fall style; an old shirt, and tight-fitting buckskin pants, extending nearly down to an antiquated pair of shoes, completed the picture—as to the dress. About his waist was a warlike looking belt, filled with cartridges and a revolver, while over his shoulder was slung a rifle of the most improved pattern.

I remarked to Mr. Abbott, that if that man should go to Italy, he would be arrested for a brigand.

Italians.

A brigand.

My Indians have not yet come in; the snow clouds are rolling up, though, just the same, and I fear, if they are much longer, I 'll have a sleigh-ride across the ranges.

This morning the agent and I are going to look after some sheep the Indians have lost. I almost wonder some of these mountains do not pour over and settle both the park and the park people.

Lost sheep

Love to father, and regards to friends.

Affectionately, your son

WILL S. STICKNEY.

Los Pinos Indian Agency, Col.,
Thursday, 7th Nov., 1878.
Mrs. Wm. Stickney,
Washington City, D. C.
MY DEAR MOTHER—

Just think of it—only three more weeks in this month, and then we 'll be in speaking distance from Christmas. I suppose father is looking up some Christmas music for the S. S. I will try and get up some little exercise for the chapel infant class, and will send it to you to give Miss Annie Wheeler. I am so isolated here, that at least for a couple of weeks I will be unable to reach any music

Preparations for Christmas.

store, so will have to depend largely on father's collection, and take his leavings. I am anxious the chapel should be decorated; as to presents, trees, &c., I 've not reached that yet.

Flowers.

While out here I have found some very pretty flowers, that will probably grow east; inclosed you will find the seeds of one of them, something like a lily. It should be started in a pot, and then transplanted. Please keep the seed, as I am anxious to see if it will grow with us.

This morning is cloudy, and threatens snow. We look for the Indians Saturday.

Give love to father, and regards to inquiring friends.

Affectionately, your son   WILL.

Los Pinos, Friday, 8th Nov., 1878.
MY DEAR FATHER—

Yours of Oct. 29th received yesterday. Sorry to hear your rheumatism is again asserting itself. This country has quite a rheumatic reputation; most every body has more or less of it; I have not altogether escaped, and the Indians are quite subject to it. Since their removal from their old agency at Coch-

etopa, mortality has been very great. The
cause is probably to be found in the large
number of hot springs that empty into the
Uncompahgre river, near the town of Ouray.
A dirty scum accumulates on these springs,
and is then carried off and dissolved in the
river. Some genuine cases of typhoid fever
have occurred, undoubtedly produced by the
poisoned water.

While I write, three chiefs are standing
by the stove. They came in about midnight;
are ready and anxious to go to Washington.
I hold a council to-morrow.

I send a package of bulbs by to-day's
mail.

Love to mother; kind regards to all.
Affectionately, your son   WILL.

Los Pinos Indian Agency, Col.,
          Friday night, 8th Nov., 1878.
Mrs. Wm. Stickney,
          Washington City, D. C.
MY DEAR MOTHER—

I have a council on the tapis (that is,
figuratively speaking, for I have not seen a
carpet for quite a while) to-morrow morning,
and I must therefore write you this evening.

Great mortality.

Indian chiefs.

Three of the chiefs have been in here (the agent's office, parlor, and reception room) all the evening. One of them (Billy) wanted to know to whom I was writing. I told him, and he wished to be remembered; said he would like to see my "piatch."—(Ute for mother.)

I have had an informal talk with these three this evening, and trust sincerely my efforts to-morrow will be successful. I should be very sorry to take the Commission any thing but a favorable report.

If I repeat myself in writing so often, you must excuse it, as I have no copying book with me.

Christmas festival.

Has father done any thing about speakers for Christmas Festival? If he has not, please ask him to write Dr. Lorimer before it is too late. Last year, you know, he had a previous engagement. We ought to be at the head of the list this year. But I am tired and sleepy, and must go to bed now.

Love to father, and kind regards to friends.

Affectionately, your son   WILL.

P. S.—Saturday morning.

A dark, damp morning; a mist—almost

a rain. Have just come from breakfast:— | Breakfast.
ham, beef hash, potatoes poorly boiled, and
sour bread, butter and tea very fair, heavy
doughnuts, and good molasses—a fair sam-
ple of our food.

Yesterday I wrote Theo, asking him to
look up some Christmas music for the chapel.
So if he comes round to talk music, you will
know what started him.

The way things look now, unless permitted to take some of these Indians to W.,
I doubt if I can finish up my Secretary's
work before the middle of Dec., and in that
event can only assist in carrying out any
plans for our Christmas Festival. W. S. S.

Los Pinos Indian Agency, Col.,
Monday, 11th Nov., 1878.
Mrs. Wm. Stickney,
Washington City, D. C.
MY DEAR MOTHER—

Another council on hand for this morning. The weather is very disagreeable, and
I am in doubt whether it will meet the pleasure of these "noble red men" to keep their
appointment this morning. They are as
fickle as the weather.

23

A dreary day.

Yesterday was a long, dreary day. I did n't feel very vigorous, and it was not till late in the afternoon I felt like reading any thing. Outside it was snow and rain, mixed and separate. In the evening I found a book containing a sketch of Savonarola, and sat up till half past ten to read it through.

Indian Sabbath.

The Indians have little regard for the Sabbath, and the agent has no service; not even Bible reading. Even if he had the disposition, it would be difficult to find a room here. The office is not larger than our library, and the chiefs and head men fill it up as they sit around on the floor, desks, boxes, and wherever they can.

A good sized room, combining a chapel, school room, and council chamber, should be provided.

Indian service.

But I have made so many suggestions about the Indian service, here and elsewhere, I fear you will think me a regular fault-finder.

By to morrow's mail I will try and send a pen-and-ink sketch of the agency and surrounding mountains, made for me by Mr. Flint, a Dartmouth graduate, and an ex-employée.

Love to father; kind regards to friends.
Affectionately, your son

WILL S. STICKNEY.

Los Pinos Indian Agency, Col.,
Tuesday, 12th Nov., 1878.

MY DEAR FATHER—

Council No. 1 is a thing of the past; but
as a memento, I have the signatures of all
the Indian men in this vicinity to a paper
giving their consent to whatever disposition
the southern Utes might make of the "L"
part of the Reservation.

After signing, the head chief said, "We
bear no ill will towards the Great Father,
but we do n't want the presents he sent."

I tried to find out the reason for this
unusual conduct, and from what I could
learn—First, they did n't want the Great
Father to think he must send a lot of presents to the Utes every time he wants them
to do any thing; and, secondly, those Utes
not here might think it was the purchase-
money for the lower land.

Yesterday I felt very miserably, and
would have spent most of the day on the
bed but for the council; but when we were

Council
No. 1.

fairly started, I was so interested, in the chief especially, that I forgot my indisposition. When the council convened, I was alone with the Indians and interpreter; the rest of the white folks being at dinner. I opened with a speech, and never had a more attentive audience. Twenty-three Indians were in the room, huddled together as best they could. When I finished, the head chief. Sapovoneri, made a speech to his people; it was natural eloquence; though spoken in an unknown tongue to me, I could not but feel that his utterances were those of an Ute Webster.

I wish I could describe this man. His face something like grandfather Kendall's, a very bright eye, high forehead, and an expression of intelligence that many of those who legislate for him would be proud to have. His build is strong, medium height, wears a light felt hat, high crown, with an eagle's feather. This king of the Utes rules wisely, and his word is law.

I wish you could see the beautiful view from the piazza. The range is covered with snow, and in the clear, thin air seems but a little way off, though it is 30 miles distant.

Speech to the Indians.

The Ute Webster.

Beautiful view.

Hope your rheumatism is on the mend, and that you will be in good condition for Thanksgiving dinner and Christmas preparations.

Love to mother, and kind regards to the bank folks.

Affectionately, your son   WILL.

Los Pinos Indian Agency, Col.,
        Thursday night, 14th Nov., 1878.
Mrs. Wm. Stickney,
        Washington City, D. C.

MY DEAR MOTHER—

I have had a peculiar experience to-day, and do not feel particularly in the mood for writing, but as I expect to go to Ouray to-morrow, will write a few lines to-day.

As yet I have heard nothing from Washington in regard to taking the Indians on; hope something will come soon, as I am anxious to start.

To-day the goods were issued. The agent said it was impossible to secure the names of the Indians receiving supplies, and he has not done it at any time. I requested the Lieutenant and the Doctor to remain at the door of the blacksmith shop, where the

A peculiar day.

issue was made, and we have a name—in a few cases manufactured by the Indians—but at all events a name for every head of a family that received any of the presents.

I was discouraged from attempting it, both by the agent and the escort, but the Will brought the way this time. During the issue, one of the ex-chiefs began to fight one of the plebs., but the result was not serious.

This pugilistic fellow is Chavano, a great rascal. He ought to be hung to the nearest tree, and if I can secure the evidence, of which there is plenty, against him that will put him in prison for life, you may be sure I will do so. He has boasted that he has killed a white man, and I have no doubt he has killed many. The Indians dislike him, and the whites hate him.

Each Indian received fourteen yards of calico, two pairs stockings, five yards flannel, two spools of cotton, two papers needles, two flannel shirts, four yards ticking, two handkerchiefs, and the chiefs, flannel, shawls, shirts, and socks extra. Every one seemed satisfied and happy. When the tickets were given out I passed around about fifty pounds of candy, and you should have seen how the young ones enjoyed it. I was real glad to see the little folks have such a good time; these poor little things do n't wear much, and have a pretty hard time.

I saw one real pretty squaw. She has just had her photograph taken. If I can get one, you shall have it. Wass, her husband, is one of two who are bigamists; the other is one of the proposed delegates to Washington. *A pretty squaw.* *Bigamists.*

What are you so busy about? I have n't heard from any of you for several days. I quote father's words:—"A postal, even, is very comforting." But I must go to bed.

Love to father, and kind regards to friends.

Affectionately, your son

WILL S. STICKNEY.

Los Pinos, Col., Sunday, Nov. 17, 1878.
Mrs. Wm. Stickney,
Washington City, D. C.
MY DEAR MOTHER—

Your letter of the 4th inst. reached me at Ouray yesterday. I am very sorry to hear father has been sick; but suppose he is improving, or you would have telegraphed.

Headache.

High
prices.

Unexpect-
ed twist.

In good
spirits.

I am glad every day that he did not venture this Rocky Mountain country. The altitude is so great that few persons escape being affected. The whole time I was in Ouray, my head ached hard; but it is all right now.

I had quite a good time in Ouray, but was considerably put out by the high prices —always higher to those purchasing for the Gov't.

One man amused me very much, by saying people could live in this country who could n't live any where else. I replied, such were my sentiments, judging from the specimens I had seen. The unexpected twist from the sanitary to the moral, that I gave his statement, was most too much for the gravity of the listeners.

Only a few people remain in town, living is so costly—sugar twenty-two, pepper seventy cents per pound, and other things in proportion. We daily see people leaving, expecting to return in the spring.

Some surveying friends dropped in on us last night. They leave to-day for the east; wish I could go with them.

There is nothing new about here. I am in pretty good spirits; not much congeniality with the people; so my life may be described as "staying." I hope to leave by the last of the week.

Thanks to friends for kind inquiries. Please remember me to all such.

Love to father. Hoping by this time you are *both* well, I will rest easy till I hear again. Affectionately, your son

WILL S. STICKNEY.

Los Pinos, Nov. 18, 1878.
MY DEAR FATHER—

I am still waiting to hear from the General. If he does not answer soon, I shall leave for a warmer clime.

Have had an informal talk with the chiefs, and with two of them visited the four mile square, twenty-five miles off. They said they would agree to the sale, but are anxious for a delegation to Washington.

I still think this the best thing to do. They will have their present notions very much modified by the sight of civilization, and a better comprehension of the strength of the Government. It will be easy to select men of good judgment, who have the confidence of the tribe.

Delegation to Washington.

24

Mental
capacity.

The mental exercises of these sons of the forest are very simple. They can scarcely do more than draw conclusions from premises that appeal to the senses; to *tell* them of the strength and resources of the Government has but little effect; to *show* it to them, is to convince.

I certainly hope word will soon come about their going. I want to leave this country; the altitude is altogether too great.

Love to mother, and kind regards to inquiring friends.

Affectionately, your son

WILL S. STICKNEY.

Los Pinos Indian Agency, Colorado,

Tuesday, Nov. 19, 1878.

Mrs. Wm. Stickney,

Washington City, D. C.

MY DEAR MOTHER—

While waiting for the team to be hitched up that will probably take me to Ouray, I will report to you and father. Rather than carry the silver back to Lake City, I am going to take it to Ouray (twenty-five miles distant), and have checks and greenbacks instead, and if all is well, hope to leave this part of the country on Thursday for Garland. *Expect* to eat my Thanksgiving dinner there; but do n't pretend to know any thing about my movements so far ahead.

Last night I went down, by invitation, to an Indian dance. I do n't know when I have laughed so heartily; the odd music (?) and the peculiar figures would have nonplused a Saratoga belle. I joined the orchestra, and then had to laugh at my own music. I hope you will be able to see some of these fellows exercise their heels; it will take you back to the queer manners of the Orientals. Would n't it be odd if I had played last night for one of old Jacob's sons to dance? and yet, the more I see of these people, the more I am convinced that they belong to other stock than ours.

Love to father, and kind regards to friends.

Affectionately, your son

WILL S. STICKNEY.

Fort Garland, Colorado,
Monday, 25th Nov., 1878.

Mrs. Wm. Stickney,
Washington City, D. C.

MY DEAR MOTHER—

Your letters of Oct. 28 and Nov. 12, and postals of 9th and 15th inst., came to hand last Friday night in Lake City.

Last Monday some of the chiefs wanted to go back to their camps for a week or so to see how matters were progressing. I immediately told them, if they left I should come here, where I could be comfortable and in telegraphic communication with Washington.

Good news   Hurrah!! Telegram from General Hatch this moment received. Says I am to take the delegation to Washington. Now I feel quite sure of being with you Christmas. But, *retournons nous à nos moutons.*

Left the agency Thursday, and rode thirty-five miles to the Cimaron River, Col., (there is another in New Mexico.) The road was very muddy and hilly, but we made good time, and reached the cabin before night. The meal would have been pretty scant had I not brought some canned baked beans and tomatoes with me.

After supper I spread my bedding on some hay in one corner of the room, and there slept. At four o'clock the next morning we were on the way to Lake City in a buckboard. As this team only went to Indian Creek, I hired a "private conveyance" to take me to my destination.

The aforesaid conveyance was an old farm wagon, and we were seven hours and a half going twenty-two miles: that made fifteen hours for that day.

Saturday I left Lake City at half-past six in the morning, and had another beautiful ride across the range; had little or no snow, reached Del Norte about eight in the evening, and then took a "jerky" and rode all night, reaching Alamosa about half-past three. A very severe snow storm set in about nine and lasted during the night. I had a buffalo robe given me at White River; this did me good service. Do not think I caught the least cold. One of the passengers was very drunk, and his soliloquies and incoherent babblings rendered sleep impossible.

The train left Alamosa at 6:20 A. M., so I had about two hours' sleep on the sofa in the hotel. Arrived here at 7:30, having traveled about two hundred and twenty-five miles from Thursday morning to Sunday at half-past seven. Yesterday slept nearly all day, and now feel quite rested.

Corres-
pondence.

Have written eleven letters to-day, and am getting tired. This business gives me a large official correspondence.

Telegraphed you yesterday of my arrival; thought you would be glad to hear of my safe return.

Did the bulbs reach you safely? But I must stop, as I have three more letters to write to-night, besides some copying that should be done.

Give lots of love to father. Expect to be in Washington about the 15th prox., and want him to *see* me. So he must tell Dr. Marmion to hurry and cure those eyes.

Kind regards to friends.

Affectionately, your son　　WILL.

P. S. Inclosed you will find the card of Mr. ——, a gossipy gas-bag, masculine gender, singular number, and invariably first person; agrees best with whiskey, unqualified.　　W. S. S.

Fort Garland, Colorado,
Last day of Nov., 1878.

Mrs. Wm. Stickney,
Washington City, D. C.

MY DEAR MOTHER—

As I have received no news from home | No news.
for several days, suppose you must be expecting my return.

Have been at work all day copying the remainder of my minutes; no small job. This evening am feeling quite well, though very tired. Am anxious to hear how father's eyes are.

The church letter business is no more than I expected; regret very much the spirit that prompted it. No church can prosper if the spirit of jealousy or what not receives more attention than that holy strife—I might call it—to verify the exhortation of Holy Writ, "Brethren, see that ye love one another with a pure heart." But 't is not for us to remonstrate. No load is ever given us greater than we can bear. Let us try and "do the duties that lie next us," and the result will be all right.

The mail has just come, but brings nothing from home.

Love to father and yourself.

Affectionately, your son   WILL.

Fort Garland, Colorado,
Tuesday P. M., 3d Dec., 1878.
Mrs. Wm. Stickney,
Washington, D. C.

MY DEAR MOTHER—

You see I am still here, though likely
to pull out in a few days. This P. M. received despatch from the Commission, saying I was to bring the Indians on with their
share of the money due them; but I have n't
any of their money; Gen. Hatch has it all.
Have telegraphed the General, and guess
he will transfer without any further trouble.
Will try hard to reach home by the 15th.

Hunting small game.

This morning, for recreation, I went with
Maj. Shorkley hunting jack rabbits; something like a hare, only four or five times as
large. It was my first hunt for a good many
years. Enjoyed the tramp ever so much.
Think I will do more hunting; it exercises
a body all over. The next time I come into
this country, will bring my own gun.

For a game country I never saw a better;
though on the line between Wyoming and

Colorado it is said to be magnificent—deer, elk, antelope, and mountain sheep, sage-hens, and trout three times a day!

Love to father and yourself.

Affectionately, your son   WILL.

Fort Garland, Colorado,
Saturday night, Dec. 7, 1878.
Mrs. Wm. Stickney,
Washington City, D. C.

MY DEAR MOTHER—

I rather guess another Saturday night will pass before seeing you once again, but trust it will be only a few days over.   Am so glad to hear father is better; not hearing for so long, feared he was worse.

My plans are all made to leave for home, but they may be changed.

Most of the time here is occupied in copying the minutes, making out reports, .&c.

Christmas must not go by without some demonstration.   Tell father I'll be all ready to help him and myself out in a little while; but he must have something to start with; have not been able to lay hands on a thing here.   Will see if the Indians have any performances sufficiently dignified for

Christmas preparations.

25

such an occasion. Billy might make a speech; he knows a little English. But we will see.

Good night. Love to father and yourself.

Affectionately, your son   WILL.

Denver, Dec. 14, 1878.

MY DEAR FATHER—

You know the "best laid plans of mice and men gang aft aglee," and though I left every thing at the agency in such shape that half a day's notice would start my delegation, now they are debating again who should go, and I am *waiting* for their sluggish minds to come to a conclusion. Communication is so slow in that country that it is impossible to tell the result for three or four days at least. Had rather wait than go after them across the mountains in an open wagon.

The Com'r, in his dispatch, says nothing as to how I am to pay the expenses of the delegation. Of course I declined to budge an inch till this was provided for, and there have several days been consumed in telegraphing, mailing, &c., between the Com-

Waiting.

missioner of Indian Affairs, General Hatch,
and myself, which ought to have been avoided. The Com'r asked me, by telegraph, if
the Indians would consent to have the expenses of the delegation paid from their
funds. The Indians were at Los Pinos, I
at Fort Garland, seventy-two miles distant,
two mountain ranges between, and no telegraph!

I occupy myself reading Gibbon and Occupa-
superintending the manufacture of a pair of tion.
boots.

Will telegraph when we leave, and if
the delegation is too slow, will put them in
charge of an interpreter and go ahead.

Love to mother.

Affectionately, WILL.

Denver, Col., Dec. 16, 1878.

MY DEAR FATHER—

Just one more letter from Denver, and
then I'll try a change of base, and call it
Topeka for a while. Topeka.

This morning started Curtis, the interpreter, after my Indian delegation, and to-
morrow I expect to take the train for Topeka,
where I will assist the Judge in preparing

the report; that means about three days' hard work. Am trying to fix matters so I will not be specially needed. Will ask the Judge to accompany them from Topeka, and if he will, please have the carriage at B. & P. dépôt at nine o'clock, P. M., Dec. 24.

Last night heard a first-rate sermon from the Baptist minister on "Manliness;" enjoyed the service very much.

To-day we have had more snow, and I have spent the time reading, with the exception of my morning walk.

Good health.

Health first-rate; never better; but will be glad to be home once more.

Kind regards to the bank friends. Love to mother and yourself.

Affectionately, your son   WILL.

Christmas announcement.

P. S.   I have a Christmas announcement for you and mother: After very careful and prayerful thought, have concluded not to go west to live. Will remain in Washington, and practice law there—at least, there will be my home.   WILL.

Topeka, Ks., Dec. 20, 1878.

MY DEAR FATHER—

You see I have at last made a start. Am detained here, having a good time, waiting for my wards. They left the agency day before yesterday, I suppose, so you may expect us all before long. Hope to be with you on the eve of the 25th, Indians or no Indians; but trust we may all arrive together, and that I may, together with you, celebrate the *dies dierum.*

I have almost lost my patience waiting for these Indians. One day they would say "Yes," and the next, "No,"—unable to decide who should constitute the delegation.

Had I been there, think I would have brought them to a decision *subito.*

About fourteen inches of snow here. and splendid sleighing, though the sleighs are most all improvised.

The Judge will leave here with me. Love to mother.

Affectionately, your son   WILL.

On Christmas eve our hearts were made glad and thankful by the safe return of the dear boy, who had been absent so long, and

[marginal notes: Indians or no Indians. Snow. Home again.]

who had labored so faithfully and energeti-
cally, amidst some trying embarrassments, to
discharge, to the satisfaction of the Government and the Commission, the arduous duties of his position.

The experience and duties were all new,
and the members of the Commission were
strangers; yet with that self-reliance which
always characterized him; with an honest
determination to devote his best energies to
the work; stimulated by an honorable ambition to deserve well of his associates; unde-
terred by obstacles which might have discouraged one of less enthusiasm; conscious
of the responsibilities he had assumed; he
entered with characteristic vigor upon the
expedition.

Success.   His success was equal to his expectations.   His associates were captivated by
his courteous deportment, obliging disposition, executive ability. and his wonderful
energy and resources so frequently brought
into requisition during the trip.

Notwithstanding his unaccustomed ex-
posure and hardship; his night and day
travel by rail, wagon, and horseback; his
hard fare and poor accommodations while

in the Indian country, he returned in im- *Improved health.*
proved health, with a decided gain in flesh.

His spirits were never better. He was
enthusiastic over the success of the Commission; had gained useful information concerning the extent and resources of the country; was becoming more and more interested
in the Indians, for whose amelioration he
made many useful suggestions to the Department; he had looked upon the "Ocean of
Peace" through the Golden Gate, and he
now declared himself ready to work for the *Ready for work.*
church and Sunday School. or wherever he
could do the most good.

Just here it may not be out of place to
insert the following Report to the Hon. Ute
Commissioners, not only for its inherent interest, but also for the evidence it gives of
careful study of the situation, and thorough- *Faithful-ness to his trust.*
ness of execution in the trust committed to
him. Indeed, the manner in which he did
his work, on the several occasions on which
he was called to do public service, justify
the remark, often made, that his death was *A com-mon loss.*
more than a loss to his family and imme-
diate friends.

REPORT.

Fort Garland, Colo.,
November 27, 1878.

GENTLEMEN —

At a meeting of the Commission held in Denver September 11, and also by a supplemental telegram dated September 24, 1878, the Secretary, accompanied by Lieut. C. A. H. McCauley, as escort, was instructed to ·'proceed as speedily as possible to the White River agency, to complete arrangements already made with U. M. Curtis, interpreter, to report as to the condition of the Indians and the agricultural capacity of the country, and to secure from the Indians, in writing, their consent to the sale of that part of the Reservation immediately south and west of the San Juan mining district," and then "to proceed to the Uintah agency with the same instructions."

In pursuance of these instructions, I beg leave to present the following as my report:

Thursday morning, September 12, 1878, Lieutenant McCauley and myself took the Denver Pacific Railroad to Cheyenne, and thence the Union Pacific to Fort Steele, in all about 284 miles, reaching the last-named place at midnight.

Major Thornburg, commander of the post, received us and kindly accommodated us at his own table.

The following day was occupied in securing an outfit with which to make the trip. The officers of the post placed at our disposal a buck-board and a pair of mules. At Rawlins, some sixteen miles distant, I hired a guide and an extra pair of horses, which were sent ahead as a relay.

Saturday, September 14th, we left Fort Steele for the agency, riding that day about sixty miles. From the Fort to Pine Grove, the ranch where the relay awaited us, is an alkali country; generally rolling, and with very little vegetation save sage-brush and grease-wood. After leaving Rawlins we passed but one house, and that is about sixteen miles out. From the Grove to Snake River the road crosses the Continental Divide, a series of high mesas separated by arroyas of greater or less depth. These table-lands abound in game, and furnish good summer ranges for cattle. Grass and sage-brush are the products of the soil, ex-

Continental divide.

26

cept on the banks of an occasional stream, where the cotton-wood seems to flourish.

The second day we rode about fifty-one miles, crossing Snake River Valley to Fortification Creek. This valley, about two miles wide at the crossing, is beautifully located, partially protected by high plateaus, and with good mountain pastures at its head. The river is lined with cotton-wood and the bottom-land well covered with grass. On our return, about eight miles above the river-crossing, we passed a mild soda-spring; the only mineral development of the valley reported.

Quite a number of settlers have already located along the river, an Indian trader, still doing a flourishing business, being the **Stock raising.** pioneer. The principal occupation is stock-raising; the cattle ranging about the mountains in summer, and sixty or seventy miles west and south in the winter, where the grass is not covered with snow. Little is done at farming, the settlers having no chance to grind their wheat nor market for their vegetables. But most of the usual crops, except corn, so far as they have been tried, seem to do well.

The third day we crossed the Bear River, known on the map as the "Yampa." Like the Snake, this valley, though sparsely settled, is used principally for cattle-ranges. The season being short and the demand small, little or nothing is done in the way of farming. The Indian trader at this post, the nearest to the agency, has a small garden, and supplied us with fresh tomatoes and very fine potatoes of his own raising.

From this valley to the agency, about sixty miles, the road crosses mountain ranges of no mean height; but before sundown Tuesday, the 17th, after riding in four days about two hundred miles, we reached the White River Valley and the Indian agency.

The agent, Mr. N. C. Meeker, received us very cordially, and introduced us to the scanty quarters and poor fare of the agency boarding-house.

Wednesday a council was convened, and, as a result, I have the pleasure to submit herewith the written consent of the most of the chiefs and headmen, viz., thirty-four in number, to "whatever disposition the Capotes, Muaches, and Weeminuches may make" of the southern and western strips of the Reservation.

The Indians were very friendly, and wished the Great Father to distinctly understand that they, the White River Utes, do not want to fight nor in any way incur the displeasure of the whites. In regard

to the late murder in Middle Park, they disclaim all connection. Washington, who was present at the murder, claimed to have advised Piah against it, but his counsel was disregarded. Piah has not yet returned to the agency. If he could be caught and punished by the government authorities, the effect on the Indians would unquestionably be for the best, and would have a tendency to prevent an early repetition of the crime.

Mr. Curtis, employed as interpreter by the Commission, presented his report as to the arable land between the Los Pinos and the White River agencies. It is submitted herewith. I also approved his action in proceeding to Middle Park so promptly with seven of the leading Indians to prevent any further trouble by an apprehension on the part of the settlers that a general outbreak was imminent.

The presents ordered by the Commission for these Indians had not arrived, and as the agent has no interpreter, I instructed Mr. Curtis to remain until they came, and with the agent to distribute them to the Indians who had assisted the work of the Commission.

On my return, the goods having reached Bear (Yampa) River, I stopped a day at the trader's store to inspect them and approve the bill.

The condition of the White River Indians and the agricultural capacity of their country seem to be but little known outside of the agency and its vicinage. The old distinction of the Yampa and Grand River bands is rapidly disappearing, and they all call themselves "White River" Utes. The chief no longer has absolute authority, but acts only in accordance with the will of a majority of his councilors. They are all well off; hardly an Indian has less than twenty-five ponies. All have good guns and an abundance of ammunition. Game is plentiful, and the Indians are rich from their hunting. They hunt *off* the Reservation. going two. three, and four hundred miles

White River Utes.

north, preferring to keep their own game intact until the rest is gone. They also own in common fifteen hundred head of cattle, from which herd the beef is supplied. None of these cattle are supposed to be killed without the consent of the agent.

The White River Valley is so mild and so well protected in winter that the herd can graze within sixteen miles of the present agency during the whole season. This is the place to which the honorable Commissioner of Indian Affairs has ordered the removal of the agency. There the valley is wider, and the fall of the river so great that irrigating ditches are being easily constructed, and a fall of sixty feet for milling purposes can be secured. The agent is already breaking up the ground, and hopes to obtain a wheat crop at least by next season.

The settlers on Snake and Bear Rivers regard this valley as far superior to their own, and better adapted for grazing and agricultural purposes than any other part of this country. All seemed to concur that at least five thousand Indians could be supported there; the agent, a professional far-

mer, claiming that he can support ten thousand people in that valley and its subsidia-
ries. He also says: "This White River
range on the Reservation is unequalled in
the west, and it possesses the great advan-
tage of not being trespassed upon by any
other herds; a condition that diminishes the
labor of herding and reduces the losses by
estrays and stealings. This range has a
money value of at least $50,000. There is
no section comparable with it south of the
.divide between White and Grand Rivers."

This country seems much better adapted
for cultivation than the Uncompahgre Valley. It lies south of the mountain ranges,
which protect it from the extreme cold; it is
fully as near a railroad, about 175 miles over
a good natural road, and is well removed
from the settlers. Should it be thought best
to consolidate the Los Pinos with the White
River agency, there certainly would be no
difficulty in supplying them; the White Rivers probably have not more than 400, certainly less than 500, and your honorable
body has already approximated the number
in Ouray's band as about 1,000, making a
total of, at most, 1,500 Indians.

Police
necessary.

In reporting as to the needs of these people, I would beg leave to call attention to the necessity of a police force. The agent has not secured his quota allowed by law, deeming such a small number insufficient to compel obedience. Some of these Indians need something more than moral suasion. While the majority mean well, and would probably prevent any open outbreak, the few who are ill-disposed can make great trouble for the agent, and commit depredations in the vicinity of the Reservation with little fear of being punished. A Ute police could do much toward preventing a repetition of the Middle Park calamity, and be of great value in securing the guilty should any insubordination occur.

Another want now felt at the agency is a trading-post. At present the nearest is sixty miles, and the next fifty miles beyond. If these trips of one and two hundred miles for barter could be checked, it would undoubtedly help to keep these people on the Reservation and localize them. Certainly some good might be effected by allowing any and all traders to build first-class buildings at the agency and do their trading

there. Liquor should, of course, be prohib-
ited, but to make the experiment a success,
ammunition will have to be sold, though
that may be easily regulated by the order
of the agent or the chief of police. So long
as the present system of the Government
obtains in regard to the rations of the Indians, they will have to hunt, and it seems
but fair that under certain restrictions they
be allowed to buy their powder and lead at
reasonable prices, and that, too, on the Reservation.

The Indians had considerable to say
about the money that was due. They seem
less anxious for the money itself than to
have the debt in some way discharged.
There are a few things they would be benefited by having, and I will ask your permission to enumerate them:

First. A grist-mill. It will be difficult
to make these Indians self-sustaining without such a mill; and if it were built with
their own money, they would probably take
a greater interest in learning how to manage
it. At present, I am informed, the Government pays nine cents a pound for flour delivered at the agency; the agent estimates it

Powder for In-dians.

27

would cost three cents a pound if he had a mill.

Secondly.   About twenty - five short-horned bulls. Most of the cattle belonging to the Indians are of the long-horned Texas stock, and an infusion of the short-horned breeds would not only improve the milking qualities of the cows, but also increase their average weight. If the other band is located here, the herd, without great expense, could be enlarged sufficiently to meet the demands of all the Indians without the aid of beef contractors.

Thirdly.   About twelve stallions, well adapted for draught purposes. The Indian ponies are of very little use, except under the saddle, and if work-horses will be needed for farm purposes, either they must be purchased and taken into the country or else the native stock must be improved. The Indians think much of their ponies, and any effort tending toward their improvement would be gratefully appreciated.

Fourthly.   A good stock of farming implements and seeds. The agent reported that several families had expressed their willingness to work, but he had no tools for them. They do not need expensive articles, but something strong and durable, likely to stand the hard knocks novices will give them. Of seeds, the staples are most needed.

Fifthly. An increase of the police force allowed by law. This agency would, under the general act, be allowed eight or nine policemen. At the start, if the agencies are to be consolidated, it would probably be well to have the number increased to fifty, the extra to be paid from the tribal fund. Fifty men carefully chosen, required to be at or near the agency, might help to keep the rest of the band from going so far from the Reservation. The first year or so such a force would need a chief, and a good man can now be secured for twelve or fourteen hundred dollars. I refer to Captain U. M. Curtis; he has great influence with these Indians, has lived with them for many years, speaks their language well, and has led them as soldiers. In Mr. Curtis the agent would not only have an interpreter, a want he sadly feels at present, but would also have in charge of his police a capable man, respected and looked up to by the Indians. At least, work in such a position could be easily tested by a year's trial, it being his duty not only to keep the Indians quiet and orderly, but make them remain on the Reservation; provided, of course, traders at the agency are permitted to sell ammunition, though it be in limited quantities, and subject to the order of the agent.

No time to be lost.

In conclusion, whatever is to be done should be done quickly. It is very important that they should be put to work early in the spring, and if they are henceforward to live under a new *régime*, the sooner it is introduced to them the better.

It is certainly to be desired that the buildings at the new agency will be of a somewhat more civilized character than the rude log huts at present occupied. The Indians learn only by imitation, and with the good saw-mill now on the Reservation, plenty of lumber, and the good supply of employés, there is nothing to prevent the erection of comfortable homes, and at the same time models fit to be copied.

I left the agency on my return Wednesday night, September 18, and reached Fort Steele Monday, the 23d of September.

Having received telegraphic instructions

to proceed to the Uintah Reservation, escorted by Lieutenant McCauley, I left Fort Steele September 24, arriving at Salt Lake the evening of the following day.

Thursday, the 26th, was occupied in fitting up for the trip. A wagon, warranted to carry us over the mountains, and a guide were hired.

Friday morning at sunrise we started. and had gone but twenty miles before the wagon broke down. Finding it useless to attempt the mountains with a broken wagon. to save time I hired a horse and sent our driver as courier over the trail to the agency. requesting the agent to procure of the Indians their release to the country south and west of the San Juan district. and returned to Salt Lake City. While waiting for the return of the courier I received a call from Tabby, chief of the Uintahs, and Tackawanna, sub-chief. They each expressed themselves as pleased with the work they are doing at the agency and as willing to sign the release. The courier returned with a letter from the agent, to the effect that the Indians were out hunting. but as soon as possible he would convene them and secure

Break down.

their signatures to the release. About a month later I received this document properly signed and witnessed, and take pleasure in presenting it herewith.

From the Indians met and agent Critchlow it would seem as if their needs were about the same as at White River. They particularly requested that stoves, wagons, and harness be given them, in addition to whatever stock and farming implements might be sent.

As requested, I reported on Saturday, October 20, at Fort Garland, to the Chairman of the Commission.

All of which is respectfully submitted.

W. S. STICKNEY,
Secretary Ute Special Commission.

The Hon. UTE COMMISSIONERS.

Upon reporting to the Chairman of the Commission at Fort Garland, he received additional instructions; their execution will be found detailed in his report, which follows.

INSTRUCTIONS.

Rooms Ute Commission,

Alamosa, Colo., October 22, 1878.

SIR: You will proceed to the Los Pinos agency and endeavor to obtain the consent of the Ute Indians to sale of all land south of 38°. The land now important to secure is the Uncompahgre Park adjoined to the town of Ouray.

It is believed the payment of so much of their annuities to the Tabequaches, now the only tribe whose consent is required to relinquish this land south of parallel 38° 10', can be obtained, and that the amount of $4,000, with the goods authorized purchased by the Indian Department, to be issued by the agent under the direction of this Commission, will obtain the consent of these Indians to disposal of their lands at such a sum as the Commission may believe it is the interest of the government to pay and for the Indians to receive.

You will assist the agent in the issue of the goods purchased by him, as directed by the Indian Department, in letters dated July 17, 1878.

You will obtain the signatures in the

manner designated by Department of the Interior, in letter of September 25, 1878, copy of which is inclosed. You will understand that only such Indians are to be paid the money annuity as agree to sell and remove from the Uncompahgre Park. The question of their future reservation is a matter to be hereafter decided by the President, through the Department of the Interior, on such action as Congress may take.

If the Indians will not sign an article to relinquish the land upon payment of this money *per capita*, you will return the money, or such balance as you may have on hand upon making payments under these instructions, with report of your action, notifying the Commission of your arrival at Alamosa.

Lieutenant McCauley, Third Cavalry, is ordered to report to Los Pinos Agency, to assist and witness payment of annuities, and will accompany you on your journey.

Yours, very respectfully,

EDWARD HATCH,
*Brevet Major-General
and Chairman Ute Special Commission.*

W. S. STICKNEY, *Sec'y Com'n.*

Washington, Dec. 26, 1878.

GENTLEMEN—

On the 22d day of October I received the accompanying instructions from General Hatch, Chairman of the Commission.

The following is therefore submitted as a partial report.

I left Alamosa, accompanied by Lieut. C. A. H. McCauley, on the night of the 23d of October, with $2,000 in standard silver dollars, the same amount in checks on the First National Bank of Denver, and five boxes of goods as presents for the Indians. In due time we arrived at our destination with both money and goods.

Most of the Indians were hunting when we reached the agency, but messengers were soon dispatched, and in a few days a council was convened, and as a result I have the pleasure of submitting to you the release of the Reservation south and west of the San Juan district by the Tabequaches.

For reasons which I deemed satisfactory the agent preferred that the presents purchased by the Commission at Alamosa should be paid for out of the tribal funds in possession of the Chairman, rather than by certified

Partial report.

Result of Council.

28

vouchers issued by the agent; I therefore
submit a receipt for all the goods delivered
to the Indians.

It was with considerable difficulty that
they were induced to receive the presents,
Sapovoneri, the chief, declaring that the
Great Father must not think it necessary to
send presents every time he wished a favor
of them. The money they requested me to
return to the Great Father, or with it pay
the expenses of a delegation to Washington;
they declined to receive it, as it had not
been given them when promised. They
evidently feared that it was a ruse to purchase the Uncompahgre Park, in regard to
which they declined to treat. Finding them
very anxious to have a delegation visit
Washington, I was encouraged to believe
that if a few of the leading men of the
tribe could talk with the President in person,
the sale of the four-mile square could be
effected.

Authority was requested to take such
delegation to Washington, and permission
having been granted, I sent Captain U. M.
Curtis, as interpreter, to bring them from the
agency here.

As soon as any definite conclusion is come to in regard to sale of the Park I will report it at once to your honorable body.

After Lieutenant McCauley witnessed the issue of the presents to the Indians he returned to Alamosa.

The checks and unexpended balance of the $2,000 cash, together with duplicate receipts, have been returned to the Chairman, as per his receipts.

Very respectfully,

W. S. STICKNEY,
Secretary Ute Special Commission.

To the honorable the
UTE SPECIAL COMMISSION.

An untried and unexpected experience now awaited my son, which was destined to prove the strength of his christian faith, as his late employment had tested his ability for severe mental and physical labor.

The particulars of these strange proceedings will be given in another chapter.

New experience.

CHAPTER V.

CHURCH TROUBLES.

THY friend has a friend, and thy friend's friend has a friend: be discreet.
—TALMUD.

JUSTICE to the memory of my son calls for a brief statement of his connection with the troubles which agitated the Calvary Baptist Church of this city, of which he and his parents were members, during the latter part of 1878, and early in 1879.

The pastor was receiving a salary of three thousand dollars a year; but the Trustees having been unable to provide a regular income sufficient to pay this sum, with other necessary expenses, seriously considered the necessity of its reduction.

A necessity.

While attending an International Sunday School Convention in Atlanta, Ga., in April, 1878, I received a letter from my son, dated Washington, April 18. 1878. containing the following:

"At the church business meeting last night, about sixty were present. In your absence I was chosen clerk *pro tem.*

Report.

"The Chairman of Trustees reported that, though the pastor had offered to give the church $41.67 per month (period not stated), the committee still thought it but right to report the same as heretofore, viz.: $2.500 to be the salary of pastor from 1st prox.

"The correspondence of the committee with the pastor was read, and the question was thus fairly opened.

"The arguments against adopting the report were —

"1. Under the contract we had no right to cut down the salary.

"2. That the proposed contribution by the pastor was equivalent to $500 a year; hence it was just what the proposed reduction contemplated.

"3. That it was a magnanimous offer on the part of the pastor.

"4. To reduce the salary, would be to say the pastor was worth but $2,500.

"5. That the church was never in so prosperous a condition financially as now; and if the $500 was taken, it should be paid back as a Christmas gift.

"The arguments in favor of the report were —

"1. That if we continued the salary at $3,000, nominally, and paid but $2,500, we should place ourselves in a false position before the world.

"2. That $41.67 per month was not the same as $500 per year, as the pastor could discontinue it at any time — in two, three, or six months.

"3. That the church should not become a pensioner on the pastor.

"4. That arguments one and five of the other side were not true, and three was doubtful.

"A substitute for the report was of- fered, continuing the salary at $3,000, and accepting the pastor's offer of $41.67 per month.

"The substitute was sustained by a vote of 33 to 9. The clerk, pro tem., was one of the nine. I think these were all that stood up when the vote was taken."

Several members of the church were so aggrieved by this action, that they surren- dered their pews, and a few took letters of dismission.

The agitation continued several weeks, when charges were preferred against several members, including my son.

He had not concealed his disappointment at the action referred to in his letter above, and had not hesitated to express his opinion that it was not *honest* for a church to assume

29

Amend- ment.

such a position, and not honest in the pastor to be a party to it.

He was formally charged with having said the pastor was dishonest, and resolutions for his expulsion from the church were presented.

At the trial before the church, Will appeared with his defence in writing. A friend had borrowed the manuscript before the meeting, and, without consulting him, had met several members of the church who were in sympathy with the prosecutors, and read to them his paper.

As Will was about to proceed to read his defence, on the night of the trial, a brother who had heard the contents of the paper, suggested that if the accused would omit reading all his defence, except the last one or two paragraphs, he thought the church would be ready to act favorably on his case.

Will complied with the suggestion, and after taking his seat a resolution, exonerating him from any blame worthy of church discipline, was adopted.

The following is the paper he had pre-pared, but which, for the reasons above, was not read:

DEAR BRETHREN AND SISTERS
of the Calvary Baptist Church —

On Sunday, January 12, 1879, immediately after Sunday School, I was waited upon by two deacons, and informed that charges had been made against me; was told what the charges were, and the brethren asked (I quote their words), "Will you meet us some time to-morrow?"

Fearing misunderstandings and mistakes. I requested that our communications be had in writing, and that I be furnished a copy of the charges, with the names of my accusers.

Tuesday I received an envelope, directed to me, containing an anonymous communication, addressed to the deacons of the Calvary Baptist Church.

The next day, Wednesday, about seven o'clock in the evening, I received official information from the deacons that the "matter concerning the charges preferred against you [me] would be submitted to the church this evening"—in about half an hour from its receipt by me.

I have noted these few facts, so that you might have a fair understanding of

29 B

the progress of my case before it reached you.

The gist of the accusations made against me is, that I have questioned the honesty of the pastor.

Answer.

That I have so done, except in regard to his conduct in a single instance, I most emphatically deny; but I will answer the charges separately, and in conclusion will attempt to explain what prompted my remarks.

The first charge, that I had said, "I have no confidence whatever in the honesty of the pastor," is not a fair statement of my remark, in that it does not recite the circumstances under which it was made.

The unqualified statement, as quoted, I never uttered. The circumstances were as follows:

I had met one of the brethren on the street; we walked together until reaching his house, when I was invited in. In the course of our conversation, the conduct of the pastor in regard to the salary question was alluded to. The brother expressed his views, and I mine. I characterized that conduct as wanting in openness, squareness,

Salary question.

frankness, and honesty, and in that connection, and referring to that alone, the remark charged was made.

Some time after this conversation, I concluded to go to the pastor and explain my feelings to him. I went twice to his study, but he was out each time. Soon after I met him at the bank, when I explained, at length, why I thought as I did. My father was present at that interview.

Explanation.

At the business meeting in April, during the discussion of the subject, I used language nearly tantamount to this, to which no exception whatever was taken; a strange circumstance, if this opinion was such heresy as my five anonymous accusers would now have you think.

The brother with whom I conversed, appeared to understand, at the time, the meaning and bearing of the words I used. The conversation was of a private nature, and I naturally considered that it was only necessary for me to make myself clear to him. I had no thought that my words would be repeated, and much less, so repeated as to give an impression different from that intended—for in every quotation of them that

Wrong Impression.

has reached my ears, only a portion of the conversation, and that, the portion rehearsed in the accusations, was repeated.

I submit that it is not right thus to separate a clause from its proper modifications and connections, and report it as an unqualified statement. If this is proper, King David must be charged with teaching "There is no God," though the whole passage says, "The fool saith in his heart; there is no God;" and in like manner, we might with as much propriety charge our Savior with teaching the heathenish doctrine of "an eye for an eye," &c., for he certainly *did* say that; though if we take what follows, we find his meaning just the contrary.

A man's words must of course be taken in their entirety. If the remark charged had been made in a general conversation, regarding Mr. Mason's moral character, it might be proper to introduce it here stripped of its connections; but when it was so intimately connected with what preceded, in fact only a conclusion in that one case, certainly it is but christian and "honest" that the circumstances under which the remark was made. should always accompany its repetition.

Absurdity

Connection of thought.

The second remark charged, that I "did not blame Mr. Fox for leaving the church; he dont want to belong to a church where the pastor is dishonest." was spoken just after the business meeting, nearly a year ago. in answer to a question by a lady, and after expressing my opinion so emphatically in the meeting, I cannot believe that any but wilful misconstruction would apply my expression otherwise than to the conduct of the pastor at that time.

Wilful misconstruction.

In conclusion, I will endeavor to state briefly my reasons for the opinions held on this question.

Reasons for opinions.

My Bible teaches that deception should be avoided as distasteful to God.

To my mind. it was a species of deception, when the pastor would have credit for receiving $3,000 for his services, when he knew he. at the end of the year, would actually have received but $2,500.

To me it is the same in principle if we had raised the salary to $10,000, and allowed a reimbursement of $7,500: and to me this would not have been any more of a deception.

Again. in 1 Thess., v: 22, we are told to

"abstain from all appearance of evil." Now even if the pastor's alternative was right *in itself*, the fact that others in the church thought it wrong, and that business men, *not in the church*, considered it a deception, should convince an honest mind that the proposition had at least the "appearance of evil;" and I reasoned, perhaps incorrectly, that a mind bent on doing the Master's will would be eager to change a course so at variance with the Divine teaching.

These thoughts, among others, led me to the opinions I held and expressed under the circumstances herein before set forth; and these convictions I still hold, not ignoring the consciences of my brethren who see no moral principle involved, any more than did Paul consider his conscience ignored when he declined eating meat because it was an offence to some of his brethren.

The weaker conscience.

But in reviewing in my mind the whole subject; the harsh construction put upon my words; the unkind remarks they have elicited; charging me with malice, and with wantonly endeavoring to injure, &c., &c., feelings I never have felt toward the pastor, I cannot but regard the *expression* of my opinions as injudicious and ill-advised, and I regret having given utterance to them; for I have not yet reached that higher plane where mistakes may not be made, and where life is but a faultless reflection of that *one* life — the promise of the past, the blessing of the present, and the hope of the future.

W. S. STICKNEY.

Expression injudicious.

This unworthy attempt to crush a young man, whose every word, thought, and action were as loyal to the church and the cause of Christ as he was capable of making them, who endeavored to make his conduct conform to the high standard of Holy Writ, though it might have discouraged many an older christian, did not in the least shake his confidence or weaken his faith in the truth and reality of the religion he professed. His convictions were a part of himself. I believe he would have submitted to a martyr's fate rather than renounce them or betray his Master.

Confidence in religion unshaken.

In all this there was no wilful obstinacy or unreasoning bigotry. He was willing to reason upon any subject, but must be con-

30

vinced of error before he could surrender his convictions.

The wrong keenly felt

He felt most keenly the great injustice done him by this attempt to stigmatize his character, and repress if not destroy his usefulness, sometimes referring to it with quivering lip and tremulous voice. Though the provocation had been so great, he never cherished anger or feelings of revenge towards any of his brethren—saying, on one occasion when alluding to them, "but—let us not judge."

Nobility of bearing.

The nobility of his bearing throughout this, his first taste of the contradictions of the world, is worthy of imitation. Instead of defying his accusers to do their worst, he calmly prepares his plea—a plea which the judgment of every disinterested man will accept as conclusive of innocence of the wrong with which he was charged. Then, judging himself by the same interpretation of the exhortation to "avoid every appearance of evil," which he applied to the conduct of others, he regrets the use of words which might seem evil. But his magnanimity goes even beyond this. He is willing to omit the major part of his plea—the part of all parts to which most men would tenaciously cling—and express sorrow that he had used words which had been misunderstood. If such a spirit as this were more common, there would be greater unity in the churches of Christ, and the prayer of our Savior answered—"That they may be one even as we are one."

CHAPTER VI.

BEGINNING OF PROFESSIONAL LIFE.

DILIGENT in business, fervent in spirit, serving the Lord.
—ROMANS, XII: 11.

WITH good will doing service, as to the Lord, and not to men.
—EPHESIANS, VI: 7.

HAVING completed his studies in the Law-School, Will was anxious to be employed.

The city of Des Moines, Iowa, had been recommended as an inviting field for a young lawyer, but his parents did not encourage a settlement so far from home.

He looked about in Washington for a suitable opening, but found none that was in all respects congenial. At length he was received into a law office, not as a partner, but for the purpose of obtaining a more practical knowledge of the profession, in return rendering the firm what useful service he could.

Enters law office.

He had the privilege of attending to any professional business that might come to him individually. By the influence of his friends in various parts of the country, he was entrusted with quite a number of cases — principally claims before the Departments. He was successful in the prosecution of several; some of which involved between one and two thousand dollars. He manifested the same zeal here as every where, devoting himself zealously to the business committed to him.

Entrusted with cases

He was also energetic and faithful to the interests of the firm, whose good opinion he was determined to maintain by untiring industry, fidelity, and rigid integrity.

Since his death, Mr. Johnston, one of the members of the firm, in a letter of sympathy to the parents, says:

Estimate of his character.

"We have both been much impressed, during our association with your son, not only with his quick intellect and sound judgment, but with the uprightness of his character; and we predicted for him a successful life as a lawyer, and a high reputation as a man.

"His thorough methods of attending to the confidential matters entrusted by us to him, satisfied us of his capacity as a man of affairs, and his equable temper and gentle manners have produced a genuine sorrow at his loss. His high character as a student gave ample evidence of his high character as a son."

He also found time to give much thought to the interests of the church and Sunday Schools, esteeming it his highest pleasure to contribute, according to his ability, to their prosperity and usefulness. Nothing but absolute necessity prevented his attendance upon these services; always considering it a loss if compelled to be absent.

Devotion to church.

Having been urged to transfer his connection with the Kendall Mission to the Calvary Mission School, he consented, and accepted the office of Superintendent of the latter, to which he was first elected Dec. 23, 1877. He was again chosen to fill the position in 1878 and 1879.

In his pocket he carried the name and address of each of the four or five hundred scholars and teachers, ready at all times to minister to them in cases of sickness, or distress of any kind.

Often he has come home after fatiguing duties at his office, and without stopping for dinner, has started upon a visiting tour to the scholars or their parents, to contribute to their comfort or relief. These labors were not always confined to cases of physical want. He was as deeply solicitous for their spiritual as their temporal welfare. He encouraged them in their religious life, provided company to and from church at night,

Care of sick and needy.

went out. of his way to invite them to the meetings, conversed with them on personal religion, and in every proper way sought to lead them to a nobler and higher life.

This was no perfunctory or professional service for him.   His sympathy with his scholars and their families in all their trials, was sincere.   He experienced real happiness in ministering to their happiness.   In his life he beautifully illustrated the missionary spirit which he considered essential to all true christians.   To him faith and works were inseparable, and his life was a faithful exponent of his doctrine.

Hopeful and earnest himself, he sought to inspire others with courage manfully to fight life's battles, and endure with christian resignation its inevitable trials.

During the summer of 1879 the family made their accustomed visit north, to pass the months of July and August.   Having been called west on Indian business, I wrote Mrs. Stickney to visit Watch Hill and Martha's Vineyard for a couple of weeks, and then meet me at Saratoga, our usual summer resort.

Happy in conferring happiness.

Faith and works.

In Chicago I received a letter from Will, written at New York, July 23, saying —

"Mother and I left W. this A. M. for Watch Hill. Every thing quiet in Washington. Church meetings are fairly attended. A good congregation present last Sunday night; the singing was excellent, and the sermon very good. S. S. keeps up well, considering the hot weather; 219 last Sunday, 220 week before; 192 at chapel. Rhodie Boucher [one of his scholars] I was glad to see present last Sunday. She has been living on the Island; hence her non-attendance.

"We expect to leave here to-morrow for Watch Hill, and go from there to Martha's Vineyard to attend the meetings. They have a grand programme for this year.

"I am very glad we have turned our backs on Washington for a time. The heat affects mother, and I find myself not quite so strong as I supposed; but the invigorating influences of the salt air and water will, I hope, restore us to our usual health. When do you think of joining us? Better meet us the 15th prox. at Saratoga, where I hope to have a good long visit."

Watch Hill.

A few days were passed pleasantly at Watch Hill, when the travelers proceeded to Martha's Vineyard, as narrated in the following letter:

Wesley House, Martha's Vineyard,
Monday, Aug. 11, 1879.

MY DEAR FATHER—

Martha's Vineyard.

How I wish you were here to enjoy with us the attractions of this place.

Feast for an epicure

Yesterday was a feast for an epicure. In the morning Dr. Evarts preached on the place and importance of the ordinances in religion, a most able exposition of our denominational views. As the sermon is to be printed, I will not attempt an abstract.

Angel visitation.

In the P. M. Dr. E. G. Taylor gave us a sermon on Angel visitation; a little in advance of modern thought, but calculated to do good; and I was glad to hear it.

Dessert.

And last came the *dessert*, by Mr. Gifford, of Warren Ave. Church, Boston. Mr. G. was in the seminary, while I was at college—an old acquaintance. The sermon, on the Holy Spirit, was a poem in prose. I wish you could have heard it. Though not quite so full of logic and metaphysics as Dr.

L., he is much more graceful, and his style more chaste.

Saturday, had the pleasure of meeting Dr. Taylor, who regretted your absence.

If present arrangements are carried out, we will leave here Friday, and hope to meet you at Saratoga Saturday P. M.

Affectionately,   WILLIE.

We met in Saratoga at the time designated, and remained till about the middle of September. The days were spent chiefly in drinking the sparkling waters; listening to the music by the various bands; attending the daily prayer meetings; playing croquet; visiting and receiving visits; riding and walking; reading and writing; and so regaining health and strength for future use.

About the middle of September we all went to visit our friends in Bangor.

Will, anxious to be home, preceded us to Washington. On the 30th of September he writes: "At the chapel 203 present. The superintendent conducted the review exercises without assistance; had a good time. Last night was the children's service; great success; room full; a good deal of interest. Mrs.

Saratoga.

At work again.

Jones, with the rest of us, made the armor
[the Christian Armor being one of the exer-
cises], and the young soldier (Charlie Ma-
gruder) looked very fine in his military dress.
Mr. Fuller, of Iowa, who preached for us in
the morning, was present and made a splendid address.   Programme inclosed."

At home things moved along as usual.
In December, 1879, the pulpit of the Calvary Baptist Church having been vacant
A new several months, the Rev. Samuel H. Greene,
pastor. of Cazenovia, N. Y., was elected pastor.
He accepted the position, and immediately
religious matters assumed a new and live-
ly interest.   A vigorous impulse was given
to all our religious work; meetings for
"young ladies" and "children," "young
men" and "young people," were well attended and sustained; conversions from the
Sunday Schools were frequent; the church
was united, happy, and prosperous.

The Home and Mission Schools had each
their usual celebration at Christmas.

At the chapel the room was crowded,
and the occasion was intensely interesting to
all present.   The scholars, whose names

were on the "Roll of Honor," received a
present from the superintendent, who was
never more happy than on that occasion.
His modesty of manners, considerate treatment of all, generosity in dispensing gifts.
frequent visits to the homes of his scholars,
unselfish and unremitting devotion to the
work, gave him a hold upon the affections
of his school which death alone could sun-
der.

It was while engaged so earnestly in
striving to inculcate in the hearts of these
his young parishioners a love of those principles and doctrines of the Bible in which
his soul took such delight, that he began to
question within himself whether. after all,
he was not more useful and more happy in
this work than in attending to the duties of
his profession.

He soon entertained serious misgivings
on this subject, and debated the question of
abandoning his law, and preparing himself,
by a course of theological study. for the
ministry. He expressed himself as willing
to do just what the Master would have
him. and was only concerned to know His
will.

Margin notes: Roll of honor. A faithful superintendent. Thoughts of the ministry.

A helper.

His love for the souls of the young, especially, was daily becoming deeper and more manifest. To him many confided their religious experience, gladly accepting his counsel and advice. The pastor found in him a ready and constant friend and brother, upon whom he could always depend to aid in whatever enterprise might be suggested for the good of the church.

"Where can I be the most useful to my fellow-men?" had become with him the paramount question. Had he foreseen the end of his earthly career to be so near, he could hardly have employed his time more profitably and more devotedly to the cause of the Lord than he did.

Ill health.

Notwithstanding all his activities in the church and Sunday Schools, his health was not good, and he was not unfrequently compelled to stop entirely and recuperate.

CHAPTER VII.

SECOND UTE COMMISSION.

AND the chiefs made answer, saying:
" We have listened to your message,
We have heard your words of wisdom,
We will think on what you tell us.
It is well for us, oh brothers,
That you came so far to see us."— LONGFELLOW.

AS Congress had passed a bill at its last session for the appointment of another Special Commission to the Utes of Colorado, Will thought he saw in this a most favorable opportunity for him to be of service to his Government, and to seek that recreation and change of which he so much felt the need.

Before making the application for the appointment, we discussed the question fully and deliberately. Will referred to the great benefit derived from his previous trip, which was of a similar character, and to the same country, as the one now proposed. His former experience would greatly aid him in this, and he would come back invigorated for the winter's work at the church and Sunday School.

His cousin, Charles Stickney, of nearly his own age, from Bangor, Maine, was visiting the family at this time. Will felt a deep interest in his cousin, who was in poor health, having had several hemorrhages, and who was hoping some way would open for him to go west, where, he was led to believe, he might hopefully look for recovery.

These considerations prevailed, and after

Special Commission.

Benefit to be derived

Position
obtained.

the passage of the bill, application was made
to the Hon. Carl Schurz, Secretary of the
Interior, for the position of Secretary and
Disbursing Officer, which was at once cheer-
fully granted.

Peculiar
peril not
anticipa-
ted.

It was known the duties of his office
would be arduous, and the time protracted,
perhaps for five or six months, but never a
doubt or misgiving entered the minds of his
parents that the expedition involved peculiar
peril, or greater hardship, than had been
experienced by the previous Commission.

The following gentlemen were appointed
by the Secretary of the Interior to constitute
the Commission: Messrs. G. W. Manypenny,
A. B. Meacham, Otto Myers, J. B. Bowman,
and J. J. Russell. The two former my son
had met a few times; the others were strangers to him.

Bonds.

As one of the duties of the Secretary of
the Commission would be the disbursement
of about seventy-five thousand dollars to the
Indians, the law required of him a bond.
This was given in the sum of fifty thousand
dollars.

The Commissioners visited Washington.
had an interview with the Secretary, and

received their instructions. A meeting of the Commission was appointed at Denver the last of June.

I was present with my son as he called to bid the Secretary "Good-bye." Tuesday morning, June 22d. We met Messrs. Manypenny and Meacham there. I shook them by the hand, and said to them, in the presence and hearing of my son, "I expect you to take good care of my boy;" to which both responded, they certainly would.

LAST WORDS TO HIS BELOVED SUNDAY SCHOOL.

Just before the close of the Calvary Mission Sunday School, the Sunday before his departure, the superintendent feelingly alluded to his anticipated absence for several months.

Among his papers were found the following "notes" of what he proposed to say to the School:

"Your teachers have wisely elected Mr. Taylor, who will more than fill my place in my absence. I trust you will all sustain him; be prompt and orderly: let each one try to surpass the other in doing what is right. Do not neglect the school, even if the weather is hot and some of the teachers are absent. Be proud enough of your school to be present every Sunday.

"I expect and hope the building of the new chapel will be commenced this summer. You must help every way in your power, and when fall comes let every class raise some money, that each one of you may have at least one brick in it. I want you to be interested here — willing to do without some things, if necessary, for the sake of your chapel.

"Teachers, thanks for work done. I commit the work to your hands and hearts during the days that are to come. Be faithful to your trust. Remember the object of each day's work is to lead some soul nearer the Master. Therefore, pray much; visit much. If your scholars are absent a single Sunday, I beg of you, call and see them; no matter if you know the reason; go to the house; go in and stop a little while, and manifest your interest. Be enthusiastic in your work; prompt; know your lessons; be bright and cheerful — enthusiasm is the fire to kindle zeal in others. Pray without ceasing."

Be faithful

Visit the scholars.

Then, according to his custom, he lead the school in a short, earnest prayer, in which he expressed the hope that, if they met no more on earth, they might, "every scholar and teacher, without a single exception, meet around the Great White Throne in heaven."

The engraving at the beginning of this chapter represents my son as he appeared every Sunday afternoon at the Calvary Mission School, with his singing book in one hand, the other resting upon the desk, waiting for the school to come to order.

This position was a signal for silence, and without uttering a word, a few moments sufficed for that perfect stillness which always preceded the commencement of the exercises.

The slightly-raised platform, desk, and piano are faithful copies, and present a scene familiar to many who will peruse these pages—a scene hallowed by associations that time will only render more tender and sacred in the hearts of his devoted teachers and scholars.

At the "Young People's" meeting, the

night of his departure, Will was present, as usual, leading the music by playing on the piano. He spoke seriously and earnestly to the two or three hundred young people present, exhorting them to be faithful in all their duties; zealous in their work; to honor their Master by precept and example, and to labor for the salvation of souls. He bade them an affectionate "Good-bye," expecting to be absent perhaps till Christmas.

He returned from the church to the house, kissed his mother "Good-bye," shook hands with his friends who were present, not omitting the servants, and then, accompanied by his particular friend and assistant S. S. superintendent Taylor and myself, with his cousin Charlie, proceeded to the Baltimore and Potomac dépôt.

On the way we rode to the city Post Office, where I purchased one hundred postal cards, and gave half to each of the boys, with an injunction to return every one in due time.

It had been a custom with Will from his earliest infancy to kiss his parents "Goodnight" before retiring to bed. This habit he never gave up. To strangers it may have looked odd to see a son, as tall as his father, kissing him "Good-night" as he would leave to go to bed. For this Will made no apologies nor explanation. He had always done so, and he was never ashamed to do so. It was also his custom, on leaving home, or returning after an absence, to salute his father, as well as his mother, with a kiss. So, in the car, on that eventful Tuesday night, he gave his father a cordial shake of the hand, a hearty kiss, and tender "Goodbye," and left at 10:30 for his long journey to Colorado.

No apologies.

A final "Goodbye."

Postals were received from Altoona the next day: "All well. Safe journey, so far. Beautiful morning." From "on the cars just east of Richmond, Ind., where we expect to take supper: Very warm day. Some tired, and very dusty. Country beautiful; no signs of army worm; wheat being harvested; corn from one to three feet high. Have been reading instructions. Think we can save time by going first to Southern Utès. However, more anon."

Our next is a letter, as follows;

Lindell Hotel,
St. Louis, June 24, 1880.

MY DEAR FATHER—

Father of Waters.

This morning at eight, we crossed the "Father of Waters," and at present are comfortably ensconced in the hotel above. The ride here was comfortable, and most of the way interesting. The Cincinnati Convention formed the general topic of conversation, and the guesses were as various as they were numerous. The announcement of the nominees at the hotel this noon created a little enthusiasm, but not much.

Dr. Park [his dentist friend] has given me two sittings to-day, and wishes two more.

Hope to leave for Kansas City and Denver to-morrow P. M.

Went down to the sub-Treasury this afternoon. My draft not yet received.

Ignacio first.

In reading the instructions, it seems as if considerable time could be saved by visiting Ignacio first. Then some of the Com'n could go and see Ouray and the White Rivers (now near Ouray), while one or two of us could visit the Uintahs. Then, when the agreement was signed by *all*, the Commission would be near the White Rivers, and could secure, or attempt to secure, their immediate removal to the Uintah country, and the delivery of the criminals—the next step after the agreement is signed.

If the Com'n go to the Ouray and White River Utes first, and *then* to the southern country, they would have to retrace their steps to come again to the White River Utes, to see about their removal.

I think we had *all* better go to the southern country, as the influence of numbers will undoubtedly be needed there, and then one of the Com'n and myself can do all the work necessary with the Uintahs.

Southern country.

I write thus fully, for the Secretary may receive a dispatch from the Com'n, asking permission to go south first, and I would like to have you able to give him some of the reasons.

My way will save about six days—a desideratum, when the time is so limited.

I do not think the Uintahs will require more than a representation of the Com'n before signing the agreement, and, while

Return of
prisoners.

one or two of us are on that business, the remainder will have all the more time to labor for the return of the prisoners — desideratum No. 2.

Will keep you advised.

Love to mother.

Affectionately, your son   WILL.

We next hear from him by postal:

On the cars Mo. Pacif., six or eight miles
     from Kansas City,
                         Saturday, June 26, 1880.

Pleasant ride last night; just enough rain to settle the dust. This A. M. we both feel pretty well — in readiness for breakfast.

Yesterday afternoon Dr. Park took us through some of the pleasant drives about St. Louis. Had a delightful time.

Love to mother. Aff'y,   WILL.

Out on the
prairie.

"Wallace" for breakfast Sunday, A. M., "way out on the prairies," or "plains" would be more accurate. Had a good night. Each of us feels pretty comfortable. Weather cool and delightful. Colonel Manypenny on this train. Aff'y,   W.

"Denver, June 27, 1880.
Sunday night.
Reached here at 4:30 this P. M. Heavy rain.
Both quite well, considering the long jour-
ney. No Commissioners here, except Col.
Manypenny."

Monday, Tuesday, and Wednesday Will *Purchas-ing sup-plies.* was constantly occupied in purchasing 3,300
pounds of camp supplies, outfit, &c., prepar-
atory to their long journey in the wilderness.
Wednesday he sends the following postal:

June 30, '80. Denver.
Very busy, and very tired. I leave here
to-morrow for Alamosa to look after baggage. Commissioners will follow next day.
Expect to meet Indians Thursday. Have so
telegraphed them. Charlie will not go on
this trip. Dr. Denison thinks he had better
become a little more acclimated. Please
send me copy of the treaty of '68, also one
of '72.
Love to mother. Aff'y, WILL.

The next information, is the following letter:

Hot Springs, Colorado,
    Near Wagon Wheel Gap,
        Sunday, July 4, 1880.
MY DEAR MOTHER—

To-day I will write you something of the trip so far. Though not my practice to write Sundays, think I can employ part of my time to-day better this way than any other.

The ride to Denver you have heard about. Monday, Tuesday, and Wednesday were spent in buying the outfit. Thursday went to Alamosa with Col. Meacham; a long and tiresome ride.

[Alamosa is fourteen hours, by rail, from Denver, by the Denver and Rio Grande. R. R., and the terminus of the road.]

Friday I completed the outfit at A. and went back to Fort Garland [about 30 miles] to look after some things left there two years ago. Returned with the supplies bought at Denver, and made arrangements for the freight to leave Saturday morning.

Friday P. M. Col. Manypenny and Mr.

Long ride.

Russell came, and yesterday P. M. we all left
in the coach for this place.   The ride for the
first thirty miles was very dusty, though the
roads were smooth.

The country may have magnificent possibilities; we may yet see the orange and
the palm, beautiful in foliage, and stately
in shape, growing in tropical luxuriance
through the San Luis Park, but at present
the sage-brush and grease-wood vie with
each other, and over, and under, and about
every thing is the alkali dust, so fine and
disagreeable.

The company in the coach was very interesting.   Beside ourselves, were three Cornish miners and a Mexican ranchman, Senor
Antonio.   The miners were unusually intelligent.   First, they described their sports in
England; then mining at Lake Superior and
Brazil, and finally, began to talk about the
Bible.   Their queer pronunciation and peculiar idiom were to me very fascinating.   They
did not seem to have any objective—"Do
you know *he?*" or, "Did you see *they?*" was
the usual form.   When they discussed Bible
truths, repeating unusual passages, I felt
they had learned to mine for richer ores than

*Possibili-
ties.*

*Cornish
miners.*

silver or gold, and their treasure was already great.

Never, I think, have I traveled all day with any other three men, rough or polished, when I have not heard a single objectionable word, or even hint. I was surprised and gratified at the style of these men. That kind of immigration will not hurt us; and if their American cousins would take a few lessons from them, they would be all the better for their coming.

The Senor may have done a deal of thinking, like the owl the Irishman bought for a parrot, but he did not say much.

At Del Norte we took dinner at two o'clock; thence the scenery improved, and, about six, the rocky sides of the mountain loomed up to very great heights. I cannot describe the view to you. Imagine an Au Sable chasm, one-fourth of a mile wide, and three times as high, a valley of pines and the jumping, dashing Rio Grande, with the road first by the side of the mountain, and then skirting the river, the mountains showing their bare, steep sides so high "one has to look twice" to see the top. It was grand — magnificent! and I could not but feel it was

Good kind of immigration.

Au Sable.

all made for us, that we might use them to the glory of the Creator. Perhaps the Psalmist had some such display of God's works in mind, when he asks, "What is man?"

At seven o'clock we reached the Gap. The Col's stopped at the hotel there, Mr. Russell and I came up here, two miles, and found the Saratoga, may be, of the future — three hot springs, about one hundred and ninety degrees, almost exactly like the Arkansas springs, and two cold, with just a little gas, some iron, and considerable magnesia; these are all I could taste. The hot springs have soda, sulphur, and iron.

Last night, after a trout supper, Mr. Russell and I took a grand bath in a tub twenty feet square by four and a half deep.

To-day we have been quietly resting, preparatory to another week's hard work.

The Commissioners are now all in the State, and I expect to have a very pleasant time with them. We hope to be at the agency Wednesday.

Charlie did not come along. He called on Dr. Denison, author of the "Rocky Mountain Health Resorts," and the Dr. thought the long ride, so soon after his illness, with the high altitudes, would be too much for him for two or three weeks. I have understood, since, that the Dr. thinks he can be entirely cured in four years. Expect he will accompany me on the next trip, when we come to pay the annuities.

Information respecting the Indians is very encouraging. Hope they will sign the agreement promptly, and let us get to the real work of the summer.

Hope Taylor is getting along well with the school. I believe he expected to be absent to-day. Wish I might look in on you and it.

Keep me posted, please, as to what you are all doing.

Please ask father, if he has not already done so, to send me the treaty of 1868. A new question has arisen, and I think we will need it.

How did the pic-nic come off? Thought of you at the time. Hope every thing passed off satisfactorily.

Love to father and all inquiring friends.

Affectionately, your son

WILL S. STICKNEY.

Hopes.

A new question.

Los Pinos Indian Agency,
             Thursday, July 8, 1880.
MY DEAR FATHER—

Col. Manypenny and I reached this place yesterday about noon. Col. Meacham was quite sick at Indian Creek (fifty miles from here), and we left him and Mr. Russell to stay over a day. We expect them this noon.

Every thing here is quiet. The agent says the Indians were never more friendly than at present.

The Indians have been told they are to lose all they possess, and get nothing for it. This will make it more difficult to convince them that all is right; but trust we may be successful.

False reports.

This place is just as it used to be — very dusty, and every thing as inconvenient as it could well be.

Our outfit has not yet arrived, and for the time we are boarding with the mess, and it is pretty poor eating.

We applied to Gen. McKenzie for some tents, and he answered, he did not expect any such a request, and did not think he had any to spare. What is the use of an order from the Secretary of War, if that is the

A useless order.

way it is to be treated? As it was, the agent found places for us. What we will do when all the Commissioners come, remains to be seen.

The annuities and supplies have not yet come, and things are getting pretty low in the store-house. I think the agent said he had about two more issues of flour. An omission in the issue of supplies at present, I think would be unfortunate.

Ouray is here, and the Indians are coming in slowly.

Health good.
My health is pretty good, and, when well rested, think I will feel first-rate.

Love to mother, and regards to friends.

Affectionately, your son

WILL S. STICKNEY.

Los Pinos Agency, Col.,
Sunday, July 11, 1880.

MY DEAR FATHER—

Yours of 2d and 3d inst., inclosing report of last Ute Commission, came to hand yesterday. Many thanks for your frequent writing. We have nothing to do here, and the mail is looked forward to with great interest by us all.

When in Denver, I suggested to Colonel Manypenny that he secure an interpreter; but he preferred to wait until reaching the agency. Now we are here, and there is no one who can interpret our speech into Ute.

Friday the Commission instructed me to hunt up Curtis. I staged it twenty-five miles, and that night received a courier dispatch to hire a man and send him, and for me to return. I did so, and returned the next morning. Mr. Russell thought some one else might do as well, and save me the trip; hence my recall. Now we are waiting for Curtis; it may be four days, and perhaps ten, before he comes.

The Commissioners were in such haste to leave Denver, that our beds. blankets. eatables, &c., were all left to be freighted, and they have not arrived yet; so we are bunking on tables, sofas, and the like. Last night I slept on the floor.

The fare here is just about as poor as it well can be. However, we hope soon to live under our own vine and fig tree.

The dust is so ubiquitous that it is impossible to keep clear of it; so we do not

keep ourselves quite as neat as we would
like; but it treats us all alike.

Have wished a good many times this
morning that I might look in on you at S. S.
and church.

This is a poor country for Sunday observance.   The agent has been unloading
goods; the Commission sent one of their
number to confer with Gen. McKenzie, and
when I suggested to-morrow would be as
well, so far as the urgency of the business
was concerned, Col. Manypenny and some
of the others laughed at the idea — so soon
have these gentlemen adopted the habits of
the country.

Yesterday we witnessed the issue of rations.   After the flour issue, we went to see
the beef slaughter.   If I were Commissioner
of Indian Affairs, I would certainly repri-
mand an agent who issued beef in that way,
and if he repeated the offence, would sus-
pend him from duty.

The cattle were put in a corral; theoreti-
cally, one Indian was detailed to do the kill-
ing.   He shot the first beef, then he was
assisted by fifteen or twenty others; some
of the cattle were wounded, and left to die

in their agony; one accidentally (?) escaped
through the gate, and they had a gay time
chasing and shooting at the poor animal
until it was killed; a yearling also escaped.
and they gave chase to him. Almost as
soon as the first one was killed, the women,
men, and children rushed in and commenced
to flay it, and there, in the midst of the blood
and filth of the place. the squaws chopped
off the different parts of the animal and
bore them to their ponies to be carried home.
The blood-thirsty way in which they all
acted in this brutal scene, was discouraging
to all attempts at civilization. It is no wonder they continue savages, when these scenes
are repeated every week.

We were told, that the week before some
of the men amused themselves by driving a
calf about and alternately slashing its sides
with knives until death terminated its mis-
ery. It is too bad, and ought to be stopped.

Ere this you have heard why Charlie did
not come with me; so will not repeat. Yesterday I heard from him; he seems quite
encouraged, and in good spirits; hopes to
join me the first of August.

Love to mother. Please tell her I re-

ceived her letter duly, and like O. Twist,
Esq., am looking for more.

Kind regards to friends.   Health is first-
rate.

Affectionately, your son   WILL.

P. S.   I understand there is nothing but
beef at the agency.

Los Pinos Agency, Colo.,
Tuesday, July 13, 1880.

MY DEAR FATHER—

Thanks for yours of 6th inst., with in-
closures, which came in to-day's mail.

Our interpreter has not yet arrived, and
we are consequently in a state of masterly
inactivity.

Gen'l McKenzie tells us he has no authority to furnish transportation and tents
"to the east, on any mail line, without special instructions from the Department Commander."   This will make it very expensive
traveling to the Southern Ute agency, unless
the aforesaid instructions can be obtained.

Expect the goods will be here to-morrow.

Wednesday, the 7th inst., pic-nic day, it
rained very hard here; hope you had all sun-

Expensive
traveling.

shine. Shall expect to hear all about it day after to-morrow.

Please send me some papers. Now and then we have a Chicago paper, but no New York journals. If Taylor would send his old Tribunes, they would be thankfully received.

Newspa-pers.

We are all well, and having as good a time as can be expected in such a place.

Love to mother, and kind regards to the bank folks and other friends.

Affectionately, your son
WILL S. STICKNEY.

HIS LAST LETTER HOME.

Los Pinos Agency, Colo.,
Wednesday, July 14, 1880.

MY DEAR MOTHER—

Yours of 5th inst. came to hand this noon. I heard from Charlie the other day, and he seemed to be improving. He wrote in good spirits, and with good courage.

Good courage.

Glad to hear you had such a good day Sunday, the 4th. There is so little Sabbath observance here, that it seems good to hear of a good Sunday elsewhere.

Sorry to hear about the pic-nic disappointment [it was postponed on account of the rain], but expect you had a fine time when it did come off.

Herewith please find check for ten dollars. This will pay the Hazelton bill for shoes furnished some of our Mission scholars.

I have no news to give you. Neither the interpreter, the Indians, nor the outfit have come yet; but I hope we may get to work Monday next.

I spend most of my time reading up the treaties, writing letters, stitching torn comforters, and sleeping.

The gentlemen have the same programme, varied by a game of whist every evening.

At night, and early in the morning, it is quite cool, sometimes cold, but from ten to four it is as hot, almost, as you have it. But I must fix up my bed, as some of the things are on another bed, and the occupant of the latter wishes to retire. Will finish this in the morning.

Thursday morning, [July 15, 1880.]

It is a bright, beautiful morning, promising a warm day; but the atmosphere is cool and pure. I must tell you how we sleep while waiting for our goods. Col's Many-penny and Meacham have beds, Gen. Bow-man sleeps in the carpenter shop on an old door laid on two horses, Judge Russell and I sleep.on the floor in the agent's room. This room was originally intended for a stable, but the agent thought it an improvement on his own quarters, and moved in.

Beside the Judge, myself, and the agent, Hermon Silver, a friend of Mr. Mears, and Col. Parker, chief of the secret mail service, slept in this room last night. Mr. Mears shares a bed with one of the employés. To-night I hope our supplies will be here, and we can sleep in our tents, such as we have.

Give love to father, please, and kind re-gards to all inquiring friends.

Affectionately, your son

WILL S. S.

In a letter written from Los Pinos to his friend Taylor, under date of Monday, July 12, he says:

"This place is nothing but dust—no grass, no good place even for a tent. The

Tenting.

accommodations are scarce. I sleep on the floor, and this morning came to the conclusion that I could do better out of doors; so to-night I am going to try it in a tent, if possible. Our bedding and outfit are all *on the way*, so we have to put up with what we can get.

Interest for the Chapel.

"How comes on the chapel improvement? [Referring to a project inaugurated several months previously for the enlargement of Calvary Chapel.] Is the fence up yet? I sincerely hope you will get the *foundation* for the north wall in this summer or fall; then we can go ahead in winter, if it is thought best. Kendall was to prepare some drawings, but I have not heard any thing about them since I left. Keep things moving.

Books.

"After a while I may want you to send me something to read—Lecky, Van Holst, or Stubbs; but I wont trouble you yet.

Sunday.

"Yesterday [Sunday] I thought much of you all, wishing for your success and blessing. No service here.

"A letter to father in the morning; then a little time for putting the room in order; dinner, and a very poor one; then a nap;

afterwards a reading in the Bible, then a good wash; supper; walk; some more Bible reading; then good - night.

"One of the Commissioners went to fish, put his rods on the bank, and they tumbled off, and floated down the stream — 'lost to sight, but to memory dear.' He received little sympathy."

Little sympathy.

CHAPTER VIII.

SICKNESS AND DEATH.

WHEN the righteous die, it is the earth that loses. The lost jewel will always be a jewel; but the possessor, who has lost it — well may he weep. — TALMUD.

A DIRGE.

Died July 20, 1880.

"Blessed are the dead who die in the LORD."

Do ANGEL choirs chant requiems o'er the dead
When far from friends and home they fall asleep,
No lov'd one near? or is the rhyme of Nature —
Th' unwritten, unheard music of the spheres —
The breath which wafts th' unprisoned soul to Heaven?

What stricken mourner then can say — "Thy will"?
The spirit cries for one last look and word;
Still is the answer to our rebel "Why?" —
"The LORD hath given, the LORD hath called away;
Give thanks. Thy dead is living over there!"

—T. I. K. in "MUSICAL BULLETIN," Washington.

THURSDAY morning, July 15th, after bathing in cold water, as was his daily practice, Will remarked to Commissioner Russell: "I feel so well this morning." That night he determined to exchange his floor of the cabin for a cot in the tent. Accordingly, with Mr. Russell, he retired under a small shelter tent, or fly, without pins, a short distance from the cabin. His bed consisted of blankets spread upon boards. The weather became chilly during the night, the wind blew freshly, and as the walls of the tent were not banked nor pinned, the inmates were exposed to its cold blasts. In the morning Mr. Russell observed that Will had protected his face by covering it with his hat.

Friday morning he complained of soreness of throat, and said he believed he was feverish, and thought he had taken cold. He declined to eat any breakfast. Mr. Russell gave him some quinine, and called in the physician of the agency, Dr. Lacy, who administered quinine and calomel.

Friday night a cot was placed in the tent.

Saturday morning he was worse; the fever had increased; the temperature of his

Well!

Sick!

Worse.

body was 100 degrees; but to his friends his condition did not appear alarming. He evidently considered himself quite sick, and suggested that information be sent to his parents, but was told he would soon be better. Commissioner Meacham watched with him that night.

Sunday found him no better. At six o'clock that evening, by advice of Commissioner Meacham, a messenger was sent for Dr. Brown, the army physician, who was with the military post, sixteen miles distant. For some reason, the message failed of being delivered.

Sunday night Mr. McRae, a friend of Commissioner Bowman, sat up with the patient, who appeared to be delirious at times, asking to be moved out of the sun, as it hurt his head, though it was not then daylight.

Monday morning he was visited by Ed. Jenkins, the driver of the stage between Los Pinos and Cimmaron. Will had previously made his acquaintance in his travels there, and had won his confidence and friendship. Jenkins, entering his tent, remarked, "I have come to see you." He replied, "That's right. I hope to be well in a day or two."

Delirious.

Hopes.

The driver asked if he could not bring him something from Mrs. Clines [twenty-five miles distant on his route], "some milk, or something else?" "Yes," he said, "bring me some crackers; not hard-tack, but soda-crackers."

Will renewed the suggestion that his parents had better be advised of his illness, and was informed that as soon as the fever was broken speedy recovery would follow. There can be no doubt, though he may have considered himself very ill at this time, that he did not think himself to be in any real danger.

During this day (Monday), after a general consultation, it was determined to remove him to the cabin, the sun rendering it uncomfortably warm during the day in the tent.

Two sticks were placed under the frame of the cot, and four men carried him about one hundred and fifty yards distance, into the cabin.

Mr. Curtis, the interpreter, took him in his arms and carried him into a second room, which was as comfortable as any the agency afforded. When Mr. Curtis placed him on

Thought of home.

the bed, Will thanked him for giving him "such a nice ride."

When asked by Mr. McRae, between nine and ten o'clock of this morning, how he was, he replied with some difficulty, "Not very well."

This night (Monday) an employé of the agency watched with the patient.

Another messenger was sent for the army physician, who reached the agency at two o'clock Tuesday morning. He expressed his approbation of the treatment, and recommended its continuance.

At ten o'clock the sufferer motioned to Curtis to come to his bed. Will drew him down and tried to talk, but could not speak.

Loss of speech.

From the best interpretation of his articulations and signs, his last thoughts were of his home—a home peculiarly dear to him— never forgotten, and from which he always parted with regret—

"And dragged at each remove a lengthening chain"—

to return to which he daily looked forward with the greatest desire.

That morning the fever was broken, and stimulants administered.

His friend Jenkins, the stage driver. went to see him shortly before twelve, with the milk and crackers. He swallowed with difficulty several spoonsful.

Retaining full consciousness to the last. at half - past twelve, without a struggle. calmly and peacefully his pure spirit took its flight.

Death.

Commissioner Bowman writes: "It was my sad pleasure to sit by his side, and alone. while all others were absent, not expecting so sudden a result, and to witness his peaceful, quiet departure.

"His noble, manly form lies before me at this moment, as natural as life, with that kind, bland expression which made him so attractive while living.

"Our Commission had all become greatly endeared to him, and knew well his manly, christian virtues."

Commissioner Russell: "The morning before his death, I asked if he desired to write his parents, and he said, not if we felt that he would be out in a few days. He was all the time quiet, except when spoken to;

and at no time did he express regret, or complain because of his sickness. I felt all the time, until the moment of his death, that he would recover; but it seemed to be the will of the Ruler over all that it should be otherwise."

Commissioner Meacham writes: "Willie retained full consciousness and voice until about ten this morning. Every thing that love could do was done. The Commission, the agent, and military officers have all been

Lamented.

kind, and deplore the sudden death of one so young and so much beloved.

"We sought in every way to encourage him in the hope of speedy recovery, fully believing, until the day of his death, he would soon be well again; and for this reason, he has left no message for the loved ones."

It is not the purpose of this Memorial to attempt to describe the anguish of the parents, as they were aroused from sleep at midnight, Wednesday, the 21st of July, by Mr. Bell, the Assistant Secretary of the Interior, and told that their son, of whose welfare and good health they had received almost daily tidings, lay dead at the Los Pinos agency.

He presented the following telegrams, just received:

Los Pinos, Colorado, July 20, 1880.
To CARL SCHURZ, *Sec'y Int.*,
Washington, D. C.

Telegrams

Clerk Stickney has been sick five days with typhoid fever. We have two physicians. They pronounce his condition critical. Please inform his father.

GEO. W. MANYPENNY, *Ch. Ute Com.*

Los Pinos Agéncy, Col..
July 20, 1880.
HON. SECRETARY OF INTERIOR.
Washington, D. C.

W. S. Stickney, Clerk of the Ute Commission, died at 12:30 to-day. Embalming impossible. The physicians think it impracticable to send body east at present. Will pack it in zinc coffin and charcoal, ready for removal in fall. Please inform Mr. Stickney.

GEO. W. MANYPENNY, *Ch. Ute Com.*

This was the first and only intimation received by the parents, that their precious boy, their joy and pride, was otherwise than well.

Mr. Bell, with such words of consolation as he could command, soon took his leave of a home, till then happy, but ever after to be desolate.

The parents were stunned almost into insensibility. They could not believe the dreadful tidings. It was not possible that their kind, Heavenly Father had, in an instant, without premonition, put out the light and joy of their life.

The telegraph and the mail soon extinguished the glimmer of hope that there might be some mistake, and the reality, with all its great, crushing weight, began to force itself upon their consciousness.

The sad, sad intelligence that their boy, so manly, noble, and pure; so high-minded, self-reliant, hopeful, and strong; so full of spirit and of action; upon the threshold of his manhood, was cold in death, must, however reluctantly, be accepted as true.

Wednesday, July 21, at five o'clock in the afternoon, the remains, which had been placed in a zinc casket, inclosed in a wooden box, were escorted to the hill-side about a mile from the agency, by the members of the Commission, civilians, members of the army present, and a few Indians, including the present chief, Sapovoneri, and buried beneath the pines.

Buried beneath the pines.

The Episcopal service was impressively read by one of the gentlemen present.

The physicians and Commissioners concurred in the opinion that it would be impracticable to remove the remains east before winter, and so telegraphed and wrote. But the parents could not endure the thought of having the precious remains in the wilderness of Colorado, when, in their judgment, it was possible to have them brought home.

Accordingly, Messrs. T. R. Jones and L. R. Taylor, warm friends of the family and of the deceased, who volunteered to visit Colorado and bring the precious dust to Washington, were commissioned to perform the sad office.

They were entirely successful in the discharge of their melancholy duties, and on Wednesday, the 11th of August, reached Washington.

Remains brought home.

CHAPTER IX.

THE FUNERAL.

S. T. T. L.

Sit tibi terra levis.

May the earth be light upon thee. — Inscription on Roman Tomb.

Unveil thy bosom, faithful tomb,
　Take this new treasure to thy trust ;
And give these sacred relics room
　To seek a slumber in the dust.
So Jesus slept ; God's dying Son
　Passed th'rough the grave and blessed the bed ;
Rest here, dear saint, till from his throne
　The morning break, and pierce the shade. — Watts, 1734.

THE funeral services occurred on Friday, the 13th of August, at the Calvary Baptist Church, at half-past three.

The following correct account of the obsequies was published in the National Republican newspaper:

"IMPOSING FUNERAL DISPLAY AT CALVARY BAPTIST CHURCH.

"The funeral of William Soule Stickney, Secretary of the Ute Commission, who died in Colorado on the 20th of July, took place at three o'clock yesterday afternoon from the Calvary Baptist Church, and seldom have greater honors been paid to the dead. After a prayer at the house of Mr. William Stickney, father of the deceased, at the corner of Sixth and M streets, the remains were removed to the Calvary Baptist Church. The church was already packed with people, the crowds extending out into the street. The funeral ceremonies were conducted in the Sabbath School room, which was draped in mourning. The teachers of the Sabbath School, who wore appropriate badges of mourning, were seated at the right of the pulpit, while the space at the left was occu-

Sunday
School
children.

pied by the three hundred children of the Calvary Mission School, attended by their teachers. Each child held in his hand a bouquet of white flowers, and wore upon his bosom a white silk badge, inscribed in black letters, *July 20, 1880. In memory of our beloved Superintendent, W. S. Stickney. *In solo Deo salus.*' The casket, covered with cloth, with drop black handles, with a plate suitably inscribed, was placed before the altar. A feature of the obsequies was the

Floral
offerings.

richness and profusion of the floral display—flowers being worked in every appropriate design. As the procession entered the church, a dirge was rendered by Professor Hayden, the organist. Rev. Mr. Greene conducted

Eulogies.

the services and pronounced a eulogy of the deceased. He was followed by Rev. Dr. Morehouse, of New York City, formerly pastor of the church attended by the deceased when a student at Rochester, N. Y. Dr. Welling, President of the Columbian University, also added his testimony to the worth of the deceased. During the services the children of the Calvary Mission, under the direction of Mr. David Haines, sang with

Singing.

fine effect 'It is Well with My Soul.' The

remains were then removed from the church to the hearse, Messrs. Theo I. King, L. R. Taylor, J. M. Bessey, J. H. Olcott, H. G. Jacobs, H. H. Kendall, D. A. Chambers, and D. E. McComb officiating as pall-bearers."

Impressive as was the scene at the church, the spectacle at Oak Hill Cemetery, beautiful by nature and radiant with its rich profusion of flowers, was most affecting.

At Oak Hill.

The members of the Calvary Mission School filed in solemn procession past the grave, which was about to close upon the form of their beloved Superintendent, and cast in their beautiful floral offerings—the last expression of their deep affection for a true and devoted friend.

Calvary Mission School.

The church choir sang the "Sweet Bye-and-Bye," and the pastor read the following requiem, sent by an unknown friend:

REQUIEM.

WILLIAM SOULE STICKNEY.

LAID TO HIS REST AT OAK HILL, AUGUST 13, 1880.

BROUGHT home, where the dust of his kindred reposes,
To sleep 'mid the dew and the breath of the roses —
In summer, the season the sweetest and fairest —
Himself, of its blossoms, the purest and rarest.

Requiem.

He sleeps his last sleep — while all nature reposes,
And melody breaks from earth's thousands of voices;
Like distant sweet chimes, o'er evening's winds singing,
The music he breathed is in echoes still ringing.

Life's silver cord loosed, and the golden bowl broken;
. We bow to the mandate Jehovah has spoken;
God's promise proclaims, o'er the lov'd and lamented,
The silver cord loosed, shall again be cemented.

We lay him in love 'neath the rose and the willow—
Peace sits by his ashes — Peace breathes 'round his pillow;
How well that such graces and gifts should be given,
Like precious first fruits — an offering to Heaven.

God gave — and we bless him!   God took — and though parted,
Still trusting — still loving — we yield, broken-hearted;
Again in the home of the blest we shall greet him,
And youth bloom immortal, when joyful we meet him!

A short prayer and benediction, and the mournful company slowly retired, leaving all that is mortal of their precious friend among the flowers, the "purest and rarest," and loveliest of them all.

CHAPTER X.

MEMORIAL ADDRESSES, LETTERS OF CONDOLENCE, AND RESOLUTIONS OF SYMPATHY.

THERE is a way to get the kingdom; get the people, and the kingdom is got. There is a way to get the people; get their hearts, and the people are got. The people turn to a benevolent rule, as the water flows downward. — MENCIUS.

ADDRESS BY THE PASTOR.

Rev. Samuel H. Greene.

SOME lives, when they terminate here, go out in utter darkness; others in the twilight of doubt and obscurity; while to others it is given to depart like the setting sun, when, having finished its daily course, it sweeps through the western gates, leaving us, under skies resplendent with its touch, to recount its kindly ministry. Such a life, it seems to me, was this, the sudden termination of which so many mourn to-day. I am prompted to no words of eulogy as I stand beside this precious dust. No words of mine can add to your appreciation of the beauty and value of the life which was so marked in the purpose and toil. His record is his best eulogy. What he has been to us in the past, what he is to us to-day, these tear-dimmed eyes and quivering lips about me speak more eloquently than words can tell.

I need not in this presence speak of him as the affectionate and dutiful son; the thoughtful and devoted friend; the thorough and enthusiastic student; the vigorous and

independent thinker; nor need I impress upon your minds the memory of one so earnest
in his religious convictions and labors as to
subordinate all else to these; of one who was
a wise, generous, anxious Sunday School
Superintendent, a tender hearted and prayerful teacher. Nor yet is there occasion to tell
you how earnestly he prayed; how tenderly
he entreated the lost; or how he preached
the gospel from house to house, often with
tears, ministering to the sick and afflicted,
and stretching out his hands generously to
the poor. Of these things you have been
the fortunate and appreciative witnesses.

Ye are the witnesses.

And while we would bring no fulsome words
of praise to this sad place, yet we instinctively feel that honesty and gratitude demand the recognition of the life which
touched so many of us only with blessings.
I shall simply attempt to recall some of the
traits which peculiarly marked this dear life;

Some traits.

and first let me speak of his INTELLIGENCE.

Intelligence.

The agreeableness and worth of human
friendship is always largely measured by its
intelligence. Nature gave him from out of
her choicest gifts. From infancy these
found a congenial sphere for development in

the home life. The natural desire for knowledge found here a wise and healthy stimulus. The privilege of native city and land were supplemented by months of study abroad, and what he gained was devoted to a high and worthy purpose. Not in a single department was he intelligent, but in many. Literature, art, and science found in him an enthusiastic student and friend. But he had a knowledge of more than was taught in the schools. He learned to know men, and more than most young men he came to know his race—its sin, its need, and its grand possibilities; his ministry, consequently, was tender, appreciative, and sensible. How largely he was successful in approaching, leading, and blessing others, let these hundreds who shared in his ministry give answer to-day.

But again. I was impressed with his HONESTY—not a mere legal or business honesty, but much more. There was in his nature an utter abhorrence of all pretense or shàm. He was an honest thinker. His convictions resulted from his thinking, and they represented to him intelligence, conscience, and judgment. To these convic-

Honesty.

tions he was loyal, cost what it might, and no man can say that ever, for a single day, did he turn aside from the course to which those convictions impelled him. If mistakes were made, they were mistakes of judgment and not of heart. He believed in the triumph of the right, and consecrated himself to it. I cannot better describe his position than to give one of his favorite quotations:

"Truth is ever on the scaffold,
    And wrong is ever on the throne;
Yet that scaffold sways the future,
    And behind that great unknown
Standeth God within the shadow,
    Keeping watch above his own."

Honest with himself.

He was as honest with himself as with others. A fault was not less a fault because he discovered it in his own life. I remember how tearfully it is told in his home now, that, when but a little child, having transgressed the commandment of his mother and felt no punishment for it, he came to her, bringing in his little hand a stick, and asking that he might receive the punishment he merited. Whatever it might cost of open confession and tears, the consciousness of an honest life was worth infinitely more to him than every other consideration. This honesty made him a model of untiring industry and left upon his work the marks of thoroughness throughout. He was too honest to expend the time, strength, or means which God had given him, in any thing but the highest and best of purposes. In the social, religious, and business life his sincerity was every where apparent, and constituted one of the peculiar charms with which his character was invested.

But again. He came so near us and blessed us so largely in his SYMPATHY. No nature was more susceptible to touch of joy or sorrow than was his. His delicately constituted senses quickly comprehended and took hold of the experience of others, and the unfortunate, the suffering, the bereaved, found in him a warm and practical sympathy. I well remember, when not a week had elapsed since I had entered on my duties here, of his calling to tell me of an afflicted family in his Mission School. I remember the impression made upon me as he said, his eyes filling with tears, "It seems to me we shall save this family for God." He shared their sorrows, and used whatever

Sympathy.

To save for God.

influence he had to bless their affliction to the salvation of their souls. He was in profound sympathy with his race, and his happiest hours were when he served it. Generous, self-forgetful, he imitated the example of his Divine Master, and sought "not to be ministered unto, but to minister."

But the characteristic which impressed us most strongly, was the fact that he was PIOUS. His intelligence, honesty, and sympathy were laid in consecration at the feet of Jesus, where these earthly gifts were sanctified and guided by the Holy Spirit, and used for the highest possible good of his race. His entrance upon the religious life was not the result of any sudden emotion, but from the commencement to the close bore the mark of intelligent and decided conviction. It was fidelity to his conscience, his judgment, and the Word of God. But while he was moved by principle rather than emotion, it was not the coldness of a merely intellectual piety. There was a tenderness and depth of religious life. We felt in his presence that he had been with Christ. He was honest in his spiritual life. It meant vastly more than a nominal church member-

Piety.

Fidelity to conscience.

ship to him. It meant submission to Christ; union with Him and His people in their spirit and work; the laying on God's altar of all that was most precious and dear to him. It is pleasant to feel that the first money ever earned by him was given to build this edifice to God, and that the last time he ever lifted a pen—among the mountains of Colorado—was to write a note enclosing a check which should help to bring happiness to the scholars of his Mission School.

His piety was progressive. He grew in grace, and believed in it for himself and others. He was peculiarly happy in his religious work. Its ways to him were ways of pleasantness, and all the paths were peace. Over the intense earnestness of his religious life, strengthened by profound conviction, there broke the sunshine of his great heart and greater hope. I think none of us who walked beside our brother and shared in his work, have ever seen an hour when we could gather, by any sign or expression, that the duties of his religious life were not pleasant ones to bear. There seemed to be to him no stronger, richer satisfaction than that of

Growth in grace.

Symmetry

Desire.

being in submission to the will of his Master, and giving his life to His service.

The elements of character which we have mentioned were happily blended, giving symmetry and strength to his life. Here was ability with modesty, zeal tempered by intelligence, and faith lighted by works. That such a life was attractive, inspiring, elevating in its tendencies, we cannot wonder. His last days with us were filled with Christ-like work. He fell at his post, and away from us, but found Heaven just as near and sweet from Los Pinos as if he had gone up to it from out his own beautiful home. He learned long ago in whom he trusted, and the "valley and the shadow of death" had no fear for him. "I should like to experience for myself what lies beyond." he said but a few weeks before his departure. There was no morbid fear in his heart, but a longing to see the land to which his kindred had gone and to which he had pointed those he loved the best.

The clouds are heavy over us to-day. We had hoped to hear his voice and take his hand again this side of the river; but God had better and greater blessings in store for our brother, and to-day, I doubt not, his foot-fall is heard within the pearly gates, and a "Welcome home," grander and sweeter than ours, is sounding in his ears, and the hands we hoped to clasp are casting the crown at the feet of Him we love. The home call has sounded. The brother has entered into rest. Let us not mourn as do others. We shall not lay him in the grave to-day. This is but the casket which held the jewel. And now, while we thank God for this true, sweet life; for what it was to himself, his family, the church, and the world, let us bow in submission to the will of Him "who is too wise to err, too good to be unkind." We have left to us the precious memory of what he was, the gracious promise of what he is.

Called home.

Submission.

To these stricken parents and kindred, the bereaved church and Sunday School, and mourning friends, there come the consolations of the gospel he believed and loved. We shall meet him again when the night has past and the morning has come. "Wherefore comfort one another with these words."

No language of mine can portray to you the overwhelming loss which has fallen upon

Loss to his home.

the home dear to all our hearts. No language can express the sympathy which goes out from every true christian heart to those who mourn over so great and sore an affliction. The highest ministry we can bring is the promise of the Master we love, who bids us to find peace in Him. I cannot describe the loss which has come upon the Church of Christ in being thus bereft of one of its most vigorous and devoted laborers, whom God has gathered to Himself. And yet, while we mourn, there is greater reason for rejoicing, that in the hour of earthly loss there is triumph over pain. Our brother joins to-day in Alleluias "over there."

Personal loss.

I cannot close without giving brief expression to my own sense of personal loss in the death of this brother beloved. When I came, a total stranger to this city, these folded white hands were the first outstretched to bid me welcome. When I came at a later time, to enter upon official relations to this church, those hands again gave me welcome. and I came immediately into the strong and beautiful influence of that sweet life. To many of you who have recently put on Christ, he first called my attention. You had shared long in his love and prayers. I shall miss his affectionate words of sympathy and cheer; his counsel and prayers; his earnest, tear-wet face as it looked up to me from the sanctuary pew. I am sadly conscious that one who prayed for the success of the gospel, through my humble ministry, has left us when I seemed to need him so much. But I would not murmur; no, rather would I join hands with those who mourn, and seek with them those spiritual heights from which we can catch glimpses of the land to which he has gone, and rejoice with him in his victory. Here are crushed hopes and a darkened home; yonder, thank God. are hopes realized and the "Father's house." The inspiration of his precious life is upon us, and it calls us not to his grave, but to his work. Upon whom shall his mantle fall? I look over the young men of this congregation and ask myself, upon whom shall the mantle of our brother fall? Who shall take up the words of the prayers now ended; the testimony that has been given for the last time? Beside this silent sleeper I ask you to pledge yourselves to the work he laid down. Let us remember that he became

Missed.

His mantle.

what he was only as he followed Christ, and we can only hope to enter into his toil here and his rest hereafter, when Christ becomes to us the "all and in all."

Loss to Mission School.

I know I speak to many who mourn, outside of his home and family and kindred, the loss of our brother. The tears would come as these children filed in from the Mission School, and I thought how, to some of them, he had been more than father and mother, and I asked who should care for them now? But the, God he loved abides: though the teacher, the superintendent depart, yet the Savior, whose image he bore. dwells with those who love Him forevermore. Let your hearts find comfort in that source of consolation and comfort to which he pointed you. Let the last words he uttered in your hearing come to have a deep place in your hearts and home. For listen to what he said as he bade you what then

Last words.

promised to be but a brief farewell: "Let us all so live that, if we do not meet here again, we may meet around the Great White Throne in heaven." How little he knew how near his feet were to the pearly gates.

We take leave of him amid the flowers.

in the place full of sacred associations, to which he has come. We shall lay his body down beneath his native skies, in the midst of the community where his prayers and testimonies shall still be sounding in our ears; and beside this precious dust let us learn to know how good a thing it is to follow the Lord Jesus. How sweet and blessed it is, when life's work is ended. to sleep in Jesus!

Dead, yet speaking.

> "Asleep in Jesus; blessed sleep,
> From which none ever wake to weep."

So he goes from us in the impress and beauty of his first manhood. We shall not forget him. His memory shall cheer us in our toil; and when the toil shall be ended, and we go out from these Sabbath School classes and missions, and the places which our work and duty have made for us, it will only be into a heaven richer and sweeter because many of those we love have gone before. By the precious dust we shall write. "Blessèd are the dead who die in the Lord. Yea, saith the Spirit, that they may rest from their labors, and their works do follow them."

Not to be forgotten.

"It is well
with my
soul."

And now the dear scholars who loved
him so well, shall bring to us their tribute
and offering as they sing to us, "It is Well
with My Soul," from out those sweet songs
in which our brother so often led them before
he passed over to the other side.

ADDRESS

By Rev. H. L. Morehouse,

Secretary American Baptist Home Mission Society.

THIS, to me, has been an unusually sad week. On Tuesday last I mingled my tears with those of the friends of that great and good man, Dr. Bishop, of N. Y., whom we laid away in Greenwood Cemetery, and now I meet with those who weep the loss of an only child, and a justly beloved son. Dr. Bishop was an honored member of the Board of the American Baptist Home Mission Society, of which this sorrowing father is President, and I am here, as I was there, as a representative of that society, to express, so far as my presence enables me to express, not only my own personal sympathy, but also the sympathy of my associates, with my brother, and all who are smitten by this affliction. But I am here in more than a representative capacity. I am here because my own personal regard for him who has gone prompts me to be here. In that loss to which I have referred, and in this, a personal friendship has been sundered. The one had passed his three score and ten years

Sad week.

Personal regard.

Contrasts.

of a life filled with usefulness. The other left us before he had finished his one score and ten years — years, however, that had already yielded rich fruit, and given promise of even greater productiveness for Christ in the later life. Such are the contrasts of the week — age and youth gathered into the grave. That the aged should be called to rest was according to the divinely appointed and natural order of things. That this youthful servant, our beloved friend, should be smitten down thus, when thoroughly equipped for life's work, when so many of his stamp are specially needed in the church

Parental hopes.

and world, and when so many parental hopes centred about him, is one of those mysteries that no one can fathom. Only a strong faith can say, "It is for the best;" "All things work together for good to them that love God." Only a strong faith at such a time can say, "Thy will, O God, be done."

Life transferred.

That life, however — that higher life — has not ended. It has simply been transferred to the higher, nobler, purer world, where the redeemed of all ages unceasingly sing the praises of Him who redeemed them.

Our departed friend and brother, William S. Stickney, was indeed a servant of the Lord Jesus Christ. It was my privilege to know him and the character of his service during the important period of his life, when he was a student in the University at Rochester, New York. When, in January, 1873, I assumed charge of the church in Rochester, to which I had been called, I found him, student as he was, variously and earnestly engaged in christian service for that church, and as devoted to its service as the very best member. He was organist and chorister, having charge of a large volunteer choir, which he diligently and patiently drilled on Saturday evenings, and successfully led on the Sabbath day. For a time he conducted singing in the Sabbath School, wherein, also, he was a most faithful and successful teacher. He was a regular attendant at the Wednesday evening prayer meeting, and on Friday evening, when the Young People held their meeting, or the monthly covenant meeting was observed, he was usually present; coming in after attending the meeting of the Y. M. C. A. of the University, which met half an hour earlier. He frequently took part in these meetings, and well do I

Important period.

Activity.

remember his thoughtful, soulful, and tender utterances on these occasions. During the winter of 1874 and '75 there was a special religious interest, and I recall his assiduous labors in behalf of the unconverted, both in the Sabbath School, the congregation, and the University, and it was largely through his influence, I am sure, that several, including some students in the University, professed their faith in Christ. His fine social

Social powers.

powers were dedicated to christian service, and thus, unlike many, wherever he went he carried his religion with him, for it was in him and of him; it was ingrained, and it would manifest itself; it could not be hidden. How much richer that church was because of his presence!—how much richer those circles of friends among whom he moved!—how much richer that University because of his pronounced religious charac-

Results unknown to us.

ter, who can tell? Only God can know; only in eternity will be gathered up the results of his work and influence. When I came to know his antecedents, his culture, his refined tastes, and then saw him give his heart and strength to a church organized after he came to the University, and which, neither as to its house of worship nor general character, could be as attractive or gratifying to his tastes as other older and stronger churches, I felt the sincerest admiration for his character, and I thought, there was one who was religious not merely because it would minister to his own needs, but one who would look over the whole field and say, "Where am I most needed? Where can I do the most good? Where will my work tell the most for God?" and finding that field, would give himself wholly to it. From January, 1873, to July, 1875, he was to me a friend and helper in my pastoral work, such as few young men have been in the whole course of my ministry, and I never can forget him, and his worth, and what he accomplished, while scores of his associates, who were also christians, have faded from my memory, because they did nothing particularly worthy of remembrance. Verily, as the Psalmist says, "The righteous shall be in everlasting remembrance."

Not alone in church matters were his thoughts and efforts enlisted. The religious principle ruled in all he did. He was chiefly instrumental in establishing a University

Friend and helper.

paper, through which the institution should be represented. I remember with what earnestness he threw himself into it. He was its chief editor for a time, and ever aimed to give the paper a high character, and was especially anxious that nothing in its pages should cast any reflection on the institution, or be detrimental to the reader. Among the students he was a leader—a leader not for the sake of distinction, but to use his influence for good. He was independent in judgment and in purpose—not following the current tendencies of college life, but aiming rather to direct college sentiment and opinion into right channels. I may say here, that, by both the President and Professors of the University, he was held in the highest esteem for his thorough christian bearing and manliness, as well as for his work as a student.

If I were to sum up his character, I would say that he impressed me then as a man of profound earnestness, great sincerity, and marked conscientiousness, with simplicity of character, humility, and special consecration to Christ. His ruling purpose, I am sure. was to learn how best to serve

A leader.

Independence.

Manhood.

Christ; how, while he lived, he could do the most good for the world.

During the closing months of his college course, he reflected seriously what his call in life should be, and conversed with me freely about a call to the ministry. He was impressed with the greatness of the minister's work, but was not anxious to assume the responsibilities of the office. For several months he debated the question whether he should enter the ministry, and I am convinced that his decision not to preach the Gospel was the result of thoughtful consideration and prayer. His convictions were not sufficiently positive, and he could not think of going forward in such a serious matter uncertainly.

Question of duty.

But I must not linger on what we love to think of in him who has now gone from us. Were he to speak, would not he say: "If there was any thing good in me, the praise thereof belongs to Christ, through whose grace I am what I am?" To wise and loving parental christian training, and to the direct influences of the Holy Spirit, would he refer as the efficient causes in the formation of his christian character. So, while we mention what he was, we remember that the ultimate praise is due to Christ, who can so change, beautify, and conform to his own likeness this poor human nature of ours on which and in which He works so mightily. Though our dear friend was possessed of many natural endowments which rendered him lovable and admirable, yet all these were lighted up, mellowed, and beautified by the grace of God, as the colors and figures in a stained-glass window are brought out into beauty by the sunlight of heaven.

Some of the lessons of this life, that particularly impress me, are these: In the first place, there is in his life a lesson to young men pursuing a course of study, or engaged in any profession that calls them from home and from their usual religious associations. We have here a demonstration that the religious life need not deteriorate, while one is engaged in a course of study, as it too often does. That need not be so with any young man. The education of the head need not, should not, interfere with spiritual development. And in the second place, I wish to call your attention to the importance of youthful devotion to Christ. Our brother

His life a lesson.

did not wait until he should become old and influential before he gave his service to Christ. What ability he had as a young man he used as a young man for Christ.

Youthful devotion to Christ.

When we remember that the great harvest-field of souls is in the younger period of life, and that none can reap so well in that harvest, as young men and women, whose experiences are of the same kind as those among whom they labor, what a wonderful incentive it is for young men and young women to put all they are, all they have, all they are worth, into the cause of Christ! What a wonderful influence a christian young man

Influence of the young.

has in college, in the church, in the Sabbath School; and to-day what an influence goes out from that life, and from this place!— How the nobility of such a life stands out in

Nobility of his life.

contrast with that soulless and aimless life of multitudes. As we recall what he has accomplished for Christ, and for souls on this earth, what inspiration has gone forth from him to others, and how many noble impulses have been generated by contact with him, we can say: "Truly his life has been productive of great things."

"We live in deeds, not years ; in thoughts, not breaths ;
In feelings, not in figures on a dial. He most lives
Who thinks most, feels the noblest, acts the best."

I have spoken of these things in the hope that some one of those present may be led to seek Christ; that some one of you, troubled with faults, with passions, it may be with some besetting sin, may be led to look to Him who can impart heavenly power which will transform your character and make it beautiful, as that of our friend was beautiful. He was a standing witness to the power of God's grace to keep a soul from falling, and to render a life eminently useful.

Character transformed.

What an unspeakable consolation it is to these parents to remember his affectionate character; his deep love for Christ; and his decided religious life—a consolation which I can only illustrate by reference to an incident that occurred during my pastorate. In the same college class to which our brother belonged, was a young man who was taken sick and died near the completion of his course. He, too, was an only son. During the religious interest which prevailed in the institution, both our departed brother and myself were deeply interested in his welfare.

Consolation.

He had imbibed skepticism from books, was materialistic in his views, but being troubled on account of his sins, publicly asked prayers for himself, and honestly endeavored, as I think, to believe in Christ as his Savior. He made no positive public profession, however. So he died. When his parents came, they sought me and said, with tears, "Can you give us any evidence that our son professed faith in Christ?" and I never saw two christian hearts yearn so for some evidence on which to hang their hope of his eternal welfare—something which would afford consolation to the soul in that trying hour. I could only tell them what he had said, and how he had felt, and how he had tried to exercise faith in Christ; but how I wished for something more that I could tell them, with which their hearts might be comforted. But to-day I need say nothing to these afflicted parents to assure them that he who has gone is at rest. Theirs is the great consolation, which his pronounced christian life gives, that Christ has taken their son to Himself. And so we bid our brother farewell, feeling that he has entered into the "rest that remaineth for the people of God."

Contrast.

ADDRESS

BY JAMES C. WELLING, LL.D.,

President of the Columbian University.

I AM here to-day to attest simply by my presence, for my words must be few, not only the sympathy which is due to a stricken father and mother, who feel that the light of their eyes has been quenched, and that the gladness of earth has fled from their hearts, but also the sympathy due to a church which, in the death of our young and beloved brother, has been called to mourn the loss of a loyal and earnest christian worker, and the sympathy due to a Sunday School weeping over the sudden and, as it seems to us, the untimely fall of a Superintendent who was faithful, energetic, and devout. And I am also here to take my part in a great affliction.

It has been my fortune, and I count it my good fortune, to have known our friend and brother from his early youth down to the day of his death. I saw him as he grew up, a bright and gleeful boy, in the sacred precincts of home, diffusing joy and gladness among all with whom he came in contact. I saw him as he sat on the forms of the

Sunday School, a diligent student of the Holy Book, and as he entered the sanctuary to learn from its ministrations the way of life. I saw him as he went from among us to dwell in college halls, and as he came back from them, laden with their highest honors—the academic diploma in his hand, the academic laurel on his head. And better than all these, I have seen him, too, as he wore in the presence of this whole community the christian's crown of righteousness—the ornament of a meek and quiet spirit. and yet of a spirit which was noble, generous, and brave in every manly impulse.

The christian's crown.

And now I am here to join with you in this tearful tribute to his memory, as with reverent hands we bear his body to the burial, when, in the order of nature, it would be so much more fitting that he should help to perform these last sad offices for me. Surely, in the presence of a spectacle like this, when a young man falls in the full flush of his athletic strength, we are called to read with a new pathos the lesson of our mortality, while a new emphasis is given to that sublime declaration with which the Apostle Paul transfers our unfading hopes

Tribute to his memory.

and our unfailing expectations to the "Blessed and only Potentate, the King of kings
and the Lord of lords, *who only hath immortality.*" Change and decay are indeed written on every created thing, and the choicest
emblems of human frailty are found in that
which is brightest and fairest — in the grass
which withers and in the flower which fall-
eth away. We all do fade as a leaf. Alas!
in this vale of tears there is nothing so common, nothing so universal, as death, and
when one of our own poets would gather
the phenomena of earth into a single view,
which should be at once the most comprehensive and the most striking, it was a
"Thanatopsis," a "Vision of Death," which
unfolded itself to his sight.

> "All that tread
> The globe are but a handful to the tribes
> That slumber in its bosom."

And yet, compared with death, there is
nothing of which we can say that it is so
singular, so individual, so unique. This
King of Terrors is unique in the solemn
grandeur with which he comes to every living soul; unique in the personal summons
which he sounds in every human ear: "It

*Death not
a strange
thing.*

is appointed unto men once to die, and after
that the judgment"; unique in the demand
he makes on the tenderest of human sensibilities and the most sacred of human affections.

And standing as we do to-day around
a bier which reminds us of all that is most
inevitable, and all that is most touching in
human calamity—of hopes blasted in the
bud just as they were ready to burst into
blossom, and just as they gave rich promise
of the fullest fruitage—it only remains for
us to decide the point of view from which
we shall survey this great affliction. For
there are two very distinct points of view
from which it may be contemplated; as in
the physical world there are two very distinct horizons within which we may bound
our vision—the horizon of earth, and the
horizon of the sky. Beyond this horizon of
earth, within which are comprised the toil
and trouble of human conflict, the sights
and sounds of human woe, we can project
our thoughts to that wider and higher horizon which moves among the stars—the
unsetting stars in the infinite dome of the
sky. And so, as a French christian has

*Two
horizons.*

From
earth to
heaven.

reminded us, our life in the moral world is
hedged about by these same two horizons —
the horizon of earth and the horizon of
heaven.   Within the former of these horizons we see to-day nought but the signs
of grief—garlands laid upon a coffin, a
family clothed in the habiliments of mourning, a whole assembly dissolved in tears.
But within the latter of these horizons we
see a christian pilgrim who has laid down
the staff of the exile to bear the victor's
palm in the streets of the New Jerusalem,
"where there shall be no more death, neither
sorrow nor crying; neither shall there be
any more pain, for the former things are
passed away." I am sure, then, that I do
but speak the word which springs unbidden
to your lips, as the sentiment of its truth
lies deep and strong in your hearts, when
I say that we must find our consolation
to-day within the realm where our young
brother, whom we mourn—but whom we
strangely mourn—has found his rest and
peace—within the horizon of heaven.   For
when, by the eye of faith, we perceive the
joy unspeakable, and the peace passing all
understanding, into which he has entered,

now that he has passed "within the vail,"
we can mingle our praises and our thanks-
givings with these our tearful regrets. He
will never again come back to us, but we can
go to him.

FROM THE CALVARY BAPTIST SUNDAY SCHOOL.

Washington, Aug. 15, 1880.

DEAR FRIENDS—

As officers and teachers of the Calvary Baptist Sunday School, of which your son was so long a loved and honored member and teacher, we desire in this informal way to convey to you some feeble expression of our sympathy and condolence in this the deepest, saddest bereavement of your lives.

We remember with tenderest regard the unselfish interest of our departed brother in all that pertained to the best welfare of those around him—more especially those in the church and Sunday School—and we can never forget the many acts of kindness and benevolence with which the days of his life were filled, nor the earnest and untiring zeal he ever manifested in the furtherance of the interests of Christ's kingdom. He worked well for the Master while it was day, and now that he has gone to his reward, his works live after him.

We are thankful for the precious life that was given us for so short a season, and for all its sweet and blessed influences. And we do earnestly pray that the consolations of that religion and of that hope which made so bright and joyous the life of your loved one, may still comfort and sustain you and help you to look forward with joyful anticipations to that blissful reunion in a happier and better land, where there is no more sorrow nor tears, and where we shall forever be with those we love.

MARCUS M. BARTLETT,   E. B. CURTIS,
H. G. JACOBS,   MRS. W. M. KING,

Committee.

HENRY BEARD,	JOHN H. HOWLETT,
D. A. CHAMBERS,	ANNA G. DELONG,
L. R. TAYLOR,	GEO. S. PRINDLE,
ALICE WÜRDEMANN,	COLUMBIA E. NOYES,
JOHN L. HAZZARD,	KATIE A. STICKNEY,
D. HAYNES,	B. F. BIGELOW,
F. H. STICKNEY,	A. N. CONDRON,
L. GILSON,	E. J. GIFFORD,
EMMA HIGGINS,	S. C. BENEDICT,
M. A. QUINCY,	MRS. J. E. DEXTER,
ANNIE B. ROSE,	MRS. H. E. ALBEE,
S. M. PLUMLEY,	M. J. LYNCH,
H. M. BRUSH,	LIZZIE B. JONES,
ANNA S. WHEELER,	CARRIE A. CLAPP,
W. H. SLATER,	T. R. JONES.

To Mr. and Mrs. Wm. Stickney.

(margin notes: May the hope which cheered him comfort you. Officers and Teachers.)

FROM THE CALVARY MISSION SUNDAY SCHOOL.

IN MEMORIAM.

IT has pleased the Most High God, in furtherance of His wise and loving. though to us, inscrutable purposes, to call our dearly beloved brother and Superintendent, W. S. Stickney, from a sphere filled with christian activities, to join that great multitude, which no man can number, who stand before the Throne and before the Lamb.

Mourn his loss.

While reverently we confess the Judge of all the earth doeth right, our hearts are sad and our eyes suffuse with tears, because we shall see his face among us no more.

Cherishing the remembrance of his earnest admonitions, his wise counsels, his unwearying labors, his broad charities, his deep sympathies, his cheerful and beautifully symmetrical religious life, we promise.

A solemn promise.

by God's help, to show in our faithful attention to the interests of Calvary Mission Sunday School a reverence for his memory which language may not here express.

We sorrow with the afflicted parents in their sudden and painful bereavement, the severity of which can scarcely be mitigated by earthly remedies — for earth has nothing to offer lacerated hearts, blighted expectations, darkened homes; yet is our sorrow turned to joy, as we see in their lives evidence of that strong faith which led Job to exclaim, "Though He slay me, yet will I trust Him," and which enables them to endure, "as seeing Him who is invisible," and this to the honor of God and the glory of His church.

Sorrowing yet rejoicing.

Resolved, That the foregoing is tendered by the undersigned officers and teachers of Calvary Mission Sunday School to Mr. and Mrs. Stickney, parents of our late Superintendent, as a feeble expression of the love we bore him, and the sincere sympathy we feel for them.

L. R. TAYLOR, *Ass't Supt.*
J. MORTIMER BESSEY, *Secretary.*
T. R. JONES, *Treasurer.*
Teachers.

Officers and Teachers.

JOHN L. HAZZARD,	ANNIE R. BURNSIDE,
MARY A. QUINCY,	LILLIAN SPIGNUL,
MARY J. BESSEY,	ELLA DeMOTT,
WM. M. FLETCHER,	ELLA M. FRASER,
MARY L. BISCHOFF,	MARIAN E. SNOOK,
REUBEN PERRIN,	NETTIE B. COLLINS,

Eva S. Brooks,	Sallie S. Davis,
Mary A. Holbrook,	Amanda McMurray,
G. H. Judd,	James J. Brooks,
Mary A. Lerch,	Susie F. McKnew,
Minnie M. Moran,	Katie M. Wells,

A. M. Webster.

FROM THE COVENANT BAND OF THE CALVARY BAPTIST CHURCH.

Washington, August 20, 1880.

DEAR FRIENDS—

In His infinite wisdom our Heavenly Father has removed from us a dearly beloved brother and companion in christian work. We mourn the loss of his earnest words and wise counsels, yet instinctively our hearts turn in sympathy to you whose loss is so much greater, and the burden of whose grief is so much heavier.

Loss to the Band.

We cannot refrain, as a Band of which he was one of the covenant members, and for whose success he labored so faithfully, from expressing to you the deep sense of loss we feel in this separation, and in the knowledge that we no longer share his earnest prayers. Yet, in the midst of our sorrow. we rejoice that we have known such a life, and trust that the memory of his kind, persistent, faithful labors shall serve us as an inspiration to more faithful, more consecrated living for the Master.

His memory an inspiration.

To many of us his life was a new revelation of christian experience, and we have

all found new incentives to faith and duty
in reviewing his words and acts among us.
To you, who so much better than we, knew
and valued this life, this Covenant Band of
Calvary Church tender their most sincere
and heartfelt sympathy, and unitedly pray
that He who gave and hath now taken away
may prove a never-failing source of comfort
and consolation.

Members.

H. G. JACOBS,	THEOPHILUS BRAY,
L. R. TAYLOR,	HENRY H. KENDALL,
FRANK S. BLANCHARD,	WM. D. HENRY,
W. E. SEBREE,	FRANK H. JACKSON,
J. M. BESSEY,	J. H. ELDRIDGE,
R. PERRIN,	CHAS. F. PLUMLEY,

GEORGE S. FRASER.

To Mr. and Mrs. Wm. Stickney.

From the Officers and Teachers of Kendall Chapel.

WE, the Officers and Teachers of Kendall Chapel Sabbath School, remembering the affectionate interest and faithful labors of our christian friends, Mr. and Mrs. William Stickney, desire to express our sympathy with them in the death of their only son, WILLIAM S. STICKNEY.

Knowing him as an earnest and successful worker in the Sabbath School, and especially endeared to us by the helpful influence of his sweet music, as well as by his efficiency as a teacher, through years of service in our own school, we feel that the cause of Christ has lost an able and conscientious advocate. How great that loss, time only can show us. Yet we pray that he, being dead, may yet speak, and that his works may follow him, so that they who best loved him may find a comfort and a joy in hearing of the glorious things GOD has been pleased to work through his instrumentality.

Again we tender the assurance of our sincere and heartfelt sympathy, and pray

An earnest worker endeared by his sweet music.

Sincere sympathy.

that in this, as in all our lives, we may see GOD's goodness, and that He may be, in this time of trial, a Comforter indeed.

Officers
and
Teachers.

THEOPHILUS BRAY,
W. E. SEBREE,
CHAS. A. MUDDIMAN,
MARY A. McMAKIN,
C. A. MAHONEY,
FRANK S. BLANCHARD,
MRS. S. M. YEATMAN,
HENRY H. KENDALL,
MRS. H. S. SAYRE,
FLORENCE B. TOWERS.
SARAH F. LIVINGSTON,
J. H. JOHNSTON,

H. G. JACOBS,
FRANK H. JACKSON,
JOHN H. OLCOTT,
E. J. GIFFORD,
L. J. WHITE,
MARY HATCH,
S. BRAY,
CARRIE A. CLAPP,
ANNIE B. ROSE.
EFFIE BURR,
ALICE C. REYNOLDS,
ANNIE E. MUDDIMAN,

EMMA A. GENZERODT.

From the Superintendents' Union.

Washington, D. C., Aug. 13, 1880.

AT a meeting of the Sunday School Superintendents' Union, held August 9, 1880, a committee, consisting of Messrs. Simpson, LeDuc, and Gatley, were appointed to prepare resolutions expressive of the sense of the Union at the loss sustained by us in the death of William S. Stickney.

The committee appointed reported the following, which were unanimously adopted:

Whereas, it has pleased the Supreme Ruler of the Universe, by his inscrutable but all-wise decrees, to remove from a sphere of usefulness here on earth to the enjoyments of his home in heaven, our respected friend and co-laborer, William S. Stickney, therefore be it—

Resolved, That by the death of Mr. Stickney this Union has been deprived of a member whose sympathy and aid were ever enlisted in the advancement of the interests of this Union, and the cause of Sunday School work in this city has lost the services of one who in a signal manner possessed the ability to render efficient service in this branch of

Loss to the cause.

our Master's work, and whose heart and hand were ever ready to carry forward the work of christian education among the young of this District.

Resolved, That we tender to his bereaved family and friends our heart-felt sympathy, and while we mourn with them our loss, we would point them to Him who is the mourner's hope and joy, and comfort them and ourselves with the full knowledge that our departed friend is now enjoying the bliss of dwelling in the presence of Him whose service on earth was his chief end and joy.

Resolved, That these resolutions be entered upon the minutes of the Union, and a copy transmitted to the family of the deceased.

A true copy.

HENRY K. SIMPSON,

Secretary S. S. Supt. Union.

Mourner's hope.

LETTER FROM M. B. ANDERSON, D. D.,

President of Rochester University.

Rochester, Aug. 26, 1880.

MY DEAR SIR—
The exhaustion consequent upon
a year of unusual labor, has prevented me
from expressing sooner my deep and heartfelt sympathy with you and Mrs. Stickney
in your great and irreparable loss. I knew
your son as none but a college officer could.
He passed his four years of college life without giving me one moment's anxiety regarding his character or conduct. He was always and every where the christian gentle-
man. He had an unusual amount of the
rarest of capacities—administrative power.
This capacity prepares a man for the service
of his fellow men better than any of the
forms of what is ordinarily called genius.
I confidently expected for him a large and
honorable career in life—a career worthy of
his descent, and one which would do honor
to his Alma Mater. But God in His Provi-
dence has seen fit to take him early to the
rewards of a blessed life.

I have no children nor near relatives,

The chris-
tian gen-
tleman.

Adminis-
trative
power.

and though I cannot understand your loss, I can sympathize with you and Mrs. Stickney in the sense of loneliness with which you look forward to a childless old age. May God in His mercy give you both the grace to bear up under this terrible trial of your faith.

I need not say that Mrs. Anderson joins with me in all that I have written in regard to the moral excellencies of your son, and in sympathy for your suffering.

Not dead.

Your son is not dead. He lives in the respect and love of all who knew him. He will always hold an honorable place among our Alumni.

Sincerely yours,

M. B. ANDERSON.

Hon. William Stickney.

LETTER FROM JAMES C. WELLING, LL.D.

The Pitney House,
Saratoga, Aug. 4, 1880.

MY DEAR MR. STICKNEY —
Your letter came to take away my last ground of hope, for until it came, I still hoped there might be some mistake in the newspaper paragraph which fell under my eyes.

And now what shall I say to you in the presence of this great sorrow? You are spending your days and nights in measuring the length and breadth and depth of the chasm which has so suddenly opened at your feet, and in vain may the voice of friendship hope, in an hour like this, to divert your gaze from the dimensions of your unspeakable loss.

It has always seemed to me that the friends of the stricken patriarch Job acted wisely when, in sight of the wreck and ruin which had come to darken his life, they sat down by his side and opened not their mouths. The best homage, perhaps, which I can pay to your affliction, would be the homage of a tender and respectful silence;

A deep chasm.

Sympathy of silence.

for words can bring no solace to the heart that is withered and smitten like the grass of the fields.

And yet, even in this hour of your anguish, I may whisper in your ears the words of an old German hymn which always come to my thoughts when the grave opens to swallow my own hopes or the hopes of my friends. The purport of the lines is this: "Our pathway in life lies over the graves of those most dear to us, so long as we keep our eyes fixed on the earth, but when we lift our eyes heavenward, we see that it also lies beneath the unsetting stars of the Divine promises."

Stars of promise.

You have indeed been greatly afflicted in the death of your beloved boy, in the full flush of his manly youth, but God has also greatly honored you both in his exemplary christian life, and now, in saving him from the heat and burden of a long life, by giving him at once an early entrance into the kingdom of heaven. We shall all soon be called to lay down the burden of life's sorrow at the portals of the tomb, and happy will it be for us if the portal of our graves shall have, like his, an outlook on the cross.

A blessing

and the open gate of the Father's house,
with its many mansions. Earth has no longer any sorrows for him whom you mourn,
and earth has no sorrows for you "which
heaven cannot cure." Meanwhile you must
try to walk through this thick darkness by
the light of the stars which are still shining
over your head, albeit you can scarcely see
them while your eyes are filled with tears.

No sorrow
for the
dead.

Of course I shall wish to stand by your
side when you are called to place the remains
of your dear son in their last resting place.
I can reach Washington in a day from Saratoga, and I pray you to give me timely notice of the funeral.

Convey, I beg, my heartfelt sympathies
and words of condolence to Mrs. Stickney,
and invoking for you both the consolations
of the great All-Father, who is most kind
when to the eye of sense he seems most
stern, I remain, my dear Mr. Stickney,

Your sympathizing friend and brother,
JAMES C. WELLING.

LETTER FROM JAMES J. BROOKS, ESQ.

Washington, D. C. Sept. 4, 1880.

M Y DEAR MR. STICKNEY —
Your unexpected but welcome
letter, dated Sept. 2, is this moment received.
I have read it with weeping eyes, and if, in
writing on the spur of the moment and out
of the depths of a sorrowful heart, I should
appear incoherent or heterodox in my utterances, I beg you to impute it not to my lack
of faith in God's justice, wisdom, love, or
mercy.

That I have not had one word of comfort
to utter either to you or your dear wife, is
solely due to the fact that I was awe-stricken
and, shall I say, confounded at this unlooked
for, mysterious phase of God's dealings with
those who love Him. The more I thought
over it, the more my head and heart ached,
and as I stood facing the sad dispensation,
I confess I discovered how very weak my
faith was, nor could I, in such a frame, dare
to mock your grief by uttering words of comfort that were not born of an intelligent,
whole-souled trust in the Almighty God.
So, I say it, at the same time praying for

Bewil-
dered.

An aching
heart.

forgiveness of God, I laid my hand upon my mouth and only wept and wondered.

I lost a sweet little girl, Mary, in her fifth year. As she sickened, I prayed God to take me and spare her. I did not ask that His will be done. The instinct that prompted the prayer was of His planting. I cannot think He saw sin in the petition, but He took the child. I have lived to firmly believe that His way was the *best* for her and for me. I know what have been your thoughts. How gladly would the parents have relinquished *all* except immortal life to save the now sainted one for a few more years of labor here for Christ. But He for whom your boy labored saw all; He knows all; He marked his seed-sowing, his prayers, his charities, his mature christian life, and He said, "Come up higher!" And may it not be in reserve for the dear parents of the departed to realize, even on this earth, that His ways, though now inscrutable, are the best?

God knows all.

I cannot hope to increase your knowledge of the commands or the promises of God as given in the Scriptures, yet I am moved to request you to read Ezekiel, chapter 24, verses 15, 16, and 18, and may you be led to feel that it is a message from God to you.

Earnest-
ness and
self-sac-
rifice.

I loved your boy for his earnestness and self-sacrifice in the christian work, and as I sat and listened to his expositions of the great truths embodied in the plan of Redemption through the crucified One, I felt as though they were such revelations as only the Spirit of God could impart—so simple, yet so convincing. I felt it a great privilege to be admitted as a co-worker with him. I knew he loved me, and I asked for nothing but to do his bidding as a teacher in the Calvary Mission Sunday School.

Should it please God to restore you and your dear wife to us in health, and with that peace in your hearts "which passeth all understanding," do not think, when you see cheerful faces and hear resonant voices in praise, that *he* is forgotten. His memory

Not for-
gotten.

will long remain as a sweet fragrance in the hearts of old and young who have ever been in school and church fellowship with him. while the extent of the influence of his godly life shall be fully known only in the Judgment of the Great Day.

I fear to weary you with my words, but I cannot close without assuring you of the blessed influence already exerted by your deportment before the church and the world since your affliction came.

.While the lines of sorrow have ploughed deep into your soul, people see that your faith is still centred in the living God, and He evidently intends you shall honor him in teaching by example what that living faith is which enabled Job to exclaim— "Though He slay me, yet will I trust in Him."

I thank you for so kind a remembrance of mine and me. Your affliction was a household sorrow with us. Commending you to Him who "doth not afflict willingly, nor grieve the children of men," I am

Your sympathizing friend,

JAMES J. BROOKS.

Lake Mohonk, N. Y.

My family will be pleased to hear your letter.

Lesson of affliction.

LETTER FROM HON. LOT M. MORRILL,

Member of the First Ute Commission.

Augusta, Oct. 20, 1880.

HON. WM. STICKNEY—

MY DEAR SIR—I read in the paper you sent, with deep regret, the sad news of the death of your son, and wrote you a letter of condolence for the great sorrow that had overshadowed your house.

I had had but slight acquaintance with William until associated with him on the Ute Commission, when I soon came to know and appreciate those qualities of disposition, temper, and character which shone through and revealed his moral life; and to know one void of sensuality, malignity, and misanthropy, and whose life ran on a plane above that of vanity and conceit.

The sense of bereavement in the death of a life so young and full of promise, will, indeed, be most poignant in the home he loved so well, and in which he was so greatly beloved, and will find expression, also, wherever he was known, for the gentleness, the refinement, and courtesy of his nature. I am, my dear sir,

Very sincerely and truly yours,

LOT M. MORRILL.

Rare qualities.

The desolate home.

FROM THE UTE COMMISSION.

AT a meeting. of the Ute Commission, held at Los Pinos Agency, July 21, 1880, J. B. Bowman, A. B. Meacham, and J. J. Russell were appointed a committee to give expression of the feelings of the Ute Commission in regard to the death of W. S. Stickney, Secretary of the Commission. The following were adopted:

The death of our friend and associate. occurring so unexpectedly, so far from his home and kindred, while in the faithful discharge of duty, and amid hopes and promises of an active and useful manhood, impresses us with a profound sense of our loss and of the uncertainty of human life, and of our obligations to the Supreme Ruler of the Universe. *Profound sense of loss.*

Resolved, That we can but express our admiration for his manly qualities and christian virtues that had endeared him to every member of the Commission. That we deplore his loss as a friend and an officer of the Commission. *Admiration for manly qualities.*

Resolved, That we deeply sympathize with the bereaved parents and friends of

the deceased in the irreparable loss, which,
we trust, may be alleviated in some degree
by the assurance that he was surrounded by

friends and physicians who did all in their
power to alleviate his sufferings in sickness
and perform for him the sad office of placing
his body to rest in a quiet grave.

Resolved, That a copy of these resolutions be transmitted to the parents of our
deceased friend, and that they be spread upon the records of the Commission, and a
copy be furnished to the Washington *Republican*, Washington *Star*, Washington *Post*.
and the *Council Fire*.

J. B. BOWMAN,

A. B. MEACHAM,

J. J. RUSSELL.

It would swell this volume to too large
proportions, if all the letters of tender sympathy, and resolutions of respect for the
memory of our son, received from kind
friends were inserted. Suffice it to say, that

the tribute to his worth thus given, as well
as in the many references to him in the
public prints, is a consolation to his sorrowing parents.

CHAPTER XI.

WILL'S BIBLE.

"'I AM WITH YOU ALWAY.' These words have volumes of meaning and worlds of comfort to me."

—Extract from one of his letters, August 15, 1873.

> HERE is the spring where waters flowe,
>   To quench our heate of sinne;
> Here is the tree where trueth doth grow,
>   To lead our lives therein;
> Here is the judge that stints the strife,
>   Where men's devices faile;
> The tidings of salvation deare
>   Come to our eares from hence;
> The fortress of our faith is here,
>   And shield of our defence. — 1594.

HIS diligent, critical, systematic, and thoughtful study of the Bible is well known. He began to read it in his early youth, and continued until the close of life.

The habit was formed, when young, of reading it morning and night, which neither the presence of company, engagements, nor any thing but absolute necessity was permitted to interrupt.

The marginal annotations, corrections, references, historical allusions, varied interpretations, and comments made upon the copy he constantly carried since 1866, give evidence of careful research and thoughtful study.

He loved to feed upon its precious promises; meditate upon its sublime utterances; and learn its practical lessons, that he might be thoroughly furnished for daily duties.

Pasted on the top of the inside cover is this line:

"What have *you* done for Christ to-day?"

Following this, is the line of descent of the Herod family.

Upon the top of the first blank leaf, and directly opposite the question, "What have

Study of Bible.

Evidences of research.

Admoni-
tion and
promise.

you done for Christ to-day?" are the words,
always precious to him—"I will never leave
thee, nor forsake thee." - Thus exhortation
to service for his Lord, and promise of His
presence, are placed side by side, for the
direction and the joy of his life.

Next comes a printed slip, pasted in, on
which are the following precepts:

Precepts.

"Keep good company, or none.

"Never be idle; if your hands cannot be
usefully employed, attend to the cultivation
of your mind.

"Always speak the truth.

"Make few promises.

"Live up to your engagements.

"Keep your secrets, if you have any.

"When you speak to a person, look him
in the face.

"Good company and good conversation
are the very sinews of virtue.

"Good character is above all things else.
Your character cannot be essentially injured,
except by your own acts.

"If any one speaks evil of you, let your
life be such that none will believe him.

"Drink no intoxicating liquors.

"Ever live (misfortunes excepted) within your income.

"When you retire to bed, think over what you have been doing during the day.

"Make no haste to be rich, if you would prosper. Small and steady gains give competency, with tranquillity of mind.

"Never play at any game of chance.

"Avoid temptation through fear you may not withstand it.

"Earn money before you spend it.

"Never run into debt, unless you see a way to get out again.

"Never borrow if you can possibly avoid it.

"Do not marry until you are able to support a wife.

"Never speak evil of any one.

"Be just before you are generous.

"Keep yourself innocent, if you would be happy.

"Save, when you are young, to spend when you are old."

To the above is added, in his own writing, "Be polite."

On the next blank page is a printed slip. containing "Facts about the Bible."

Written on the margin:

"He who walks according to God's words acts wisely and happily; but he who goes according to his head, acts unwisely and to no profit."—*Luther's Bible.*

The "Eureka chapter."

The first chapter of John he designates the "Eureka chapter."

At the beginning of Psalm cxxxi:

"A proud heart and a lofty mountain are never fruitful."—*Gurnall.*

On margin of Psalm cxlv, verse 13:

"Inscription over door of great mosque at Damascus: 'Thy Kingdom is an everlasting Kingdom.'"

On margin of chapter xiv. of Isaiah. 12th verse:

"Compare Milton P. L.. B. 5. Satan's rebellion:

"'O Lucifer, son of the Morning! how art thou cut down to the ground, which didst weaken the nations.'"

The following notes on the margin show the dates of his reading the Bible through in course:

Record of reading.

"Began O. T., 2, 22, '75.
"Began O. T., 4, 20, '78.
"Began O. T., 4, 1, '80.
"Began N. T., 2, 12, '78, finished 6, 21, '78.
   "   "   6, 22, '78,   "   1, 6, '79.
   "   "   1, 7, '79,   "   9, 23, '79,
   "   "   9, 24, '79,   "   6, 9, '80.
   "   "   6, 10, '80.' "

Showing he had read through the Old Testament three times, and the New Testament five times, since February 22, 1875.

On the first blank leaf, at the end, is the following, in his writing:

"There is no other actual misfortune, except this only—not to have God for our friend."

"Isaiah, xl: 31."

"Walk with the Lord! along the road your strength he will
    renew;
Wait on the everlasting God, and He will wait on you!
Aspiring eyes ye still shall raise, and heights sublime explore;
Like eagles, ye shall sunward gaze; like eagles, heavenward
    soar."

> "To thine own self be true,
> And it must follow, as the night the day,
> Thou canst not then be false to any man."

"Whatever weakens your reason, impairs the tenderness of your conscience, obscures your views of God, or takes off the relish of spiritual things—in short, whatever increases the authority of your body over your mind, that is *sin to you*, however innocent it may be in itself."

"Our sufficiency is of God."

> "The discord is within which jars
> So sadly in life's song.
> 'T is we, not they, who are in fault
> When others seem so wrong."

"I expect to pass through this world but once. If, therefore, there be any kindness I can show, or any good thing I can do any fellow-human being, let me do it now—let me not defer nor neglect it, for I will not pass this way again."

The following, which seems almost prophetical of his sudden departure, was written by him on the blank leaves of his Bible but a few months before his death:

" When far from the hearts, where our fondest thoughts centre,
    Denied for a time their loved presence to share,
In spirit we meet, when the closet we enter,
    And hold sweet communion together in prayer.

" Then why should one thought of anxiety seize us,
    Though distance divide us from those whom we love,
They rest in the covenant mercy of Jesus,
    Their prayers meet with ours in the mansions above.

" Oh, sweet bond of friendship! whate'er may betide us,
    Though on life's stormy billow our barks may be driven,
Though distance or trial or death may divide us,
    Eternal reunion awaits us in heaven! "

A large number of verses are marked in *Marked verses.* different parts of his Bible, some of which I have copied, and grouped under different subjects. To him they were precious texts. I have given them (one for each day in the year), with the hope that they may thus prove a sort of daily food to his friends and *Daily food.* former associates in the Sabbath School. In some instances, passages which he had written in the margin are given with the text:

JANUARY 1.
Thou, God, seest me.—Gen., xvi: 13.

JANUARY 2.
And thou shalt take no gift; for the gift blindeth the wise and perverteth the words of the righteous.—Ex., xxiii: 8.

JANUARY 3.
The fathers shall not be put to death for the children; neither shall the children be put to death for the fathers; every man shall be put to death for his own sin.—Deut., xxiv: 16.

JANUARY 4.
Be ye strong, therefore, and let not your hands be weak; for your work shall be rewarded.—II. Ch., xv: 7.

JANUARY 5.
Acquaint now thyself with him, and be at peace; thereby good shall come unto thee. —Job, xxii: 21.

JANUARY 6.
Receive, I pray thee, the law from his mouth and lay up his words in thine heart.— Job, xxii: 22.

JANUARY 7.
Some trust in chariots and some in

horses, but we will remember the name of the Lord our God.—Ps. xx: 7.

JANUARY 8.

Wait on the Lord; be of good courage, and he shall strengthen thine heart; wait, I say, on the Lord.—Ps. xxvii: 14.

JANUARY 9.

Cast thy burden upon the Lord, and he shall sustain thee; he shall never suffer the righteous to be moved.—Ps. lv: 22.

JANUARY 10.

Though thy beginning was small, yet thy latter end should greatly increase.—Job. viii: 7.

JANUARY 11.

They that seek the Lord shall not want any good thing.—Ps. xxxiv: 10.

JANUARY 12.

The righteous cry, and the Lord heareth and delivereth them out of all their troubles. —Ps. xxxiv: 17.

JANUARY 13.

The Lord is nigh unto them that are of a broken heart, and saveth such as be of a contrite spirit.—Ps. xxxiv: 18.

JANUARY 14.

Many are the afflictions of the righteous.

but the Lord delivereth him out of them all.—
Ps. xxxiv: 19.

15

JANUARY 15.

None of them that trust in him shall be
desolate.—Ps. xxxiv: 22.

16

JANUARY 16.

God is our refuge and strength, a very
present help in trouble.—Ps. xlvi: 1.

17

JANUARY 17.

Call upon me in the day of trouble; I
will deliver thee, and thou shalt glorify me.
—Ps. l: 15.

18

JANUARY 18.

And he was afraid and said, How dreadful is this place! this is none other but the
house of God, and this is the gate of heaven.
—Gen., xxviii: 17.

19

JANUARY 19.

The Lord gave, and the Lord hath taken
away; blessed be the name of the Lord.—
Job, i: 21.

20

JANUARY 20.

There the wicked cease from troubling,
and there the weary be at rest.—Job, iii: 17.

21

JANUARY 21.

Behold, happy is the man whom God

correcteth; therefore despise not thou the chastening of the Almighty.—Job, v: 17.

JANUARY 22.

Thou shalt be hid from the scourge of the tongue; neither shalt thou be afraid of destruction when it cometh.—Job, v: 21.

JANUARY 23.

I would not live alway; let me alone; for my days are vanity.—Job, vii: 16.

JANUARY 24.

What is man, that thou shouldst magnify him, and that thou shouldest set thine heart upon him?—Job, vii: 17.

JANUARY 25.

I know it is so of a truth; but how should man be just with God?—Job, ix: 2.

JANUARY 26.

He is wise in heart and mighty in strength; who hath hardened himself against him, and prospered?—Job, ix: 4.

JANUARY 27.

For I know that my Redeemer liveth, and that he shall stand at the latter day upon the earth.—Job, xix: 25.

JANUARY 28.

Whom I shall see for myself, and mine

eyes shall behold, and not another.—Job, xix: 27.

JANUARY 29.

How oft is the candle of the wicked put out? and how oft cometh their destruction upon them? God distributeth sorrows in his anger.—Job, xxi: 17.

JANUARY 30.

Thou wilt show me the path of life; in thy presence is fulness of joy; at thy right hand there are pleasures forevermore.—Ps. xvi: 11.

JANUARY 31.

Oh, how great is thy goodness, which thou hast laid up for them that fear thee; which thou hast wrought for them that trust in thee before the sons of men.—Ps. xxxi: 19.

FEBRUARY 1.

I sought the Lord, and he heard me, and delivered me from all my fears.—Ps. xxxiv: 4.

FEBRUARY 2.

The angel of the Lord encampeth round about them that fear him, and delivereth them.—Ps. xxxiv: 7.

FEBRUARY 3.

O taste and see that the Lord is good;

blessed is the man that trusteth in him.—
Ps. xxxiv: 8.

FEBRUARY 4.

35

The eyes of the Lord are upon the righteous, and his ears are open unto their cry.—
Ps. xxxiv: 15.

FEBRUARY 5.

36

The sacrifices of God are a broken spirit;
a broken and a contrite heart, O God, thou
wilt not despise.—Ps. li: 17.

FEBRUARY 6.

37

What time I am afraid, I will trust in
thee.—Ps. lvi: 3.

FEBRUARY 7.

38

Whom have I in heaven but thee? and
there is none upon earth that I desire besides
thee.—Ps. lxxiii: 25.

FEBRUARY 8.

39

For promotion cometh neither from the
east, nor from the west, nor from the south.
—Ps. lxxv: 6.

FEBRUARY 9.

40

But God is the judge; he putteth down
one and setteth up another.—Ps. lxxv: 7.

FEBRUARY 10.

41

Thou didst cause judgment to be heard

from heaven; the earth feared, and was still.
—Ps. lxxvi: 8.

FEBRUARY 11.

When he slew them, then they sought
him; and they returned and inquired early
after God.

And they remembered that God was
their rock, and the high God their redeemer.
—Ps. lxxviii: 34, 35.

FEBRUARY 12.

Open thy mouth wide, and I will fill it.—
Ps. lxxxi: 10.

FEBRUARY 13.

Oh that my people had hearkened unto
me, and Israel had walked in my ways!—Ps.
lxxxi: 13.

FEBRUARY 14.

I should soon have subdued their enemies, and turned my hand against their ad-
versaries.—Ps. lxxxi: 14.

FEBRUARY 15.

Blessed is the man whose strength is in
thee.

They go from strength to strength; every
one of them in Zion appeareth before God.—
Ps. lxxxiv: 5, 7.

FEBRUARY 16.

For a day in thy courts is better than a thousand. I had rather be a doorkeeper in the house of my God, than to dwell in the tents of wickedness.—Ps. lxxxiv: 10.

FEBRUARY 17.

For the Lord God is a sun and shield; the Lord will give grace and glory; no good thing will he withhold from them that walk uprightly.—Ps. lxxxiv: 11.

FEBRUARY 18.

O Lord of hosts, blessed is the man that trusteth in thee.—Ps. lxxxiv: 12.

FEBRUARY 19.

I will set him on high, because he hath known my name.—Ps. xci: 14.

Written on the margin:

Very great is the value God sets on his name; and very great the importance he attaches to the knowledge of it. His name is the declaration of his character as the Lord God, merciful and gracious.—*Sibbs.*

FEBRUARY 20.

Harden not your heart, as in the provocation, and as in the day of temptation in the wilderness.—Ps. xcv: 8.

52

FEBRUARY 21.
For he commandeth, and raiseth the stormy wind, which lifteth up the waves thereof.— Ps. cvii: 25.

53

FEBRUARY 22.
They mount up to the heaven, they go down again to the depths; their soul is melted because of trouble.— Ps. cvii: 26.

54

FEBRUARY 23. '
Then they cry unto the Lord in their trouble, and he bringeth them out of their distresses.— Ps. cvii: 28.

55

FEBRUARY 24.
He maketh the storm a calm, so that the waves thereof are still.—Ps. cvii: 29.

56

FEBRUARY 25.
Then are they glad because they be quiet; so he bringeth them unto their desired haven.— Ps. cvii: 30.

57

FEBRUARY 26.
The Lord is thy keeper; the Lord is thy shade upon thy right hand.— Ps. cxxi: 5.

58

FEBRUARY 27.
The Lord shall preserve thy going out and thy coming in from this time forth, and even for evermore.— Ps. cxxi: 8.

FEBRUARY 28.

Lord, my heart is not haughty, nor mine eyes lofty.—Ps. cxxxi: 1.

On the margin:

A proud heart and a lofty mountain are never fruitful.— *Gurnall.*

59

MARCH 1.

Thy kingdom is an everlasting kingdom. —Ps. cxlv: 13.

On the margin:

Inscription over door of the great mosque at Damascus.

60

MARCH 2.

The Lord is nigh unto all them that call upon him, to all that call upon him in truth. —Ps. cxlv: 18.

61

MARCH 3.

He will fulfil the desire of them that fear him; He also will hear their cry and will save them.—Ps. cxlv: 19.

62

MARCH 4.

The Lord preserveth the strangers; he relieveth the fatherless and widow; but the way of the wicked he turneth upside down. —Ps. cxlvi: 9.

63

MARCH 5.

64

He healeth the broken in heart and bindeth up their wounds.—Ps. cxlvii: 3.

MARCH 6.

65

The Lord taketh pleasure in them that fear him; in those that hope in his mercy. —Ps. cxlvii: 11.

MARCH 7.

66

Let every thing that hath breath praise the Lord. Praise ye the Lord.—Ps. cl: 6.

MARCH 8.

67

A wise man will hear, and will increase learning; and a man of understanding shall attain unto wise counsels.—Prov., i: 5.

MARCH 9.

68

The fear of the Lord is the beginning of knowledge; but fools despise wisdom and instruction.—Prov., i: 7.

MARCH 10.

69

My son, hear the instruction of thy father, and forsake not the law of thy mother.— Prov., i: 8.

MARCH 11.

70

Whoso hearkeneth unto me shall dwell safely, and shall be quiet from fear of evil. —Prov., i: 33.

MARCH 12.

My son, forget not my law; but let thine heart keep my commandments.—Prov., iii: 1.

71

MARCH 13.

For length of days and long life and peace, shall they add to thee.—Prov., iii: 2.

72

MARCH 14.

Let not mercy and truth forsake thee; bind them about thy neck; write them upon the table of thine heart.—Prov., iii: 3.

73

MARCH 15.

So shalt thou find favor and good understanding in the sight of God and man.—Prov., iii: 4.

74

MARCH 16.

Trust in the Lord with all thine heart; and lean not unto thine own understanding.—Prov., iii: 5.

75

MARCH 17.

In all thy ways acknowledge him and he shall direct thy paths.—Prov., iii: 6.

76

MARCH 18.

Be not wise in thine own eyes; fear the Lord, and depart from evil.—Prov.. iii: 7.

77

MARCH 19.

My son, let not them depart from thine

78

eyes; keep sound wisdom and discretion.—
Prov., iii: 21.

MARCH 20.

79

So shall they be life unto thy soul and
grace unto thy neck.—Prov., iii: 22.

MARCH 21.

80

Then shalt thou walk in thy way safely,
and thy foot shall not stumble.—Prov., iii: 23.

MARCH 22.

81

When thou liest down, thou shalt not be
afraid; yea, thou shalt lie down and thy
sleep shalt be sweet.—Prov., iii: 24.

MARCH 23.

82

Be not afraid of sudden fear, neither of
the desolation of the wicked, when it cometh.
—Prov., iii: 25.

MARCH 24.

83

For the Lord shall be thy confidence and
shall keep thy foot from being taken.—
Prov., iii: 26.

MARCH 25.

84

Withhold not good from them to whom
it is due, when it is in the power of thine
hand to do it.—Prov., iii: 27.

MARCH 26.

85

Wisdom is the principal thing; therefore

get wisdom: and with all thy getting, get understanding.—Prov., iv: 7.

MARCH 27.

Exalt her and she shall promote thee; she shall bring thee to honor when thou dost embrace her.—Prov., iv: 8.

MARCH 28.

The path of the just is as the shining light that shineth *more* and *more* unto the perfect day.—Prov., iv: 18.

MARCH 29.

Keep thy heart with all diligence, for out of it are the issues of life.—Prov., iv: 23.

MARCH 30.

For the ways of man are before the eyes of the Lord, and he pondereth all his goings. —Prov., v: 21.

MARCH 31.

For whoso findeth me findeth life, and shall obtain favor of the Lord.—Prov., viii: 35.

APRIL 1.

But he that sinneth against me wrongeth his own soul; all they that hate me love death.—Prov., viii: 36.

APRIL 2.

The fear of the Lord is the beginning of

wisdom; and the knowledge of the Holy is understanding.—Prov., ix: 10.

93

APRIL 3.

The Lord will not suffer the soul of the righteous to famish.—Prov., x: 3.

94

APRIL 4.

The blessing of the Lord it maketh rich, and he addeth no sorrow with it.—Prov., x: 22.

95

APRIL 5.

There is that scattereth, and yet increaseth; and there is that withholdeth more than is meet, but it tendeth to poverty.—Prov.. xi: 24.

96

APRIL 6.

The fruit of the righteous is a tree of life; and he that winneth souls is wise.—Prov., xi: 30.

97

APRIL 7.

Behold, the righteous shall be recompensed in the earth.—Prov., xi: 31.

98

APRIL 8.

There shall no evil happen to the just; but the wicked shall be filled with mischief. —Prov., xii: 21.

99

APRIL 9.

Heaviness in the heart of man maketh

it stoop; but a good word maketh it glad.—
Prov., xii: 25.

APRIL 10.

100

The heart knoweth his own bitterness;
and a stranger doth not intermeddle with his
joy.—Prov., xiv: 10.

APRIL 11.

101

In all labor there is profit; but the talk
of the lips tendeth only to poverty.—Prov.,
xiv: 23.

APRIL 12.

102

In the fear of the Lord is strong confidence: and his children shall have a place of
refuge.—Prov., xiv: 26.

APRIL 13.

103

Righteousness exalteth a nation; but sin
is a reproach to any people.—Prov., xiv: 34.

APRIL 14.

104

The eyes of the Lord are in every place,
beholding the evil and the good.—Prov.,
xv: 3.

APRIL 15.

105

Better is little, with the fear of the Lord,
than great treasure, and trouble therewith.—
Prov., xv: 16.

APRIL 16.

106

The fear of the Lord is the instruction

of wisdom; and before honor is humility.—
Prov., xv: 33.

APRIL 17.

All the ways of a man are clean in his
, own eyes; but the Lord weigheth the spirits.
—Prov., xvi: 2.

APRIL 18.

When a man's ways please the Lord, he
maketh even his enemies to be' at peace with
him.—Prov., xvi: 7.

APRIL 19.

Pleasant words are as an honeycomb,
sweet to the soul and health to the bones.—
Prov.. xvi: 24.

APRIL 20.

He that is slow to anger is better than
the mighty; and he that ruleth his spirit.
than he that taketh a city.—Prov., xvi: 32.

APRIL 21.

Better is a dry morsel, and quietness
therewith, than an house full of sacrifices.
with strife.—Prov., xvii: 1.

APRIL 22.

He that covereth a transgression, seeketh
love: but he that repeateth a matter, separat-
eth very friends:—Prov., xvii: 9.

APRIL 23.

A friend loveth at all times, and a brother is born for adversity.—Prov., xvii: 17.

113

APRIL 24.

The name of the Lord is a strong tower; the righteous runneth into it and is safe.—Prov., xviii: 10.

114

APRIL 25.

A man that hath friends, must show himself friendly; and there is a friend that sticketh closer than a brother.—Prov., xviii: 24.

115

APRIL 26.

Iron sharpeneth iron; so a man sharpeneth the countenance of his friend.—Prov., xxvii: 17.

116

APRIL 27.

As in water face answereth to face, so the heart of man to man.—Prov., xxvii: 19.

117

APRIL 28.

Every word of God is pure; he is a shield unto them that put their trust in him.—Prov., xxx: 5.

118

APRIL 29.

For God giveth to a man that is good in his sight, wisdom, and knowledge, and joy.—Eccl., ii: 26.

119

120

APRIL 30.

I know that whatsoever God doeth, it shall be forever; nothing can be put to it, nor anything taken from it; and God doeth it, that men should fear before him.— Eccl., iii: 14.

121

MAY 1.

Better is the end of a thing than the beginning thereof; and the patient in spirit is better than the proud in spirit.— Eccl., vii: 8.

122

MAY 2.

Be not hasty in thy spirit to be angry: for anger resteth in the bosom of fools.— Eccl., vii: 9.

123

MAY 3.

For there is not a just man upon earth that doeth good and sinneth not.— Eccl., vii: 20.

124

MAY 4.

A wise man's heart is at his right hand: but a fool's heart at his left.— Eccl., x: 2.

125

MAY 5.

He that observeth the wind, shall not sow; and he that regardeth the clouds, shall not reap.— Eccl., xi: 4.

MAY 6.

126

In the morning sow thy seed, and in the evening withhold not thine hand; for thou knowest not whether shall prosper either this or that, or whether they both shall be alike good.—Eccl., xi: 6.

MAY 7.

127

Though your sins be as scarlet, they shall be as white as snow; though they be red like crimson, they shall be as wool.—Isaiah, i: 18.

MAY 8.

128

If ye be willing and obedient, ye shall eat the good of the land.—Isaiah, i: 19.

MAY 9.

129

Now will I sing to my well-beloved a song of my beloved, touching his vineyard. My well-beloved hath a vineyard in a very fruitful hill.—Isaiah, v: 1.

MAY 10.

130

And he fenced it, and gathered out the stones thereof, and planted it with the choicest vine, and built a tower in the midst of it, and also made a wine-press therein; and he looked that it should bring forth grapes; and it brought forth wild grapes.—Isaiah, v: 2.

131
MAY 11.
Fear not. neither be faint-hearted. —
Isaiah, vii: 4.

132
MAY 12.
For unto us a child is born, unto us a son
is given, and the government shall be upon
his shoulder; and his name shall be called
Wonderful, Counsellor, The Mighty God,
The Everlasting Father, The Prince of Peace.
—Isaiah, ix: 6.

133
MAY 13.
And a little child shall lead them.—
Isaiah, xi: 6.

134
MAY 14.
Thine anger is turned away, and thou
comfortest me.—Isaiah, xii: 1.

135
MAY 15.
Behold, God is my salvation; I will trust,
and not be afraid; for the Lord JEHOVAH is
my strength and my song; he also is become
my salvation.—Isaiah, xii: 2.

136
MAY 16.
I will make a man more precious than
fine gold; even a man than the golden wedge
of Ophir.—Isaiah, xiii: 12.

137
MAY 17.
O Lucifer, son of the morning! how art

thou cut down to the ground, which didst weaken the nations!— Isaiah, xiv: 12.

On the margin:

Compare Milton P. L., B. 5, Satan's rebellion.

MAY 18.

138

Because thou hast forgotten the God of thy salvation, and hast not been mindful of the Rock of thy strength, therefore shalt thou plant pleasant plants, and shalt set it with strange slips.— Isaiah, xvii: 10.

MAY 19.

139

In the day shalt thou make thy plant to grow, and in the morning shalt thou make thy seed to flourish; but the harvest shall be a heap in the day of grief and of desperate sorrow.— Isaiah, xvii: 11.

MAY 20.

140

And the Lord shall smite Egypt; he shall smite and heal it; and they shall return even to the Lord, and he shall be entreated of them, and shall heal them.— Isaiah, xix: 22.

MAY 21.

141

He will swallow up death in victory; and the Lord God will wipe away tears from off all faces.— Isaiah. xxv: 8.

MAY 22.

142

Thou wilt keep him in perfect peace whose mind is stayed on thee; because he trusteth in thee.—Isaiah, xxvi: 3.

MAY 23.

143

Trust in the Lord forever; for in the Lord JEHOVAH is everlasting strength.—Isaiah, xxvi: 4.

MAY 24.

144

To whom he said, This is the rest wherewith ye may cause the weary to rest; and this is the refreshing: yet they would not hear.—Isaiah, xxviii: 12.

MAY 25.

145

Wherefore the Lord said, Forasmuch as this people draw near me with their mouth, and with their lips do honor me, but have removed their heart far from me, and their fear toward me is taught by the precept of men: the wisdom of their wise men shall perish, and the understanding of their prudent men shall be hid.—Isaiah, xxix: 13, 14.

MAY 26.

146

For thus saith the Lord God, the Holy One of Israel; In returning and rest shall ye be saved; in quietness and in confidence shall be your strength.—Isaiah, xxx: 15.

MAY 27.

And therefore will the Lord wait, that he may be gracious unto you, and therefore will he be exalted, that he may have mercy upon you; for the Lord is a God of judgment.—Isaiah, xxx: 18.

147

MAY 28.

He will be very gracious unto thee at the voice of thy cry; when he shall hear it, he will answer thee.—Isaiah, xxx: 19.

148

MAY 29.

And though the Lord give you the bread of adversity, and the water of affliction, yet shall not thy teachers be removed into a corner any more, but thine eyes shall see thy teachers.—Isaiah, xxx: 20.

149

MAY 30.

And thine ears shall hear a word behind thee, saying, This is the way, walk ye in it. —Isaiah, xxx: 21.

150

MAY 31.

And my people shall dwell in a peaceable habitation, and in sure dwellings, and in quiet resting places.—Isaiah, xxxii: 18.

151

JUNE 1.

O Lord, be gracious unto us; we have waited for thee: be thou their arm every

152

49

morning, our salvation also in the time of trouble.—Isaiah, xxxiii: 2.

153

JUNE 2.

And Hezekiah received the letter from the hand of the messengers, and read it; and Hezekiah went up unto the house of the Lord, and spread it before the Lord.—Isaiah, xxxvii: 14.

154

JUNE 3.

And Hezekiah prayed unto the Lord.— Isaiah, xxxvii: 15.

155

JUNE 4.

Comfort ye, comfort ye my people, saith your God.—Isaiah, xl: 1.

156

JUNE 5.

Speak ye comfortably to Jerusalem, and cry unto her, that her warfare is accomplished, that her iniquity is pardoned; for she hath received of the Lord's hand double for all her sins.—Isaiah, xl: 2.

157

JUNE 6.

The voice of him that crieth in the wilderness, Prepare ye the way of the Lord, make straight in the desert a highway for our God.—Isaiah, xl: 3.

158

JUNE 7.

Every valley shall be exalted, and every

mountain and hill shall be made low; and the crooked shall be made straight, and the rough places plain.—Isaiah, xl: 4.

JUNE 8.
All flesh is grass, and all the goodliness thereof is as the flower of the field.—Isaiah, xl: 6.

JUNE 9.
The grass withereth, the flower fadeth; because the spirit of the Lord bloweth upon it: surely the people is grass.—Isaiah, xl: 7.

JUNE 10.
The grass withereth, the flower fadeth; but the word of our God shall stand forever. —Isaiah, xl: 8.

JUNE 11.
He shall feed his flock like a shepherd; he shall gather the lambs with his arm, and carry them in his bosom, and shall gently lead those that are with young.—Isaiah, xl: 11.

JUNE 12.
Behold, the nations are as a drop of a bucket, and are counted as the small dust of the balance.—Isaiah, xl: 15.

JUNE 13.
He giveth power to the faint: and to

them that have no might he increaseth
strength.—Isaiah, xl: 29.

JUNE 14.

They that wait upon the Lord shall re-
new their strength; they shall mount up with
wings as eagles; they shall run, and not be
weary; and they shall walk, and not faint.—
Isaiah, xl: 31.

JUNE 15.

Fear thou not, for I am with thee; be
not dismayed, for I am thy God: I will
strengthen thee; yea, I will help thee; yea,
I will uphold thee with the right hand of
my righteousness.—Isaiah, xli: 10.

JUNE 16.

But now thus saith the Lord that created
thee, O Jacob, and he that formed thee, O
Israel, Fear not; for I have redeemed thee.
I have called thee by my name; thou art
mine.—Isaiah, xliii: 1.

JUNE 17.

When thou passest through the waters, I
will be with thee.—Isaiah, xliii: 2.

JUNE 18.

I, even I, am he that blotteth out thy
transgressions for mine own sake, and will
not remember thy sins.—Isaiah, xliii: 25.

JUNE 19.

170

One shall say, I am the Lord's; and another shall call himself by the name of Jacob.— Isaiah, xliv: 5.

JUNE 20.

171

Look unto me, and be ye saved, all the ends of the earth; for I am God, and there is none else.— Isaiah, xlv: 22.

JUNE 21.

172

I have sworn by myself, the word is gone out of my mouth in righteousness, and shall not return, That unto me every knee shall bow, every tongue shall swear.— Isaiah, xlv: 23.

JUNE 22.

173

But Zion said, The Lord hath forsaken me, and my Lord hath forgotten me.— Isaiah. xlix: 14.

JUNE 23.

174

Can a woman forget her sucking child. that she should not have compassion on the son of her womb? yea, they may forget, yet will I not forget thee.— Isaiah, xlix: 15.

JUNE 24.

175

For the Lord God will help me; therefore shall I not be confounded; therefore have I set my face like a flint, and I know that I shall not be ashamed.—Isaiah, l: 7.

JUNE 25.

For the mountains shall depart, and the hills be removed; but my kindness shall not depart from thee, neither shall the covenant of my peace be removed, saith the Lord that hath mercy on thee.—Isaiah, liv: 10.

JUNE 26.

Seek ye the Lord while he may be found, call ye upon him while he is near.—Isaiah, lv: 6.

JUNE 27.

Let the wicked forsake his way, and the unrighteous man his thoughts: and let him return unto the Lord, and he will have mercy upon him; and to our God, for he will abundantly pardon.—Isaiah, lv: 7.

JUNE 28.

For my thoughts are not your thoughts, neither are your ways my ways, saith the Lord.—Isaiah, lv: 8.

JUNE 29.

He that putteth his trust in me shall possess the land.—Isaiah, lvii: 13.

JUNE 30.

I will greatly rejoice in the Lord, my

soul shall be joyful in my God; for he hath clothed me with the garments of salvation, he hath covered me with the robe of right-eousness, as a bridegroom decketh himself with ornaments, and as a bride adorneth herself with her jewels.—Isaiah, lxi: 10.

JULY 1.

Thou shalt also be a crown of glory in the hand of the Lord, and a royal diadem in the hand of thy God.—Isaiah, lxii: 3.

JULY 2.

And it shall come to pass, that before they call, I will answer; and while they are yet speaking, I will hear.—Isaiah, lxv: 24.

JULY 3.

I said, Thou shalt call me, My father: and shalt not turn away from me.—Jer., iii: 19.

JULY 4.

But let him that glorieth, glory in this, that he understandeth and knoweth me, that I am the Lord which exercise loving-kind-ness, judgment, and righteousness, in the earth; for in these things I delight, saith the Lord.—Jer., ix: 24.

JULY 5.

Thou, O Lord, art in the midst of us, and

we are called by thy name; leave us not.—
Jer., xiv: 9.

187.
JULY 6.

Blessed is the man that trusteth in the
Lord, and whose hope the Lord is.—Jer.,
xvii: 7.

188
JULY 7.

The heart is deceitful above all things,
and desperately wicked: who can know it?
—Jer., xvii: 9.

189
JULY 8.

I the Lord search the heart, I try the
reins, even to give every man according to
his ways, and according to the fruit of his
doings.—Jer., xvii: 10.

190
JULY 9.

Be not a terror unto me: thou art my
hope in the day of evil.—Jer., xvii: 17.

191
JULY 10.

But the Lord is with me as a mighty
terrible one: therefore my persecutors shall
stumble. and they shall not prevail; for they
shall not prosper; their everlasting confusion
shall never be forgotten.—Jer., xx: 11.

192
JULY 11.

Then shall ye call upon me, and ye shall

go and pray unto me, and I will hearken unto you.—Jer., xxix: 12.

JULY 12.

193

And ye shall seek me, and find me, when ye shall search for me with all your heart.—Jer., xxix: 13.

JULY 13.

194

And they shall teach no more every man his neighbor, and every man his brother, saying, Know the Lord: for they shall all know me, from the least of them unto the greatest of them, saith the Lord: for I will forgive their iniquity, and I will remember their sin no more.—Jer., xxxi: 34.

JULY 14.

195

Great in counsel, and mighty in work: for thine eyes are open upon all the ways of the sons of men, to give every one according to his ways, and according to the fruit of his doings.—Jer., xxxii: 19.

JULY 15.

196

And they shall be my people and I will be their God.—Jer., xxxii: 38.

JULY 16.

197

Leave thy fatherless children, I will preserve them alive; and let thy widows trust in me.—Jer., xlix: 11.

JULY 17.

198

He hath made the earth by his power, he hath established the world by his wisdom, and hath stretched out the heaven by his understanding.—Jer., li: 15.

JULY 18.

199

When he uttereth his voice, there is a multitude of waters in the heavens; and he causeth the vapors to ascend from the ends of the earth; he maketh lightnings with rain. and bringeth forth the wind out of his treasures.—Jer., li: 16.

JULY 19.

200

This I recall to my mind, therefore have I hope.—Lam., iii: 21.

JULY 20.

201

It is of the Lord's mercies that we are not consumed, because his compassions fail not.—Lam., iii: 22.

JULY 21.

202

They are new every morning: great is thy faithfulness.—Lam., iii: 23.

JULY 22.

203

The Lord is my portion. saith my soul; therefore will I hope in him.—Lam., iii: 24.

JULY 23.

204

The Lord is good unto them that wait

for him, to the soul that seeketh him.—
Lam., iii: 25.

JULY 24.

205

It is good that a man should both hope
and quietly wait for the salvation of the
Lord.—Lam., iii: 26.

JULY 25.

206

For the Lord will not cast off forever.
—Lam., iii: 31.

JULY 26.

207

But though he cause grief, yet will he
have compassion according to the multitude
of his mercies.—Lam., iii: 32.

JULY 27.

208

For he doth not afflict willingly, nor
grieve the children of men.—Lam., iii: 33.

JULY 28.

209

Let us search and try our ways, and turn
again to the Lord.—Lam., iii: 40.

JULY 29.

210

For I know the things that come into
your mind, every one of them.—Ezek., xi: 5.

JULY 30.

211

I will put a new spirit within you, and I
will take the stony heart out of their flesh,
and will give them an heart of flesh.—Ezek.,
xi: 19.

212

JULY 31.

That they may walk in my statutes, and keep mine ordinances, and do them: and they shall be my people, and I will be their God.—Ezek., xi: 20.

213

AUGUST 1.

When the son hath done that which is lawful and right, and hath kept all my statutes, and hath done them, he shall surely live.—Ezek., xviii: 19.

214

AUGUST 2.

The soul that sinneth, it shall die. The son shall not bear the iniquity of the father, neither shall the father bear the iniquity of the son: the righteousness of the righteous shall be upon him, and the wickedness of the wicked shall be upon him.—Ezek., xviii: 20.

215

AUGUST 3.

Behold, all souls are mine; as the soul of the father, so also the soul of the son is mine: the soul that sinneth, it shall die.—Ezek., xviii: 4.

216

AUGUST 4.

But if the wicked will turn from all his sins that he hath committed, and keep all my statutes, and do that which is lawful

and right, he shall surely live, he shall not
die.—Ezek., xviii: 21.

AUGUST 5.

217

All his transgressions that he hath committed, they shall not be mentioned unto
him.—Ezek., xviii: 22.

AUGUST 6.

218

Cast away from you all your transgressions, whereby ye have transgressed; and
make you a new heart and a new spirit; for
why will ye die, O house of Israel?—Ezek.,
xviii: 31.'

AUGUST 7.

219

For I have no pleasure in the death of
him that dieth, saith the Lord God: wherefore turn yourselves, and live ye.—Ezek.,
xviii: 32.

AUGUST 8.

220

Therefore, say unto the house of Israel,
Thus saith the Lord God; I do not this for
your sakes, O house of Israel, but for mine
holy name's sake, which ye have profaned
among the heathen, whither ye went. —
Ezek., xxxvi: 22.

AUGUST 9.

221

My people are destroyed for lack of
knowledge.—Hosea, iv: 6.

222

AUGUST 10.

Come, and let us return unto the Lord: for he hath torn, and he will heal us.—Hosea, vi: 1.

223

AUGUST 11.

Break up your fallow ground; for it is time to seek the Lord, till he come and rain righteousness upon you.—Hosea, x: 12.

224

AUGUST 12.

Who is wise, and he shall understand these things? prudent, and he shall know them? for the ways of the Lord are right, and the just shall walk in them; but the transgressors shall fall therein.—Hosea, xiv: 9.

225

AUGUST 13.

Rend your heart, and not your garments, and turn unto the Lord your God; for he is gracious and merciful, slow to anger, and of great kindness.—Joel, ii: 13.

226

AUGUST 14.

Seek good, and not evil, that ye may live.—Amos, v: 14.

227

AUGUST 15.

He hath showed thee, O man, what is good; and what doth the Lord require of thee, but to do justly, and to love mercy, and to walk humbly with thy God?—Micah, vi: 8.

AUGUST 16.

The Lord is good, a strong hold in the day of trouble; and he knoweth them that trust in him.—Nahum, i: 7.

AUGUST 17.

Return unto me, and I will return unto you, saith the Lord of hosts.—Malachi, iii: 7.

AUGUST 18.

Bring ye all the tithes into the store-house, that there may be meat in mine house, and prove me now herewith, saith the Lord of hosts, if I will not open you the windows of heaven, and pour you out a' blessing, that there shall not be room enough to receive it.—Malachi, iii: 10.

AUGUST 19.

And they shall be mine, saith the Lord of hosts, in that day when I make up my jewels; and I will spare them, as a man spareth his own son that serveth him.—Malachi, iii: 17.

AUGUST 20.

Bring forth therefore fruits meet for repentance.—Matthew, iii: 8.

233

AUGUST 21.

Think not that I am come to destroy the law, or the prophets: I am not come to destroy, but to fulfil.—Matthew, v: 17.

234

AUGUST 22.

Be ye therefore perfect, even as your Father which is in heaven is perfect.—Matthew, v: 48.

235

AUGUST 23.

For where your treasure is, there will your heart be also.—Matthew, vi: 21.

236

AUGUST 24.

Not every one that saith unto me, Lord, Lord, shall enter into the kingdom of heaven; but he that doeth the will of my Father which is in heaven.—Matthew, vii: 21.

237

AUGUST 25.

Fear ye not therefore, ye are of more value than many sparrows.—Matthew, x: 31.

238

AUGUST 26.

Blessed is he whosoever shall not be offended in me.—Matthew, xi: 6.

239

AUGUST 27.

Come unto me, all ye that labor, and are heavy laden, and I will give you rest.—Matthew, xi: 28.

AUGUST 28.

Take my yoke upon you, and learn of me; for I am meek and lowly in heart; and ye shall find rest unto your souls.—Matthew, xi: 29.

240

AUGUST 29.

For my yoke is easy, and my burden is light.—Matthew, xi: 30.

241

AUGUST 30.

Out of the abundance of the heart, the mouth speaketh.—Matthew, xii: 34.

242

AUGUST 31.

Whosoever shall do the will of my Father which is in heaven, the same is my brother, and sister, and mother.—Matthew. xii: 50.

243

SEPTEMBER 1.

And his disciples came, and took up the body, and buried it, and went and told Jesus. --Matthew, xiv: 12.

244

SEPTEMBER 2.

Again I say unto you, That if two of you shall agree on earth, as touching any thing that they shall ask, it shall be done for them of my Father which is in heaven.—Matthew, xviii: 19.

245

246

SEPTEMBER 3.

For where two or three are gathered together in my name, there am I in the midst of them.—Matthew, xviii: 20.

247

SEPTEMBER 4.

So likewise shall my heavenly Father do also unto you, if ye from your hearts forgive not every one his brother their trespasses.—Matthew, xviii: 35.

248

SEPTEMBER 5.

And all things whatsoever ye shall ask in prayer, believing, ye shall receive.—Matthew, xxi: 22.

249

SEPTEMBER 6.

O Jerusalem, Jerusalem, thou that killest the prophets, and stonest them which are sent unto thee, how often would I have gathered thy children together, even as a hen gathereth her chickens under her wings, and ye would not!—Matthew, xxiii: 37.

250

SEPTEMBER 7.

Go ye therefore and teach all nations. baptizing them in the name of the Father, and of the Son, and of the Holy Ghost;—Matthew, xxviii: 19.

251

SEPTEMBER 8.

Teaching them to observe all things

whatsoever I have commanded you: and lo,
I am with you alway, even unto the end of
the world.—Matthew, xxviii: 20.

SEPTEMBER 9.

And as many as touched him, were made
whole.—Mark, vi: 56.

SEPTEMBER 10.

Therefore I say unto you, What things
soever ye desire when ye pray, believe that
ye receive them, and ye shall have them.—
Mark, xi: 24.

SEPTEMBER 11.

And what I say unto you, I say unto all,
Watch.—Mark, xiii: 37.

SEPTEMBER 12.

Wist ye not that I must be about my
Father's business?—Luke, ii: 49.

SEPTEMBER 13.

She hath done what she could.—Mark.
xiv: 8.

SEPTEMBER 14.

Every valley shall be filled, and every
mountain and hill shall be brought low; and
the crooked shall be made straight and the
rough ways shall be made smooth;—Luke.
iii: 5.

SEPTEMBER 15.

And all flesh shall see the salvation of God.—Luke, iii: 6.

SEPTEMBER 16.

Give, and it shall be given unto you: good. measure, pressed down, and shaken together, and running over, shall men give into your bosom. For with the same measure that ye mete withal, it shall be measured to you again.—Luke, vi: 38.

SEPTEMBER 17.

Be not afraid of them that kill the body, and after that, have no more that they can do.—Luke, xii: 4.

SEPTEMBER 18.

But I will forewarn you whom ye shall fear: Fear him, which after he hath killed, hath power to cast into hell; yea. I say unto you, Fear him.—Luke, xii: 5.

SEPTEMBER 19.

For all these things do the nations of the world seek after: and your Father knoweth that ye have need of these things.—Luke. xii: 30.

SEPTEMBER 20.

But rather seek ye the kingdom of God,

and all these things shall be added unto you.
—Luke, xii: 31.

SEPTEMBER 21.

264

But he that knew not, and did commit
things worthy of stripes, shall be beaten
with few stripes. For unto whomsoever
much is given, of him shall be much required.—Luke, xii: 48.

SEPTEMBER 22.

265

He that is faithful in that which is least,
is faithful also in much; and he that is unjust in the least, is unjust also in much.—
Luke, xvi: 10.

SEPTEMBER 23.

266

So likewise ye, when ye shall have done
all those things which are commanded you,
say, We are unprofitable servants: we have
done that which was our duty to do.—Luke,
xvii: 10.

SEPTEMBER 24.

267

In your patience possess ye your souls.
—Luke, xxi: 19.

SEPTEMBER 25.

268

Watch ye therefore, and pray always,
that ye may be accounted worthy to escape
all these things that shall come to pass, and

to stand before the Son of man.—Luke, xxi: 36.

SEPTEMBER 26.

269

Why are ye troubled? and why do thoughts arise in your hearts?—Luke, xxiv: 38.

SEPTEMBER 27.

270

Search the Scriptures; for in them ye think ye have eternal life: and they are they which testify of me.—John, v: 39.

SEPTEMBER 28.

271

Whosoever committeth sin, is the servant of sin.—John, viii: 34.

SEPTEMBER 29.

272

And I knew that thou hearest me always: but because of the people which stand by, I said it, that they may believe that thou hast sent me.—John, xi: 42.

SEPTEMBER 30.

273

Now is my soul troubled; and what shall I say? Father, save me from this hour: but for this cause came I unto this hour.—John, xii: 27.

OCTOBER 1.

274

Father, glorify thy name. Then came there a voice from heaven, saying, I have

both glorified it, and will glorify it again.—
John, xii: 28.

OCTOBER 2.

275

These are written, that ye might believe
that Jesus is the Christ, the Son of God; and
that believing ye might have life through his
name.—John, xx: 31.

OCTOBER 3.

276

The sun shall be turned into darkness, and
the moon into blood, before that great and no-
table day of the Lord come.—Acts, ii: 20.

OCTOBER 4.

277

We ought to obey God rather than men.
—Acts, v: 29.

OCTOBER 5.

278

The God of our fathers raised up Jesus,
whom ye slew and hanged on a tree.—Acts,
v: 30.

OCTOBER 6.

279

Him hath God exalted with his right hand
to be a Prince and a Savior.—Acts, v: 31.

OCTOBER 7.

280

In every nation, he that feareth him and
worketh righteousness, is accepted with him.
—Acts, x: 35.

OCTOBER 8.

281

Confirming the souls of the disciples, and

exhorting them to continue in the faith, and that we must through much tribulation enter into the kingdom of God.—Acts, xiv: 22.

282

OCTOBER 9.

What if some did not believe? shall their unbelief make the faith of God without effect?—Romans, iii: 3.

283

OCTOBER 10.

For I reckon, that the sufferings of this present time are not worthy to be compared with the glory that shall be revealed in us.—Romans, viii: 18.

284

OCTOBER 11.

If thou shalt confess with thy mouth the Lord Jesus, and shalt believe in thine heart that God hath raised him from the dead, thou shalt be saved.—Romans, x: 9.

285

OCTOBER 12.

Vengeance is mine; I will repay, saith the Lord.—Romans, xii: 19.

286

OCTOBER 13.

All things are lawful unto me, but all things are not expedient: all things are lawful for me, but I will not be brought under the power of any.—I. Corinthians, vi: 12.

287

OCTOBER 14.

Wherefore, if meat make my brother to

offend, I will eat no flesh while the world standeth, lest I make my brother to offend.— I. Corinthians, viii: 13.

OCTOBER 15.

There hath no temptation taken you but such as is common to man: but God is faithful, who will not suffer you to be tempted above that ye are able; but will with the temptation also make a way to escape, that ye may be able to bear it.—I. Corinthians, x: 13.

OCTOBER 16.

By the grace of God I am what I am.— I. Corinthians, xv: 10.

OCTOBER 17.

Be not deceived: Evil communications corrupt good manners.—I. Corinthians, xv: 33.

OCTOBER 18.

Be ye steadfast, unmoveable, always abounding in the work of the Lord, forasmuch as ye know that your labor is not in vain in the Lord.—I. Corinthians, xv: 58.

OCTOBER 19.

The God of all comfort, who comforteth us in our tribulation, that we may be able to comfort them which are in trouble by the

288

289

290

291

292

comfort wherewith we ourselves are comforted of God.—II. Corinthians, i: 3, 4.

OCTOBER 20.

We should not trust in ourselves, but in
God which raiseth the dead.—II. Corinthians, i: 9.

OCTOBER 21.

For we must all appear before the judg-
ment-seat of Christ; that every one may
receive the things done in his body, according to that he hath done, whether it be good
or bad.—II. Corinthians, v: 10.

OCTOBER 22.

Knowing therefore the terror of the Lord,
we persuade men.—II. Corinthians, v: 11.

OCTOBER 23.

Therefore, if any man be in Christ. he
is a new creature: old things have passed
away; behold, all things are become new.—
II. Corinthians, v: 17.

OCTOBER 24.

Now then we are ambassadors for Christ,
as though God did beseech you by us: we
pray you in Christ's stead, be ye reconciled
to God.—II. Corinthians, v: 20.

OCTOBER 25.

Be ye not unequally yoked together with

unbelievers: for what fellowship hath righteousness with unrighteousness?—II. Corinthians, vi: 14.

OCTOBER 26.

299

He which soweth sparingly, shall reap
also sparingly; and he which soweth bountifully, shall reap also bountifully.—II. Corinthians, ix: 6.

OCTOBER 27.

300

And God is able to make all grace abound
toward you.—II. Corinthians, ix: 8.

OCTOBER 28.

301

For not he that commendeth himself is
approved, but whom the Lord commendeth.
—II. Corinthians, x: 18.

OCTOBER 29.

302

My grace is sufficient for thee: for my
strength is made perfect in weakness.—II.
Corinthians, xii: 9.

OCTOBER 30.

303

Do I seek to please men? for if I yet
pleased men, I should not be the servant of
Christ.—Galatians, i: 10.

OCTOBER 31.

304

Let us not be weary in well-doing: for
in due season we shall reap if we faint not.—
Galatians, vi: 9.

305
November 1.

For by grace are ye saved through faith; and that not of yourselves: it is the gift of God.—Ephesians, ii: 8.

306
November 2.

And are built upon the foundation of the apostles and prophets, Jesus Christ himself being the chief corner-stone.—Ephesians, ii: 20.

307
November 3.

Be filled with the Spirit, speaking to yourselves in psalms, and hymns, and spiritual songs, singing and making melody in your heart to the Lord.—Ephesians, v: 18, 19.

308
November 4.

Giving thanks always for all things unto God and the Father, in the name of our Lord Jesus Christ.—Ephesians, v: 20.

309
November 5.

Whatsoever good thing any man doeth, the same shall he receive of the Lord.—Ephesians, vi: 8.

310
November 6.

It is God which worketh in you both to will and to do of his good pleasure.—Philippians, ii: 13.

NOVEMBER 7.

I press toward the mark for the prize of the high calling of God in Christ Jesus.— Philippians, iii: 14.

311

NOVEMBER 8.

The peace of God, which passeth all understanding, shall keep your hearts and minds through Christ Jesus.—Philippians, iv: 7.

312

NOVEMBER 9.

I have learned, in whatsoever state I am, therewith to be content.—Philippians, iv: 11.

313

NOVEMBER 10.

Buried with him in baptism, wherein also ye are risen with him through the faith of the operation of God, who hath raised him from the dead.—Colossians, ii: 12.

314

NOVEMBER 11.

Forbearing one another, and forgiving one another.—Colossians, iii: 13.

315

NOVEMBER 12.

Above all these things put on charity, which is the bond of perfectness.—Colossians, iii: 14.

316

NOVEMBER 13.

And whatsoever ye do in word or deed,

317

do all in the name of the Lord Jesus.—Colossians, iii: 17.

NOVEMBER 14.

Let your speech be always with grace, seasoned with salt, that ye may know how ye ought to answer every man.—Colossians, iv: 6.

NOVEMBER 15.

Study to be quiet and to do your own business, and to work with your own hands. —I. Thessalonians, iv: 11.

NOVEMBER 16.

Rejoice evermore.

Pray without ceasing.—I. Thessalonians, v: 16, 17.

NOVEMBER 17.

In every thing give thanks; for this is the will of God in Christ Jesus concerning you.—I. Thessalonians, v: 18.

NOVEMBER 18.

Prove all things.—I. Thessalonians, v: 21.

NOVEMBER 19.

Abstain from all appearance of evil.— I. Thessalonians, v: 22.

NOVEMBER 20.

The Lord is faithful, who shall stablish

you, and keep you from evil. — II. Thessalonians, iii: 3.

NOVEMBER 21.

The end of the commandment is charity
out of a pure heart, and of a good conscience,
and of faith unfeigned.—I. Timothy, i: 5.

325

NOVEMBER 22.

Now unto the King eternal, immortal,
invisible, the only wise God, be honor and
glory for ever and ever. Amen.—I. Timothy, i: 17.

326

NOVEMBER 23.

Who will have all men to be saved, and
to come unto the knowledge of the truth.—
I. Timothy, ii: 4.

327

NOVEMBER 24.

For there is one God, and one mediator
between God and men, the man Christ Jesus.
—I. Timothy, ii: 5.

328

NOVEMBER 25.

Fight the good fight of faith, lay hold on
eternal life, whereunto thou art also called.
—I. Timothy, vi: 12.

329

NOVEMBER 26.

Our Savior Jesus Christ, who hath abol-
ished death, and hath brought life and im-

330

mortality to light through the gospel.— II.
Timothy, i: 10.

331

NOVEMBER 27.

Therefore endure hardness, as a good
soldier of Jesus Christ.— II. Timothy, ii: 3.

332

NOVEMBER 28.

Study to show thyself approved unto God,
a workman that needeth not to be ashamed.
— II. Timothy, ii: 15.

333

NOVEMBER 29.

Preach the word; be instant in season,
out of season; reprove, rebuke, exhort with
all long-suffering and doctrine.— II. Timothy, iv: 2.

334

NOVEMBER 30.

Young men likewise exhort to be sober-
minded. In all things shewing thyself a
pattern of good works: in doctrine shewing
uncorruptness, gravity, sincerity, sound
speech that cannot be condemned; that he
that is of the contrary part may be ashamed,
having no evil thing to say of you.—Titus,
ii: 6-9.

335

DECEMBER 1.

There remaineth therefore a rest to the
people of God.— Hebrews, iv: 9.

DECEMBER 2.

For he that is entered into his rest, he also hath ceased from his own works, as God did from his.— Hebrews, iv: 10.

DECEMBER 3.

Unto them that look for him shall he appear the second time without sin unto salvation.— Hebrews, ix: 28.

DECEMBER 4.

Lo, I come to do thy will, O God.— Hebrews, x: 9.

DECEMBER 5.

Let us draw near with a true heart, in full assurance of faith, having our hearts sprinkled from an evil conscience, and our bodies washed with pure water.— Hebrews, x: 22.

DECEMBER 6.

Let us hold fast the profession of our faith without wavering; for he is faithful that promised.— Hebrews, x: 23.

DECEMBER 7.

And let us consider one another, to provoke unto love, and to good works.— Hebrews, x: 24.

DECEMBER 8.

For ye have need of patience, that, after

336

337

338

339

340

341

342

ye have done the will of God, ye might receive the promise.— Hebrews, x: 36.

DECEMBER 9.

343

For yet a little while, and he that shall come will come, and will not tarry.—Hebrews, x: 37.

DECEMBER 10.

344

Choosing rather to suffer affliction with the people of God, than to enjoy the pleasures of sin for a season.—Hebrews, xi: 25.

DECEMBER 11.

345

My son, despise not thou the chastening of the Lord, nor faint when thou art rebuked of him:—Hebrews, xii: 5.

DECEMBER 12.

346

For whom the Lord loveth he chasteneth. and scourgeth every son whom he receiveth. —Hebrews, xii: 6.

DECEMBER 13.

347

Holiness, without which no man shall see the Lord.—Hebrews, xii: 14.

DECEMBER 14.

348

He hath said, I will never leave thee nor forsake thee.—Hebrews, xiii: 5.

DECEMBER 15.

349

So that we may boldly say, The Lord is

my helper, and I will not fear what man shall do unto me.—Hebrews, xiii: 6.

DECEMBER 16.   350

Jesus Christ the same yesterday, and to-day, and for ever.—Hebrews, xiii: 8.

DECEMBER 17.   351

It is a good thing that the heart be established with grace.—Hebrews, xiii: 9.

DECEMBER 18.   352

If any of you lack wisdom, let him ask of God, that giveth to all men liberally, and upbraideth not; and it shall be given him.—James, i: 5.

DECEMBER 19.   353

Blessed is the man that endureth temptation: for when he is tried, he shall receive the crown of life, which the Lord hath promised to them that love him.—James, i: 12.

DECEMBER 20.   354

Every good gift and every perfect gift is from above, and cometh down from the Father of lights, with whom is no variableness, neither shadow of turning.—James, i: 17.

DECEMBER 21.   355

Wherefore, my beloved brethren, let every man be swift to hear, slow to speak, slow to wrath.—James, i: 19.

356

December 22.

For whosoever shall keep the whole law, and yet offend in one point, he is guilty of all.—James, ii: 10.

357

December 23.

Even so the tongue is a little member, and boasteth great things. Behold, how great a matter a little fire kindleth!—James. iii: 5.

358

December 24.

Out of the same mouth proceedeth blessing and cursing. My brethren, these things ought not so to be.—James, iii: 10.

359

December 25.

But the wisdom that is from above is first pure, then peaceable, gentle, and easy to be entreated, full of mercy and good fruits. without partiality, and without hypocrisy.—James, iii: 17.

360

December 26.

Draw nigh to God, and he will draw nigh to you.—James iv: 8.

361

December 27.

The effectual fervent prayer of a righteous man availeth much.—James, v: 16.

362

December 28.

But as he which hath called you is holy.

so be ye holy in all manner of conversation.
—I. Peter, i: 15.

DECEMBER 29.

363

Forasmuch as ye know that ye were not
redeemed with corruptible things, as silver
and gold, from your vain conversation received by tradition from your fathers, but
with the precious blood of Christ, as of a
lamb without blemish and without spot.—I.
Peter. i: 18, 19.

DECEMBER 30.

364

Casting all your care upon him; for he
careth for you.—I. Peter, v: 7.

DECEMBER 31.

365

Now unto him that is able to keep you
from falling. and to present you faultless
before the presence of his glory with exceeding joy, to the only wise God our Savior, be
glory and majesty, dominion and power,
both now and ever. Amen.—Jude. 24, 25.

Other
reading.

Aside from the numerous note-books, in which, in his neat hand, are found references to the subject matter of the text he was perusing, and suggestions of further study, other records of his reading are found in carefully-marked passages of books with which he seemed to have choice fellowship. One such book was "The Blood of Jesus," by Rev. William Reid, M. A. Some of these marked passages are here given:

"In reference to the pardon of your sins, there is *no time to be lost.*

"The true gospel of God is, that when any one belonging to our sinful world feels his sin to be oppressive, and comes straight to the 'Lamb of God' with it, and frankly acknowledges it, and tells out his anxieties regarding it, and his desire to get rid of it, he will find that Jesus has both the *power* and the *will* to *take it away.*

"You are as welcome to Christ now as you will ever be. Wait not for deeper conviction of sin; for why should you prefer convictions of sin to Christ? And you would not have one iota more safety, although you had deeper convictions of sin than any sinner ever had.

"Well, here is the Bible — your invitation to come to Christ. It does not bear your name and address, but it says, '*Whosoever*' — that takes you in; it says, '*All*' — that takes you in; it says, '*If any*' — that takes you in.

"For the question is not, Will you remove these evils and then come to Christ? but, *Will you have a Christ to remove them for you?*

"Jesus, and Jesus only, is the object on which your anxious eyes must rest, for peace with God and a change of heart.

"Our conscience may well find settled rest where God's holiness finds rest.

"'Looking unto Jesus,' — Hebrews, xii: 2 — is the most refreshing exercise in which we can engage; and the shortest road to genuine spiritual revival is by the cross of Calvary.

"The reason why many real christians are harassed with doubt, fear, and darkness, is, that they leave off leaning entirely upon their beloved Savior, and rest part of the weight of their souls' eternal well-being on their own experience."

Marked passages.

OLD TESTAMENT.

NEW TESTAMENT.

CHAPTER XII.

CONCLUSION.

LET us hear the conclusion of the whole matter: Fear God and keep his commandments: for this is the whole duty of man. For God shall bring every work into judgment, with every secret thing, whether it be good, or whether it be evil. — ECCLESIASTES, XII: 13, 14.

IT now remains to bring this Memoir to a close. To the fond parents it has been a pleasure thus to live over the past; but alas! with the end of the work comes again the keen sense of loss, the unsatisfied longing for —

> "The touch of the vanished hand,
> And the sound of the voice that is still."

But they comfort themselves with the belief that the life they were permitted to give to the world, so useful here, cannot but be more useful there, whither his Lord has taken him. That they shall see him again, they know; that the time of their separation cannot be long, they are admonished. In the beautiful imagery of Longfellow, they can say —

> "Good night! Good night! as we so oft have said
> Beneath this roof at midnight, in the days
> That are no more, and shall no more return.
> Thou hast but taken thy lamp and gone to bed;
> I stay a little longer, as one stays
> To cover up the embers that still burn."

But with the hope that this brief and imperfect sketch of the life and character of one so faithful as a son, so true as a

Closing remarks.

Consolation.

Admonition.

May his deeds live after him.

christian, may be helpful in the formation of the character of the young, we send it forth with the prayer, that he, being dead, may yet speak.

Secrets of success.

If asked, What was the secret of his successful career? we should mention two things: First, the fact that it was always with him, Christ to live. "What hast thou done for Christ to-day?" indicates the constancy with which he kept the true object of life before him. Secondly, his abiding faith, that his Savior would always be with him. Had the Son of man audibly assured him—"I will never leave thee, nor forsake thee"—the conviction of its precious truth would not have been stronger, or deeper, or more influential on his life and conduct, than it was. Under the inspiration of these two

Unfaltering devotion.

incentives, from the hour when, in the enthusiasm of his new life, he wrote to his mother of his conversion to Christ, to the day of his death, he pursued his way, and faltered not in all the journey—faltered not, not because of his own inherent strength, but because his trust in his Savior was the victory which overcometh the world.

To this we may add the fact, that he

constantly sought for the most intelligent view of such a life of devotion to Christ, and of trust. He was, in a large sense, an *educated* christian. That he might be con- trolled, not by mere impulses, or repose in false security, he constantly searched the Scriptures, for in them he thought he had eternal life, and they, he knew, bore testimony of Christ. Thus, whether at home, with the conveniences of study at hand, or abroad, tenting among the Indians of the wilderness, the mountains, and valleys, with few such helps, he made his Bible his constant companion. Over its pages he bent in devout study and meditation; into its deep mines of thought he entered, to come forth loaded with its priceless treasures. Of its grace, and mercy, and peace he freely received, that he might freely give. Behold in these things, then, the secret of his life.

Educated christian.

To the questionings of distrust and unrest, which would seek the reason for the early close of an earthly career so beautiful and useful, we can only reply: In the first place, the timeliness or untimeliness of death is not to be judged by length of years, but by the realization or loss of the great end of

Questionings of distrust.

Prepara-
tion for
eternity.

earthly existence—preparation for eternity.
In the second place, usefulness is not to be
measured by the opportunities and possibilities of earth alone, but by those of heaven
also. If, to be prepared for eternity, is to
come to a timely death, then must we regard
his death as most timely; if to be useful, is
an end of our being, then has he truly attained that end, since to him the Lord has
said, "Come up higher!" In his own favorite
quotation of the words of "Festus" (Bailey),
whose truth he so beautifully illustrated in
his life—

Favorite
quotation.

"He most lives
Who thinks most, feels the noblest, acts the best."

And now, little book, embalming the life
and character of this darling son and christian for "a life beyond life," go on your mission, to teach by the printed page, as did

Living
voice.

he by the living voice, the helpful, helping
hand, and the conscious and unconscious
influence, that there is no true manhood,
no real nobility, save that which is with
Christ in God, and that such a manhood is
freely offered to all in the gospel.

❖ RODNEY. ❖

BISHOP HEBER.   W. S STICKNEY.

1 Ho - ly, ho - ly, Lord God al - might - y!
2 Ho - ly, ho - ly, though the dark-ness hide Thee,
3 Ho - ly, ho - ly, Lord God al - might - y!

Ear - ly in the morn-ing our song shall rise to Thee.
Though the eye of sinful man Thy glo - ry may not see,
All Thy works shall praise Thy name, in earth, and sky, and sea;

Ho - ly, ho - ly, mer - ci - ful and might - y,
Thou art ho - ly, there is none be - side Thee,
Ho - ly, ho - ly, mer - ci - ful and might - y,

God in three per - sons, bless-ed Trin - i - ty!
Per - fect in power, in love, and pur - i - ty!
God in three per - sons, bless-ed Trin - i - ty!

INDEX.